Bernice Rubens

YESTERDAY
IN THE
BACK LANE

An *Abacus* Book

First published in Great Britain by Little, Brown 1995
This edition published by Abacus 1996

A CIP catalogue record for this book is
available from the British Library.

ISBN 0 349 10763 7

Typeset in Ehrhardt by M Rules
Printed and bound in Great Britain by
Clays Ltd, St Ives plc.

Abacus
A Division of
Little, Brown and Company (UK)
Brettenham House
Lancaster Place
London WC2E 7EN

To Carla Strobel

Bernice Rubens was born in Wales and later read English at the University of Wales, of which she is now a Fellow.

Her writing career began when she was thirty, and around the same time she started work in the film industry. For some time, the author alternated between writing novels and making films, but for the last decade she has concentrated solely on writing. Her novels to date include the 1970 Booker Prize winner *The Elected Member*, *A Five Year Sentence*, which was shortlisted for the same award, and *Our Father*, winner of the Welsh City Council Prize. Two of her books have been successfully transferred to film: *I Sent A Letter to My Love* and *Madame Sousatzka* – the latter directed by John Schlesinger and starring Shirley Maclaine. Many of her novels are available in paperback from Abacus books.

Bernice Rubens' other love, apart from writing, is playing the cello.

'An achingly poignant book, whose triumph is the depiction of the intensely moving in the everyday, a tragedy of Greek dimensions played out in backstreet lives'
Independent

'Marvellously alert to the little daily rhythms of kinship, the mundane yet fascinating conversations about menus and bus journeys'
Sunday Times

'There are some unlikely ingredients in this coolly ironic cocktail of love, death, guilt and atonement, but they are mixed with skill and go down easily'
TLS

'Never less than surprising . . . She yet again demonstrates literary gifts of the highest order'
Mail on Sunday

PART ONE

CHAPTER ONE

My name is Bronwen Davies, and yesterday I killed a man. Well, it feels like yesterday. During the war it was. I was seventeen years old at the time, and now I am over seventy. So I must have lived more than fifty years of yesterdays. I don't know what happened to all those todays and tomorrows. It was only yesterday that mattered. And matters still.

I look in the mirror. Duw. The lines on my forehead, the crow's-feet that tread the corners of my eyes, the sorry second chin that sags because it cannot help itself, none of these were there yesterday. That day when I killed the man who tried . . . well, you know what he tried to do.

Even after all these years, I still have difficulty with that word. For in those days they didn't use the word rape, unless they meant a crop of charlock or field mustard. We used a euphemism. 'Interfered with' was the phrase current in my young years, and now I come to think of it, schooled in grammar like I am, it was a phrase used always in the passive voice. So no man interfered with me, but I was interfered *with*, like it was my fault. 'Interfered with' was a gentler phrase than the single word 'rape', that violent monosyllable. 'Rape' is a word to be screamed aloud, like 'help'. And perhaps in those days, someone would have come to my aid. But at the time, it seemed to me ridiculous to shout, 'I am being interfered with,' for I fear few passers-by would have been impressed. But I did not call for help. I was so affronted by my situation that I was more concerned with revenge than rescue. So I killed him. Yes. That's what I did. Over fifty years ago. But in my heart and in my hands and in my fingers, it was yesterday.

It was Christmas 1943, one of those war Christmases when snow came with the calendar. We lived in a terraced house, the one on the corner, so it was posher than the rest, qualifying for the label of 'semi-detached'. It was a big house, too big for my mam and dad and me, so we had lodgers on the top floor. Paying guests, or PGs, my mam used to call them. She thought the word 'lodgers' was common. It was Christmas, like I said. Just Mam and Dad and me and two of the PGs because they didn't have a family and my Mam was sorry for them. Most Christmases, our Auntie Annie used to come, but that year she was going to Abertillery to her daughter's. They'd just begun to talk to each other after twenty years of quarrelling and this Christmas was supposed to be a celebration of the peace. I had no doubt that they would probably quarrel again, and right in the middle of the pudding. What with the turkey and the bread sauce and the stuffing, their mouths would have been too busy for speech, but they would have eased by pudding time, and malice, though trimmed by sweet aftertaste, would flower. I was sure that the following year my Auntie Annie would be back with my mam and dad and me. I wondered whether I'd get a present from her, even though she wasn't coming. Every year she bought me a brooch, full of highly coloured stones, and I kept them side by side in a rainbow row on my shelf. I never wore them but I dusted them from time to time. She would bring the carving knife too, every year, because my dad didn't have one. And after Christmas dinner she would wash it herself and put it back in its leather sheath. Till the following year.

'The sharpest knife in the whole of Wales,' she always said before my dad started the carving.

'And England?' I used to say.

But she scoffed. England didn't matter to my Auntie Annie. They didn't bother to learn her language, so the sharpness of their knives was irrelevant.

'Run over to Auntie Annie,' my mam said. 'She'll be off early in the morning to Abertillery. Better go now,' she said. 'Better take the tram too. It's getting dark.'

She gave me tuppence. That would take me there and back. I was short for my age, so I could still pass as under fourteen. In any case, I wasn't going to take the tram. Betty, the owner of the corner sweet shop, sold liquorice under the counter without coupons, so that's how I spent my tram fare.

I waited for the tram to come, then I raced it all up the City Road. I got to the top and the tram was still trundling. I could hear its rattle way down the road and I waited for it to nose the bend, then I stuck out my liquorice tongue in triumph while I paused to get my breath.

My Auntie Annie lived down a cul-de-sac, but I still kept running even though there was no race any more. She was glad to see me, though not surprised.

'You've come for the knife, girl,' she said. 'And now you're here, you can take the brooch. Not wrapped yet,' she said, 'so you can wear it. Look nice it will on your blue jumper.'

Then she pinned it on me before I could look at it, putting her hand down my neck to shield the pin from my chest.

'There, looks lovely,' she said, and I took a bird's-eye view and it gave me back a rainbow wink, and I thought there'd be room for it on my shelf.

'Growing you are, girl,' she said, having sneaked evidence from her pinning. 'Be married soon, you will.'

'Not me, Auntie Annie,' I said. 'I'm never going to get married. Men are dirty things.' That's what my mam always said, and so did Auntie Annie. She stopped saying it when Uncle Gwyn passed on, but then I suppose when he was dead he was clean again.

'Not all of them are dirty,' she felt she had to say, then she quickly changed the subject because she had no confidence in her argument.

'Who's coming for Christmas dinner then?' she said.

'Mam, Dad and me.' I put the two lodgers last and then I remembered that we'd only got the four chairs and I wondered where the second lodger was going to put himself. And so did Auntie Annie.

'You've only got the four chairs,' she said.

'We'll find something.'

'Have to sit on one of their laps, girl,' Auntie Annie cackled. I shivered.

'You'll sit on worse laps in your time,' she said, and it sounded like a warning.

'Looks nice, that brooch,' she said, as she poured me a glass of pop. 'Drink it now and be off before it gets dark.'

She handed me the knife. All wrapped up it was, what with the leather holder and the paper bag. Nice and tidy. 'You've got your penny for the tram,' she said.

Then I tasted the liquorice again, just a hint of it, and I nodded my head and kissed her goodbye, and I said I loved her and I meant it because she smelt old. Then I ran. I didn't wait for a tram to outrun. I could hear one rattling down the City Road and I could catch it up and still race it to the bottom. And I did, and caught my breath again, and gripped the knife, not for solace or protection but so as not to drop it or my mam would hit me, or pretend to, because my dad was looking. It wasn't far to my house so I stopped running. I knew that if I took the short cut through the back lane, I'd be home in no time.

It was a long lane, starting at number seventy-eight on the

even side of our terrace, and I counted backwards to number two which was where I lived. Seventy-six, seventy-four, seventy-two and so on, and I measured my steps against each number. Four strides for each house.

I'd reached number fifty-four when I saw him. He seemed to have come out of nowhere. I saw him walking towards me, counting forwards instead of backwards. I was afraid. He seemed to have appeared without any beginning, and suddenly the thought occurred to me that a carving knife did not necessarily expect a turkey. I was still counting, but now it took five steps to pass a house. Soon he reached me within smiling distance, but his was not a smile that invited a return. I felt in response that I should turn and flee for my life, but I was near rooted there in fear, with now a faltering ten steps to cover each dwelling. At number thirty-six we were level. He stopped, and try as I would, I could not move at all. I watched him fumble with his trousers and allow his red stick free exit, and I stared at it with wonder because I had never seen such a thing before. But I knew what it was, and I knew too that it was not good for me. I don't know why I didn't run. There was no-one about in the lane, and at this time of night, not likely to be. From number seventy-eight to number two, they were all indoors listening to the news on the wireless. I could actually hear the six o'clock pips out of their kitchens and the voice of Alvar Liddell with the latest bulletin. I stood there thinking that I was possibly about to die, yet I was listening to the news because after so many years of family six o'clock addiction, it was a habit difficult to break. The Russians were repelling a German attack while I was on the ground with the man on top of me, and in between the litany of casualties on both sides, I whispered that I was being interfered with. I was whispering because I didn't want to miss hearing about the number of dead and injured on the battlefield. Then I thought I could well be one of them, on a more local killing field, and

I stopped listening and with my two free hands I unsheathed the knife from its nice and tidy paper and leather wrapping, and I murmured a 'sorry' to Auntie Annie. Then I just stuck it into his back, just so I could stop being interfered with. Then he became even heavier than before, and with all my might I pushed him off, sideways, so that he lay in the lane on his stomach with the knife sticking out of his jacket. He was very still, and I thought he must be dead. But I didn't care about that. I had to retrieve the knife so that my dad could carve the turkey. There was a lot of blood and I didn't want to get any of it on my new jumper, so I had to roll up my sleeves and start pulling. It came out easily, as if there were oil inside. Then I wiped it on his trouser leg and I put it back in its leather and its paper-wrapping. And I ran. Thirty-four, thirty-two, thirty, twenty-eight, and my house was at my feet before my tongue had reached its number. Inside the garden gate, I caught my breath, then I went through the back door into the scullery. I could hear Alvar Liddell in the kitchen. He was talking about Christmas in a hospital, and there were carols and bells. Loud bells that drowned the running water as I rinsed the knife under the tap. Then wiped it and put it back in its wrapping. Then laid it on the slab.

'Got the knife, Mam,' I shouted into the kitchen, and my voice was so ordinary, it stunned me.

'How's your Auntie Annie then?' she shouted back.

'All right,' I said. 'Is there water for a bath?'

'There'll be plenty,' she said. 'But leave it in. I'll get in after.'

'Waste not, want not,' I heard my dad say, then I went bold as brass into the kitchen.

'Wash my hair I will,' I said, and I went upstairs and thought about him lying in the back lane and wondered what I ought to be feeling.

The bath had a black tape inside, stuck all around, four

inches from the bottom. It was a war-time savings law. I knew
my dad would never take it off even when the war would be
over. He never saw the point in baths. 'A good wash down is
all you need, girl,' he was always saying. I let the water run,
and I watched it creep towards the black permit. It's important
not to break rules, and I shut off the tap just before the depth
would be illegal. Best to be on the safe side. It was lukewarm
anyway, so the less of it the better. By the time my mam got
into it, she would have to boil a kettle or two. I lay in the
water and busied myself with washing. My hands, mostly. I
thought of Lady Macbeth, because that was the set play for
our Higher School Certificate, and I sniffed at my hands
which smelt all right to me, and I thought, Bugger the per-
fumes of Arabia. Then I recited a lot of the play because I
knew most of it by heart, and that took up enough time to take
my mind off the body lying in the lane and postpone the
feelings of what I ought to be feeling.

I got out of the bath and I shouted, 'Mam, put the kettle
on,' then, 'I'm going to bed to read,' I added, though it was
only half past six, but I didn't want to be downstairs in case
anybody knocked at the door.

'I'll bring you your cocoa then,' my mam called.

I got into bed and I took *Middlemarch* out of my satchel.
Another set book for the exams. I know it's supposed to be
one of the best books ever written, but I think that it's just
boring and all that moralising gets on my nerves. I opened it
on page fifty-five, which after a year's reading was all I'd
managed, and I had little confidence that it would take my
mind off the back lane. I read every word, even aloud, but in
my mind I couldn't assemble them. When my mam brought
the cocoa, I could see she was impressed by my diligence.

'My little scholar you are,' she said. 'Be a teacher you will.
No doubt about it. A great success you'll be.'

And I thought to myself, I've already had a great success

because I'm still a virgin. And that thought comforted me a little. I don't know why. I tried once again with the book. I could always rely on *Middlemarch* to put me to sleep, but that night I just lay awake waiting for the knock on the door. I wondered whether anyone had found him yet. Poor bugger could lie there in the cold until tomorrow, I thought. But in the light, someone was bound to see him. It would be in the papers. In the evening *Echo*. Front page it would be, I was sure. Because it wasn't every day there was a murder in Cardiff. Might even be on the news, I thought. Not Alvar Liddell, though. On the Welsh network it would be. I tried to remember what he looked like, but his face was gone and I wondered for a moment who had murdered him. I lay there waiting for my mam and dad to go to bed and then I felt safer because we were all together and finished for the day and nobody would knock at the front door because we were closed.

But then somebody did, and it was still dark although it was morning. Ten past seven, by my alarm. I heard my dad shouting on the landing. 'Who's there?'

'Mr Thomas, it is,' came through the door.

Mr Thomas lived next door at number four, and I knew what he'd come for. And then I heard my mother go down the stairs and I got out of my bed and I joined them so that I could be part of the innocents.

Mr Thomas was red in the face, puffing and blowing like he'd come a long distance, though it was only four strides from next door. And I ought to know. But it seemed he'd come straight from the lane.

'Thought I'd put a new hinge on my back door,' he said. 'Been meaning to do it for a year. And what d'you think's there?'

'What?' my dad said, and I said the same, though with more curiosity than befitted a diligent schoolgirl.

'Murder, that's what,' he said. Then he invited himself into the kitchen.

'I'll put the kettle on then,' said my mam, who believed that a cup of tea would solve everything.

I got out the cups and the milk and sugar and there was an air of great excitement in the house. An event had evented. And what an event! But first we had to rule out any possible personal connection. We had only one relative and that was Auntie Annie, and we knew she was on her way to Abertillery. So we could all sit down and enjoy ourselves. Especially Mr Thomas, who had a finders-keepers look on his face, which that morning had spotted a treasure that he could live off for the rest of his life.

'Minding my own business I was,' he started when the tea came. 'Then I dropped a nail and I turned round to look for it. Then I saw it. Couldn't make it out at first. Just a big lump in the lane. So I went and had a look. Duw, it was terrible. A man it was. Couldn't see 'is face because 'e was lying on 'is stomach. But I knew it was a man from 'is trousers. Covered in blood, 'e was. Stabbed, I reckoned. There were 'oles all over 'im.'

You're a liar, Mr Thomas, I thought, there was only one hole, and I wondered how Mr Thomas' telling would wander, and probably by the end of the day, the man in the lane would be like a colander. But Mr Thomas didn't wait until the end of the day.

'Like a sieve 'e was, poor bugger, and all 'is blood running through 'im.'

'What'll we do?' my dad said.

And my mam said, 'Tell the police, of course. Their business, isn't it?'

'Not me,' Mr Thomas said quickly. 'I'm not getting mixed up in it. If I tell them, the next thing they'll think I did it. You know what coppers are like.'

My mam turned away to refill the pot and I was sure she was wondering exactly what the police would wonder. And I began to feel sorry for Mr Thomas who by now must have regretted he'd opened his big mouth at all.

'Gotto tell someone though,' my dad said.

'I'll tell the police,' I volunteered.

'You just stay right there, my girl,' my mam said quickly. 'Mr Thomas is right. We don't want to go meddling.'

We sat in silence then, drinking our tea.

'Old man, was 'e? Or young?' my dad said after a while. He too felt sorry for Mr Thomas whose minstrel career had so swiftly foundered.

'Middling,' Mr Thomas said gratefully. 'From what I could see of 'im. Shabby too. Not of any account, I would say.'

'That's no reason for to kill 'im though,' my mam said. Then there was silence again.

'Better go then,' Mr Thomas said after a while.

I didn't think he'd visit any more neighbours. He'd just have to go back to his empty house and tell the story to himself. Over and over again. He was all alone there. Mrs Thomas passed on before the war, and Gareth, his only son, was killed in France somewhere. Poor Mr Thomas. I was tempted to tell him the real story and to insist on the one hole, just to comfort him, but like my mam said, I shouldn't meddle. Then I thought, if nobody wants to meddle, even if they go down the lane, then no one will ever tell the authorities and he'll simply rot there and on a Thursday the dustman would come and take him away.

Mr Thomas thanked my mam for the tea and he made for the door.

'What are you doing for Christmas, Mr Thomas?' my mam asked.

'Nothing special,' he said. 'I'll just listen to the wireless.'

'Duw, you can't be alone for Christmas,' my dad said. 'He can come to us, can't 'e, Mother?'

That's what my dad always called my mam. Or missus. Always did. Betty was my mam's name, but I'd never heard him use it. She didn't call him 'Father' though. Dai he always was to her.

'Better bring your chair,' I said.

'Duw, that's kind,' Mr Thomas said. 'I'm ever so grateful.'

We took him to the door and we noticed that, early as it was, the street was dotted with doorstep meetings and we all could guess at the subject of their chatter. Someone else must have brought back ill tidings from the lane.

'D'you hear about it then?' Mrs Evans shouted from across the road.

'Mr Thomas found 'im,' my dad said proudly.

'No, really? Get away,' Mrs Evans said, and she crossed the road with her gathering. Then in no time half the terrace was on our doorstep and Mr Thomas was well into his colander tale. And still not one of them had told the police because nobody wanted to meddle. And for the same reason. Most of them hadn't seen the body in the lane though each one of them had a gross appetite for viewing.

'Let's all go and see.' Mrs Evans could hold herself no longer.

They decided for safety's sake to go in a body, and to take the roundabout route to the end of the terrace, skirting the side of our house to arrive at the top of the back lane. So we trooped along, with Mr Thomas in the happy lead, but at the lane's end, a police cordon forbade access. The Law had arrived, many handfuls of them, and a pitched green tent was the only sign of quarry.

Mrs Evans was very cross. 'It's that Mrs Griffiths,' she spat, first ascertaining that the culprit was not amongst the viewers. Mrs Griffiths was the only person in the terrace with a telephone, so it figured. She was the chairwoman of many committees and her husband was in charge of the local

fire-watchers' brigade. They made sure that they knew everybody's business and such knowledge found its telephonic
route to those in authority, so that the odd black-market deal
in the terrace or the showing of a light in the blackout was
quickly reported and dealt with. The Griffiths were not popular in the terrace. They were people who did their duty so
ostentatiously that duty acquired a bad name.

I stood at the back of the cluster of neighbours. I was glad
that we were not allowed to go further, for I did not relish a
second viewing. My contribution was to echo the neighbours'
comments.

'Duw, there's terrible it is,' said Mrs Evans.

'In our own back yard too,' my mam said.

'Duw, who'd have thought it?' was all my dad could say,
and Mr Thomas, full of Griffiths fury, could only mutter,
'Saw it first, I did.'

It was clear that the show was over and we all returned to
our houses with no offers of a cup of tea from anybody
because tea was rationed and so was hospitality. We idled
round the doorsteps for a while, then having exhausted what
small information was available, the street slowly emptied and
went back to the wireless, hoping for local news. But the air-
raid siren wailed and gave us all something else to do. I prayed
fervently for a direct hit on the back lane so that all evidence,
including the body, would be destroyed once and for all. We
hadn't had a warning for four days and we thought that the
Germans were lying low for Christmas.

'Bugger them,' my dad said. 'No respect for Jesus, those
bloody huns,' and he put on his fire-watcher's coat and my
mam and I went to the Anderson shelter in our garden. Our
PGs didn't bother to come down. 'If a bomb's got your name
on it,' they said, 'there's nothing you can do about it.' So it
was just me and my mam in there, with our thermos and broken biscuit ration.

'Your dad'll hear the latest,' my mam said. 'Mr Griffiths will have all the details. Seems odd though,' she said, 'a murder in war-time. You'd think there was enough killing now, wouldn't you? Seems illegal like.'

My mam could have funny thoughts at times.

'They'll catch 'im though,' she said. 'They always do.'

'Why does it have to be *him*?'

'Don't be daft,' my mam laughed. 'Women don't do that sort of thing.'

She made me feel safe. I smiled at her as I poured her tea. We heard the anti-aircraft guns.

'Must be the docks again,' my mam said, as she always said, and as it always was, but afterwards it could be anywhere, as they dropped their surplus to lighten their load on the way home. I suppose our men in aeroplanes did exactly the same. Then the all-clear went, and my dad came back and said, 'We got three down. One in Landaff fields, would you believe.' That night, the *South Wales Echo* confirmed it, though one of them, it turned out, had nothing to do with anti-aircraft fire. It was flying home, it seemed, and ran into cloud, a cloud that was stuffed with Caerphilly mountain. But that news took second place to the banner headline of 'MURDER IN THE BACK LANE', and my dad was reading it with his lips moving.

'Read it aloud then,' my mam said crossly, but I knew he didn't want to, so he handed the paper to me.

'You do it, luv,' he said. 'You're quicker.'

I wished he hadn't asked me. I was worried about my voice. So I decided to read it quickly and without expression, but the lack of expression only served to heighten the barbarism of the deed. 'The body of a man was discovered early this morning in the back lane of a terraced street in Splott. He had been stabbed.' I took a breath. 'The victim has not yet been identified. He was in his thirties, of medium height and build, with

ginger hair which was closely cut. The body was discovered by
Mr Samuel Griffiths, Air-raid Warden of the Splott area, who
informed the police.'

'Mr Thomas won't like that at all,' my dad said.

'Not fair it isn't,' said my mam. 'It's Mr Thomas should
have his name in the papers. Is that all there is?'

'Yes,' I said, and I was relieved. I was glad they didn't know
who he was and I hoped they'd never find out. I didn't want
to know whether he was the son of some grieving mother, or
brother to an adoring sister, or God forbid, a father to
orphaned children and a husband to a bewildered wife. I
wanted him anonymous for ever. The most identity I was
willing to grant him was that of 'interferer'. I wondered at the
steadiness of my voice. I wondered too for how long I could
keep my secret. I knew it would never come from my mouth,
but my body had a mind of its own. A blush, a trembling, a
faint even; I had no control over any of those. And for the first
time since the killing, I began to be afraid.

'What's the matter, luv?' my mam said. 'You've gone white
as a sheet.'

'Stomach-ache,' I said. It's useful being a woman sometimes. My mam understood. I just hoped she wouldn't
remember that I had claimed the same pain, genuine then,
only two weeks before. But my mam wasn't very good at
arithmetic. 'Time flies,' she said.

At six o'clock we turned on the news and we wondered
whether our back lane murder would merit national coverage.
But there was no mention of it. But Cardiff figured and the
bombing of the docks, and the three aeroplanes that were
brought down. But there was no mention of Caerphilly mountain, and I began to wonder who we could trust and whether
any of the news was true, even that of our back lane murder.
And I began to feel I had dreamt it all.

We had our supper and then my mam and dad went to the

pub to pick up some more information. I wasn't allowed in there because I was under age. But that didn't worry me. I didn't want to hear any more news. I just dreaded the time when somebody would give the man a name.

But they came home with it a couple of hours later.

'Peter Thorne,' my mam said.

No daffodil or leek name.

'From London 'e was,' my dad confirmed.

I said I was tired and I went to bed because I didn't want any more details. I knew it would be in the *Echo* the next night and maybe even the *Western Mail* in the morning. And after that there would be no papers because it was Christmas, and any news would have to be on the wireless.

I lay in bed and I thought about Peter Thorne. It was still only a name and it didn't yet connect to anything or anybody. I was told he was thirtyish, of medium build and with ginger hair, but each of those details was as unknown to me as was his name. I didn't remember looking at him, though I must have looked but I never saw. The ginger couldn't have helped. Every pigmentation has its own particular smell. White, black, yellow and red. I have always found red less pleasurable than the others and perhaps because of it, I was quicker on the draw. But I didn't want to think about that. I couldn't go to sleep until I heard my mam and dad go to bed. Then I would feel safe because they would be close enough to look after me.

In the morning my dad went out before breakfast to buy the *Western Mail*. The *Echo* didn't come out till the evening, and he couldn't wait that long.

'Hurry up now,' my mam said. 'We'll read it for breakfast. Part of the meal like,' she said, as if it was an extra-special dish.

He came back soon enough and the tea was already brewed.

'You read it to us, luv,' my mam said to me as we sat down, and I dreaded what tone of voice would drop from my mouth.

It was on the front page, underneath the slaughter on the Russian front, and I read a bit of that first, in the hope of tuning my voice to a fitting pitch.

'Not that bit,' my dad said crossly. 'You can save that for later.'

I understood him. The death of an individual, especially one in our back lane, was far more believable than that of thousands on a distant foreign field. I took a deep breath.

'The body of a man was found in a lane in Splott early yesterday morning. He has been identified as Peter Roger Thorne of London. He was a soldier on Christmas leave and he was visiting a friend in Cardiff. He was thirty years old, and leaves a wife Mildred, and two children, aged six and eight.'

My voice must have faltered at this juncture, for I felt my mam's hand on my shoulder.

'Oh, there's terrible it is,' she said to comfort me.

There was mercifully no more to report.

'Is that all it is?' my dad said, disappointed.

'There'll be more tonight in the *Echo*,' my mam said. Now she was comforting *him*. 'Why don't you go out and tidy up the garden a bit? I've got to get on with the turkey.'

The mention of turkey did not please me, but I offered to give her a hand with the stuffing. I vainly hoped it would take my mind off whatever it was I didn't want to think about.

'That poor Mildred,' my mam said as she took the turkey out of the pantry. 'Won't be much of a Christmas for her now, will it? And those poor kiddies. Six and eight years old.'

Although after only one hearing, she already knew the report by heart. I kneaded the stuffing with fury. It was crumbly and could have done with an extra egg for binding. But I knew there was no egg to spare, so I poured some water on it and kneaded away. I wished my mam would shut up, but she was going on about those kiddies, six and eight, and old Mildred, and I began to hate that name and I convinced myself that anybody with a stupid name like Mildred deserved to have a husband murdered. And in any case, if she had a husband like Peter Thorne, she should be glad to see the back of him.

'I've finished the stuffing,' I said, though I hadn't, but I had to change the subject.

'Get me the needle and thread then,' my mam said.

I was glad to be alone for a while and I spent some time fiddling with the sewing box in the breakfast room. I knew the colour of the thread was irrelevant, but I chose that which was nearest to turkey skin, because I liked things to be nice and tidy. I am like my Auntie Annie in that respect. I threaded the needle and tied a knot in the cotton and then I decided that I'd offer to sew up the bird myself. It wasn't a job I'd ever volunteered for but I thought to myself that if I could thrust a knife into human flesh, a gentle needle stab into a bit of turkey skin would be child's play. My mam was grateful for my offer. She had so many other things to do. I sang while I sewed, snatches of songs, but I avoided carols or any form of God-reminder, but even so, neither singing nor stuffing nor sewing could take my mind off the back lane. I dared not think of the consequences of my deed. All I was sure of, and absolutely certain, was that whatever happened, I would never confess. Never. I would bear the stain on my conscience for ever. I would suffer for it. I would allow it to deprive me of pleasure for the rest of my life. But I would never ease my conscience with confession.

'Can't take my mind off those poor kiddies at Christmas,' my mam was saying. She was back to Mildred again, and she wasn't going to let her go. I could understand her. In our house, we didn't talk very much. We never quarrelled but neither did we laugh very much, and we seemed to have talked about everything there was to talk about. Now my mam had found a subject, and no doubt she was going to milk it dry. So would my dad. So, no doubt, would all our neighbours. Apart from the bombing, which we were getting used to, we lived in a monotonous and eventless terrace, and who could blame them for trapping a happening, even one so sordid, with such relish and appetite.

'Hope they've got an auntie or something. Or a gran.' The notion of uncle or grandfather did not occur to my mam. In her vision they were not sources of solace. 'Put the wireless on then,' she said. 'Bound to have some news.'

I turned it on in time for the ten o'clock pips. But there was nothing. Not even war news, leave alone our back lane. Everything stopped for Christmas and the bulletin was simply a recital of festival news.

'Haven't found anyone yet,' my mam said. 'Police are probably on holiday.'

I let the matter rest, and vainly hoped she would do the same.

'Get started in earnest after Christmas they will,' she assured me, or rather herself, for her constant filleting of the news had become more soliloquy than conversation.

I finished sewing, both the neck and the stomach of the bird, and I patted it into shape. I was pleased with my work. I had used cross-stitch and loop-overs, and had I had more skin to spare, I would have attempted a French seam.

'You've made a good job of that, girl,' my mam said.

'What else is there?' I asked.

'You can crumble the bread for the bread sauce.'

A benign job. Just with the hands. No instruments. So I crumbled and crooned and my mam joined in, then my dad came in from the garden and he joined in our singing and he touched my mam's shoulder, and they were a happy couple who had sired a crooning murderer between them. And then my dad started on Mildred as well, and I left the kitchen and went out for a bit of fresh air. I walked around the garden,

round and round, preparing myself to make straight for the
back door. After many turns, I walked towards it, and rested
my hand on the latch. I held my breath, and I opened the
door. The lane was empty. I thought that if I walked the
length of it, stopping for a while on the spot where it had happened, it would help take my mind off it, because now that
there was nothing there, I could pretend there was nothing
special about the place. I walked in my normal fashion. Four
strides to a house. When I reached number thirty-six, I
stopped. There were chalk marks on the ground, the outline of
a body, and I pretended it had nothing to do with that thing
I couldn't get off my mind, but that it was the faded markings
of hopscotch that I'd seen children play in the lane. I actually
hopped around it, recalling the rules on my one leg, and I
longed for those hopscotch days when there was no blood in
the back lane. I hopped all the way back to the house in time
for Alvar Liddell and the one o'clock news. No battleground
or back lane bulletin. It was 'Heilige Nacht' time and a
Christmas truce, and Alvar Liddell assured us that there were
enough turkeys to go around. Despite rationing, no one would
go hungry for Christmas.

'Food isn't everything,' my mam said. 'What about that
poor man's wife and kiddies?'

She was back to Mildred again.

'And all those soldiers,' my dad said, 'the ones that have
been killed or missing? What about their wives and kids?'

I was glad my dad was making a distinction between legal
and illicit deaths. It sort of put Mildred in her proper place.

'We're lucky,' my mam said as she put our dinner on the
table. 'Only the bombs to worry about. And we've got our
shelter.'

'Fat lot of good that'll be with a direct hit. I've seen it
myself,' dad said. 'Two in Splott a few weeks ago.'

'Get on with your dinner,' my mam said. She didn't like

war talk. She was more comfortable with Mildred and the back lane. It was within her orbit and manageable. I wished she'd forget about it as I was trying to do. I convinced myself that they would never catch the culprit since I had left no clues and had no intention of confessing. It never occurred to me that they could arrest the wrong man. I wanted everybody to forget all about it and never mention it again so that the whole sorry episode would fade and go away. But my mam was carrying the Mildred torch, in blissful ignorance of the fact that it might well set her own daughter on fire. For a moment I thought I might confide in her, but I loved her enough not to burden her with my guilt. I would have to live with it, and in time I might even forget it myself, and in forgetting, let it sink into myth or legend, a tale I could tell to my grandchildren, with ease and detachment.

CHAPTER TWO

I must have eaten over fifty Christmas dinners since that time, but that post-murder meal is the only one I can remember. As if it were yesterday.

Mr Thomas arrived at one o'clock, bringing with him his chair, a whole week's sweet ration, and one egg. He was dressed in a suit, probably the only suit he had ever possessed, for it had an old-fashioned look with its wide lapels and even wider turn-ups. The cloth, though shiny now, looked of good stock, and I had the feeling that he had worn it at his wedding, and had I been able to look in his pockets, I might have found traces of faded confetti. He hung on to his chair, holding it close to his body like a shield.

'Put it down by the table, Mr Thomas,' my dad said. They'd known each other all the years they'd been in the terrace, but in all that time, neither man, nor their women for that matter, had offered their Christian names. It was the same with our lodgers, even though they shared our bathroom. Mr Travers and Mr Philips they were. As paying guests they were entitled to their surnames. My mam insisted on it. Christian names would only do for lodgers.

We had sweet sherry before dinner. There was the half a bottle over from last Christmas, together with half a bottle of brandy which Auntie Annie had brought two Christmases ago. Mr Travers and Mr Philips had brought an illegal bottle of wine each, and their gifts were accepted with the silence granted to bootleggers. The parlour had not been used since the Christmas of last year and the paper loops and streamers still hung from the ceiling, heavy with accumulated dust.

The guests had all arrived promptly. My mam wanted our dinner over by three o'clock so that we could all listen to King George and his Christmas message. I used to feel sorry for him. All over England and Wales people would switch on the wireless at three o'clock and only for to listen to his stammering. Would the poor bugger make it to the end of the sentence? Men who never gambled in their lives would lay a Christmas bet on the poor King's articulation. Whatever he had to say went unheeded and unheard. All that mattered was whether he managed or not to spill it out at all. Cruel it was, I thought, and not like my mam and dad at all. Especially my dad. He was a shy man, and gentle. He didn't say very much but I know he had deep feelings. He was always so kind to everybody. Except to poor King George on Christmas Day. On every other day of the year he thought the King was special, there by divine right, he used to say. I suppose he needed to find some flaw in that perfection, and the stammer would do for the feet of clay. We sat around sipping our sherry and nobody said anything, as if sherry-sipping was a full-time occupation. I noticed that Mr Philips' glass was empty but he went on sipping anyway so as not to look out of things. My dad was taking his time. He didn't like sherry very much, not so much for the taste of it but for its class, which he equated with a more affluent setting than our own. He saw it in a decanter, with cigars and *The Times* newspaper within its reach. He hated the sherry classes and all that they stood for. But my mam sipped it with relish and wished that every day was Christmas.

We settled ourselves around the table, and my mam brought in the big tureen of soup. Tomato it was, our favourite. Tinned soup, and the very best. Gold it was in those days. Canned food wasn't rationed but it was in short supply. But the corner grocer had a soft spot for my mam. Or that's what my mam thought. But I knew otherwise, because it was me he had the soft spot for. 'Send your girl in,' he'd say to my mam. 'I'll have something for her.' And then my mam would send me to the corner and in exchange for a tickle in the nether folds of my pleated gymslip, I would be rewarded with a tin of couponless nourishment. I didn't mind really. Over the weeks my pleats became shamelessly frayed, but it was a small price to pay for the heaven of tomato soup.

My mam ladled it out with reverence. She sprinkled a little parsley on the top, her sole contribution, apart from the tin-opener, to the first course. It looked pretty, the green and the red, and I viewed my portion for a while because it seemed a pity to disturb the pattern.

'Get that soup down you now,' my mam said, 'before it gets stone cold.'

I was the last to finish the soup and I felt all their eyes on me, and my soup spoon began to tremble with embarrassment. But I did not hurry myself. When I look back on it now, I suppose I must have been doing my bit to postpone the turkey and the carving knife, though at the time I was conscious of no troubling thought in that direction. I felt them waiting for me around the table. In time I finished the soup, but a scattering of parsley still lay around the bowl and rim of the plate, irre-trievable by spoon. Only a finger could gather them. This I used while my mam gasped, 'Manners!' and my dad smiled at the lodgers and Mr Thomas to prevent their censure. I gath-ered the bowls into a pile and took them to the kitchen. 'Manners,' I heard my mam say again and I waited for its echo to fade before I returned to the parlour.

As I sat down my dad said, 'Are you ready then?' and my mam, knowing his meaning said, 'You can get the knife then. It's on the sideboard.'

'Shall I help, Mam?' I asked.

'You sit right there, girl,' she said.

I was not offended. My mam considered the turkey and all its trimmings as her own sole production, despite the fancy stitching I'd sewn on the stuffing, and she didn't want me to steal any of her Christmas thunder. I understood, and I sat with my hands folded as my dad laid the knife on the table and stood up to perform his annual duty. If one of us had had a bugle handy, now would have been the time to give it a blow, and in my mind, 'The Last Post' would have been more than suitable. And for the first time that day, my nerves trembled as I recalled in awesome detail how, why, and where the knife had been. I dreaded the turkey's arrival at the table. I shut my eyes and resolved to keep them tightly closed until the serving ceremony was over. Then I heard a great gasp around the table, and the steam and smell of the bird brushed my nostrils, and my eyes, if not my mouth, watered, and I had to open them to wipe the tears away. And in so doing, I caught sight of the bird as it landed in all its brown and shining glory on the head of the table. I joined in the gasps of admiration, but only to please my mam, and I stared at the bird with as much resolve as I had hitherto ignored it, for I feared that if I failed to acknowledge it, it would take sudden wing and fly its rude reminder into my face. So I stared at it and saw, on its periphery, how my dad raised the carving knife and gently placed it on the brown-skinned breast. I held my breath as I waited for the first incision and for nothing less than the sudden end of my life, for I knew that with that cut, my secret would be out and with it my heart, with the breath I could no longer hold. A silent, dry and winded prayer dropped from my lips as my dad guided the knife into the white flesh. And again and again and again until half the breast was shredded to the bone. And still nothing at all had happened. I had heard no confession splutter across the table and my heart and my pulse were secure.

And then I saw my comeuppance. Right under my nose. Slap bang in the middle of the patch of white damask in front of me. A small and symmetrical circle of blood. I stared at it and noted how shortly it was joined by another, and yet another, hard upon. All eyes around the table were on the turkey, so that at first nobody noticed the minor sacrifice at my place setting. And then my mam handed around the tureen of vegetables and she noticed it and quickly found its source.

'Duw, girl,' she said. 'What have you done?'

Cross she was, concerned with the white damask that would cost the earth to send to the laundry. 'Get up quick,' she said. 'Lie yourself down. I'll fetch you a hankie.'

'Have mine,' my dad said, and he took a white spotless handkerchief out of his breast pocket, and handed it over to my mam. 'Pity to spoil that,' she said, once more with laundry thoughts.

'I'll go and get a flannel.'

'Duw,' my dad said, and went on carving.

I didn't remember ever having had a nosebleed before, and what disturbed me was not the thing itself, but its disturbing timing. I wondered how many carving Christmases and nosebleeds it would take to bleed me to death and thus, in long-winded fashion, my punishment would be served. Then my mam came back and roughly clamped a cold, wet flannel on my face. What with my parsley harvesting and nosebleeding, she was not well pleased with my manners.

'Not my fault, Mam,' I said, but of course it was, but my mam wasn't supposed to know where the knife had been.

'Sit there quiet,' she said, 'while I get on with the serving.'

I knew instinctively that once my dad had stopped carving,

the bleeding would stop too, and I prayed to God that no one
would ask for a second helping.

'Everybody had?' I heard my dad say, and after a pause I
heard the click of the knife on the table and I was tempted to
get up and snatch it and wash it and sheathe it and paper-bag
it away until I could take it back to my Auntie Annie. I took
the flannel off my face and gently sat myself erect. I knew the
bleeding had stopped but I gave myself a moment to make
absolutely sure.

'It's stopped, Mam,' I said.

'Then come and eat your dinner, girl.'

Her voice had softened and went with the beam that she
spread around the table in happy satisfaction of another
Christmas achieved.

'There's tasty it is, Mrs Davies,' Mr Thomas said.

'You've done wonders, like always,' Mr Philips added.

'Here's to the missus then,' my dad said, raising his glass,
and my mam's face went very red with embarrassment.

The clock on the wall struck two.

'Now we've plenty of time to eat,' my mam said. 'It'll be an
hour before the King so we can eat as much as we like. But we
mustn't listen to the wireless with our mouths full.'

'That would be disrespectful,' Mr Thomas put in.

I was nervous of my mam's invitation to eat heartily and I
scanned the plates around the table and found them mercifully
overfull. My dad had been very generous with his carvings.

'Plenty of vegetables,' my mam was saying, but I didn't
mind vegetables, for a serving spoon was benign. I tasted the
turkey. I had no problem with cutting it with my blunt knife.
It was dead already and I had had no hand in its killing.

'It's lovely, Mam,' I said. 'So is the stuffing.'

She smiled at me, my manners forgotten. 'And so are the
stitches,' she said.

Then we all settled down to eating. My dad kept the wine

glasses full. He was giggling and we knew he'd already had too much.

'Be careful with that wine now, Dai Davies,' my mam said. She always used his full name when she was cross with him. 'We don't want you to get drunk in the King's hearing.'

My dad gave a weak coda giggle and was not heard from again. Until he broke the silence some time later by asking, 'Anyone for seconds?'

I trembled. I felt my nose listening, and I held my breath, and to my relief, there was a general silence around the table. We had all eaten our full, and as if to mark an interval, the clock struck the half-hour.

'Time for a fag, luv?' my dad asked. 'All of us I'm sure would like a bit of a smoke before the pudding.'

'Well, since it's Christmas,' my mam said.

So my dad lit up and so did the others and each, in view of the tobacco shortage, from their own pockets, while me and my mam cleared the table.

'Better wash that knife and put it by for your Auntie Annie,' my mam said in the kitchen, and I did exactly that with the greatest pleasure and relief. And when it was done and safely put away, I felt I could begin to enjoy Christmas. I started to do the washing-up.

'That was a great dinner, Mam,' I said.

'Wait till you taste the pudding,' she said, and she levered it out of the boiling water and unwrapped the cloth that sheathed it. She put it on the dish and stood back to admire it. Since the beginning of the year, she had begun collecting ingredients, sultana by sultana, candied peel by candied peel and she'd hoarded the miniature bottle of brandy that some years ago had been a *Reader's Digest* free offer. She took the box of matches from the shelf, then she poured the brandy over the pudding. 'Ready now,' she said, as she struck the match, and turning her face away, she hovered the flame over the dish. A mauve and gentle fire combed the pudding's dome and she held it before her like an offering, pleased with her work, yet humbled by it too. Her tread to the parlour was hesitant with pride and shame.

I followed her and as she entered the room, I heard a cheer and I was happy for her. Then my dad started singing, 'I wish you a merry Christmas' and we all joined in so that his unreliable pitch was less disturbing. The pudding fire had died by the time the song was finished, but its pungent aroma spread across the table and we all savoured it for a while.

'Now mind the sixpenny bits,' my mam said as she cut into the first slice.

'How many are there, Mam?' I asked.

'Enough for all of us.'

I looked at her steaming, happy face. I was sure that she had forgotten Mildred's name. The back lane hadn't been mentioned the whole day. I was confident that by the new year, the whole episode would have sunk into the forgotten past. But for me it would always be yesterday, and yesterday's too young for history.

We ate our pudding portions with great care. Mr Thomas was the first to unearth a treasure and carefully he mined it out of his dentures and held it up as a trophy.

'Good luck then, mun,' my dad said. 'It'll be a good year for you.' And as he said it, his mouth half full, he too chewed on a silver piece. 'Me too,' he shouted. He licked it free of sultana and laid his booty before him. I prayed that the lodgers would strike silver too, though I was confident that my mam knew where the bits were and she had sliced accordingly. And sure enough, both Mr Travers and Mr Philips struck lucky at the same time. So now there was only my mam and me left, and I was sure she'd measured the quarry for both of us. Then I bit on my silver share, and my mam shortly afterwards.

'That's the lot then,' my mam said, having accounted for

the half-dozen pieces of the treasure hunt. 'Finish up now. Ten minutes to go for the King. Then we'll have our tea and mince pies.'

'You've done well, missus,' my dad said. He'd sobered up a little. Now he was just merry from the brandy in the pudding. And so were they all, and Mr Thomas suggested using their winnings for to place a bet on the King's stammer. Sixpence on the first sentence, or the second, or the third. But my mam would have none of it though she was laughing at the suggestion.

'It's disrespectful,' she said. 'Poor bugger. Can't help his speech. Turn the wireless on, Dai,' she said.

'Can't move, luv,' he said. 'I am replete.'

It was a word he brought out for every Christmas. It came with the streamers and the pudding. He never used the word at any other time. He relished it and he didn't intend to wear it out.

'Replete I am,' he said again.

Twice a year was his ration of the word. Now he'd put it by till the next Christmas pudding.

So I got up and put the wireless on. Five minutes to go and they were carolling over the airwaves. Despite the few armchairs in the room, and the sofa, none of us chose to leave the table. We felt we should not sit easy to listen to the King. You sat with your back straight and in a slight discomfort as token of your respect and obedience. We all sang along with the carol. 'We Three Kings' it was, sung by a boys' choir, but what with our shaded participation, the choir's gender was rudely blurred. When the song was finished we clapped ourselves until the clock struck three. My mam shouted 'shush', but the clock took no notice and was chiming the hour as the announcer introduced the head of the nation and the Empire in a voice that suggested he was clothed in black. We all turned in our chairs to face the wireless, as if the King's features would materialise on the brown Bakelite sun of its casing.

'The Queen and I,' he began, 'are happy to wish all our subjects a very merry Christmas.'

So far, so flawless. Anyone who'd laid a bet on the first sentence would have lost his shirt. But on the second, he would have made a small silver fortune. For the poor soul could hardly begin it. Having started with such a triumph, he completely lost his nerve, and there was a terrible silence as we suffered for him and prayed for him to continue. And prayed and waited. And then at last, his reluctant words obliged. 'In these troublesome times,' he said, 'we send our thoughts and prayers to all those who struggle for our great country.' The word 'struggle' was most loath to take the air and reflected the awful strivings of the man himself. 'Our men and women on foreign fields,' he went on, 'and all those on the battlefields at home, let us give our thanks to them.'

I looked around at our little audience and I noticed a tear in Mr Thomas' eye. The others were simply staring at the Bakelite and there was no trace of a smile on any of their faces. What they had all hoped for, and indeed were prepared to bet on, was resounding in their very ears. But unlike in previous years, none took any pleasure in it. I thought perhaps it was the presence of Mr Thomas and the recall of the death of his son, that bereavement on their very doorstep, that stifled their laughter, and I understood then that nothing is real until it happens to you. Or perhaps to somebody next door. Or someone unknown in one's own back lane.

The good King stammered along. He told us nothing that we didn't already know and nothing that we had not already heard on Christmas Day in years before. Finally he prayed for peace, his most reluctant word of all, and to which he donated at least six painful syllables. His struggle was so overwhelming that it sounded like a prayer for war. His Majesty must have sighed with relief when it was all over, a sigh that was echoed by millions across the land and in the wastes of foreign fields. As was the off switch on the Bakelite and the return to a good cup of tea and mince pies.

'I'll put the kettle on,' I said. I wanted to get away from the silence in the parlour. I knew that it was due to the heavy presence of Mr Thomas and his shredded coat of grief. I could hear the silence from the kitchen and I made sure to put the whistle on the kettle to manufacture a sound of sorts to break into all that unspoken sympathy. By the time I'd pre-pared the teapot and the tray of cups and saucers and mince pies, the kettle had boiled and I allowed it to whistle its heart out. I carried the tray through the kitchen and into the hall, and still no sound came from the parlour. I noticed the relief on all their faces as I entered, for my appearance was an event which offered them something to do.

'That's my girl,' my dad said, and the silence at last was broken. They shifted in their seats, and that movement made noise too and what with the clatter of the cups in the tray it seemed as if that mysterious silence would be forgotten. And then my dad said, 'A cup of tea will do us all good.'

He should never have said it. It inferred that we were all in a very bad state, which was not exactly true, but even if we were, such a state was private, and needed no reference. And not surprisingly, poor Mr Thomas burst into loud sobbing. He sobbed in a stuttering fashion, not unlike our King, with the same struggle to muffle his impediment.

'Have a cup of tea now,' said my mam, who was convinced that a cup of tea could make everything better. She thought that the rationing of such a remedy was a stupid and cruel manoeuvre and that if we were to lose the war, the blame would lie squarely in the lap of the Minister of Food. She handed a cup to Mr Thomas and he took it in a quivering hand, then he placed it on the table, fearful of his unsteady hold. My mam served the others in an unbroken silence, while everybody stared at the floor and with such concentration that it is possible that my dad took note of the carpet pattern for the first time since it had been laid over ten years ago. The rattle of cups was all my mam could offer and it had to do for conversation.

In an effort to restrain his sobs, Mr Thomas had begun to hiccup and I knew that someone had to say something, however irrelevant or trivial, just to break the now unbearable silence. I scratched in my mind for something to say, but nothing, appropriate or otherwise, obliged.

It was Mr Travers who came to our rescue. 'My brother was shot down over Bremen.' He allowed a pause. 'Dead,' he said.

I don't know why, but I was sure Mr Travers was lying. He'd been our paying guest for over a year and he'd never mentioned a brother. Then Mr Philips opened his mouth and I prayed that he would not offer a family death simply to keep company with the bereaved. But he did, the liar, though at least his offer was marginal. His sister-in-law's mother had been killed in a raid over Birmingham. I dared to look at my dad. I could always tell when he was trying to think of something. His brow would furrow and his lower lip would tremble. In our family we had no deaths to offer, at least none on the battlefield, and I hoped to God he was not going to invent one. My mam had the same hope, and she gave him a look that stopped him thinking.

But a battlefield strewn with corpses could not comfort Mr Thomas. Only one body he mourned. His wife's passing had been in the natural order of things, but his son, dead at the age of twenty, was out of nature.

'I'm ever so sorry,' he managed to say, then he took a sip of his tea. 'It's because it's Christmas,' he offered. 'Always a bad time.'

I'm sure that the silly name of Mildred crossed my mam's mind at that time and the sorry widowed Christmas she was enduring with her orphaned children. But if the name did cross her mind, she did not utter it. There was enough bereavement on the table, real or imagined, to satisfy the most ghoulish of appetites. Mildred would have festered the white lily of mourning.

Mr Thomas had, by now, pulled himself together and he asked for a mince pie. This my mam gladly passed him and his renewed appetite gave everybody licence to get on with Christmas. 'These are good, missus,' my dad said, and through full mouths, everybody agreed.

'Poor bugger's getting worse,' Mr Philips said. 'The King, I mean,' he clarified.

If the monarchy were nothing else, it was a subject for conversation and would tide them over the tea and mince pies towards the gathering dusk and home time.

'You can't help having a bit of a laugh though,' Mr Travers said, having quickly recovered from his brother's questionable demise.

'He's a good king in my opinion,' Mr Philips claimed, as if he had had dire experience of bad ones. 'So's she. The Queen, I mean. The way they walk around the bomb sites. Worth every penny of my money.' Every penny of Mr Philips' money wouldn't have kept the royal couple in broken biscuits, but it was a gesture, which was all he had meant it to be.

'If we didn't have them, we'd have someone like Hitler,' my dad said.

'God forbid,' Mr Thomas muttered. 'King and country, that's what we're fighting for. A war against tyranny.' He was echoing the words that Mr Churchill had used in a Bakelite Christmas message only a few days before.

'To rid the world of Satan.' Mr Philips put in his penny-worth.

'Well, here's to peace and freedom,' my dad said, raising his almost empty glass.

None of them knew what they were talking about. They'd picked up bewildering phrases from the papers and the wireless and they repeated them while fighting fires, or clearing rubble or in the pub during the lulls. It would not be until after the war was over that those phrases would slowly acquire meaning, when the actual nature of the enemy was fully revealed. Then they would justify their overused slogans, and understand in hindsight what they had been fighting for. But for now, slogans would have to do.

With my dad's last toast they had clearly finished with their war talk, and I knew that the only thing left that they all had in common was the back lane. And to forestall that topic I had to think of something else to engage them in conversation. But I heard myself say, 'I wonder if they've found anybody yet.'

'Who?' my dad asked.

'The police. Whether they've found anybody yet for the murder.' I don't know why I said it. Perhaps it was because I needed to be in control. I needed to dictate the tenor of their speculation. But it was more than that. I needed to find some reason for the curdling knot in my stomach, in the hope that talking about the back lane would somehow unravel it.

'Nothing happens over Christmas,' Mr Travers said. 'But don't you worry. They'll find him.'

I marvelled at his assumption that the killer had to be a man. But it offered me no relief. My mam was glad to be given a cue for poor Mildred and she wondered yet again how the wretched lady could swallow her Christmas pudding. The subject of Mildred took up a little time, with offerings from all the guests as to the nature of poor Mildred's bereavement, and her lack of Christmas decorations. And by the time that subject was exhausted, the dusk had begun to gather, and the twilight was a clear hint that the party was over. But still the knot in my stomach persisted.

'Any more tea, Mam?' I said, in the vain hope that some liquid might melt it. If mental stress can result in physical pain, then there's no reason why it should not respond to physical remedy.

'I'll make a fresh pot,' my mam said.

But Mr Thomas had risen from the table. 'Not for me,' he said. 'I must get back home.'

He said it as if a certain urgency awaited him there, and we all knew that that imperative was simply to be alone, to weep and to hiccup as much as he wished, and perhaps to hit what bottle he had, to take his mind off his mind. For Mr Thomas was known to be a bit of a drinker. In the old pre-war days, with son and wife safely installed, you could hear him through the walls, shouting and swearing in drunken fury. And probably beating up that wife of his, who had died out of sheer revenge, and the son who had perished to punish him. Poor Mr Thomas.

'Thank you ever so much, Mrs Davies,' he said, nodding his head. 'It was really very kind. Best Christmas I've had for a long time.'

'You must drop in more often,' my mam said. 'No need to be lonely.' My mam didn't understand that being alone was a need sometimes, and it didn't have to mean that you were lonely. Mr Thomas was going home to company, to the painful memories of his wife and son and a little beer to make them bearable.

When Mr Thomas had gone, Mr Travers and Mr Philips saw fit to leave too. They didn't have far to go, just up two flights of stairs. Then they would get out of their Sunday best and into their working clothes and down to the pub and normal behaviour.

When they had gone, the house felt strangely isolated, as if, far from being part of a terrace, it was a lone dwelling in the middle of a field, with no back lane to anchor it to reality.

'I'll wash up,' I volunteered. 'You two go down to the pub.' Like Mr Thomas, I wanted to be alone. I wanted to root myself once more in our terraced home and to connect that home with the out-back site of my terror. I wanted to acknowledge my fears, wholly and even heartily, and then perhaps they would go away.

CHAPTER THREE

We were well into January of the new year, and I'd gone back
to school at the start of the spring term. I was having breakfast one morning and my mam was at the front door seeing my
dad off to work. I could hear some conversation on the
doorstep. Then my mam rushed back into the kitchen and
turned the wireless on. I heard the start of the local news.

'They've got someone,' my mam said. 'Heard it from Mrs
Powys. Shush now.'

There had been a raid on Cardiff docks the night before and
the announcer was giving details of the damage and the number of aircraft we had shot down. He gave a decent pause after
that piece of news, and then informed us that a breakthrough
had been made in the investigations into the murder of a man
in Splott a few days before Christmas. A man had been
arrested and had been taken to police headquarters where he
was helping police with their enquiries.

'They've got the murderer,' my mam shouted, with
absolutely no evidence at all. 'Be hanged he will. And serves
him right.'

I wondered about the phrase 'helping police with their
enquiries'. It was a euphemism, of course, like the phrase
'being interfered with'. But I knew for certain that the poor

devil was being more than 'interfered with'. If he was 'helping the police with their enquiries', it meant that they were beating the shit out of him. I was sorry for him, of course, but I was not unduly worried. I knew with absolute certainty, and with plenty of good reason, that he was innocent, and at the same time, I had enough faith in British justice to believe that shortly he would be so proved.

I picked up my satchel and set off for school. I went down the back lane. It was my routine route to school, but whereas before the episode, I had taken it as a mere short cut, now it was as if I was going for a fix, and no matter how much time I had, I would never think of going any other way. I stopped at number thirty-six, as was my wont. Not that I needed any reminder, but it was, I suppose, by way of memorial. Then I hurried. My school was not far from my house, in all, about a ten-minute walk. As I turned the corner, I noticed a bevy of girls converging on the school, and seeing them, I realised that I had forgotten my gas mask. It was not an oversight one could get away with. Old Miss Berryman would stand every morning at the gate like a stern sentry, and check on our compulsory baggage. There was another entrance at the back of the school, but that too was cunningly screened. I turned back and ran for home. When I reached the top of the lane, I stopped. From where I stood, I could see two policemen and a man between them, hovering around number thirty-six. I hesitated, wondering whether the lane was still available to the innocents. And with this thought, I braved it, and practically strutted past them. I noticed that the man and one of the policemen were curiously joined at the wrist. I was tempted to shout, 'He didn't do it,' but my nose began to tickle and I cursed it, for in the end, I knew it would be my nose that would give me away and see me forever damned. I wiped the blood on the sleeve of my blazer. There was not much of it and by the time I reached home, it had stopped. I grabbed my gas mask and went out by the front door. Although I was late, I took the longer route. I'd had enough of the lane for one day. I was late for school, of course, but Miss Berryman was still duty-rooted to the gate. I flashed her my gas mask with some defiance. I was in a bad mood, and it suited me to think that she was the cause of it.

I was restless at school that whole day. That term the work-load intensified, in preparation for the Higher Certificate exams in the summer. I hoped to do well enough to get into university, but I was wary of my powers of concentration and of what role the back lane would play in my earnest revisions. To make matters worse, my period started mid-morning. A week early, if I reckoned correctly, and it occurred to me that the back lane episode had thoroughly overturned my nature and that I was full of blood that oozed from every orifice. I wanted to go into a corner and cry. I went to the sick room to get myself some protection. I complained of a stomach-ache and the nurse advised me to lie down for a while. Thus I was able to skip Assembly and the Lord's Prayer, of which I was sorely in need, but too ashamed to give voice to. I wondered about my future and how I would survive it all. I had a fleeting thought that with luck, I would be killed in an air raid.

I must have fallen asleep, for I was sharply awakened by the bell that signalled the start of lessons. I rushed to my class-room. I felt no better, and the French lesson that faced me would in no way improve my condition. I simply couldn't con-centrate. I kept thinking of that innocent in the lane. I'd only seen the back of him and his handcuffed wrist. But I didn't need to see his face to smell the fear and bewilderment in that outline. I tried to put myself in his shoes and to feel his offended innocence. He looked such an ordinary man. Round about forty perhaps, a bit younger than my dad. How many times would he have to say 'I didn't do it' before they would believe him? My dad would buy an *Echo* on the way home from work and it would be the talk of the doorstep terrace all evening. They couldn't keep him long. By the morning they would have to charge him. That was their time limit, unless they got an extension. Or else they would have to let him go. I knew the law. I worried that they might beat him into a confession of sorts. From the back of him he looked enfeebled and submissive enough for that.

'Bronwen? Bronwen Davies?'

I heard my name called. Or, rather, shouted. My lack of attention had been noticed.

'Are you with us this morning?' Miss O'Brien had a tendency to sarcasm, a trait which I normally appreciated as long as I was not the target, but now I found it hurtful.

'Sorry, miss,' I said, though I wasn't sorry at all. I wanted to tell her I had more important things to think about than the French Romantic poets. I turned my mind to de Musset whose poem she was reading at the time and I read it silently and in unison with her voice in an effort to re-enter her teaching. And soon enough, and miraculously, I was with her and the back lane had dissolved in the man's innocence. I put it out of my mind for the rest of the day. I took the long route home and I decided to spend the rest of the evening in homework and revision. I hoped that a period of intensive work would not allow me to indulge in any unrelated thoughts. But my dad was already at home and with the *Echo*, and they were both of them in the kitchen poring over the latest news.

'Read it out, Bron,' my mam said, though by now she must have known it by heart. She handed me the paper and pointed out the appropriate place. It was only a few sentences and it lay on the bottom of the front page. I read the headline. 'Police interview a man.' The anonymity was clear from the start. 'Early this morning,' I read, 'a man was taken to police headquarters in connection with the murder in Splott on the twenty-third December of last year. He has not been named.

For the moment' – I paused before reading that time-honoured phrase – 'he is helping police in their enquiries.'

'Well, there's no smoke without fire,' my dad said. He too had found him guilty, whoever he was. And no doubt the whole street was thinking likewise and preparing to attend the gallows. I went to my room and tried to settle into working, but the *Echo* report had put me off my resolve. I prayed for the morning when the innocent might be released and things would go back to normal, whatever that meant any more. But on the other hand, they could decide to charge him and I dared not think of the consequences of such a monstrous decision. I picked up *Middlemarch*, in the certainty that it would send me to sleep, for that was what I needed. A dreamless oblivion. But it didn't work. The boredom of that novel simply kept me awake, so I put it aside and picked up a collection of English Romantic poets, a sure escape route into matters that did not refer to the back lane. In this manner the evening passed very quickly and by the time my mam called me for supper, I had inadvertently revised a goodly part of the English syllabus.

The air-raid warning went early that night, and my mam and I were in the shelter before we could finish our supper. My dad went out on his duties, checking that no chink of light was showing through windows, and helping to put out fires if called upon. His area covered our terrace and three parallel streets. We were not afraid for him. Although we were on the air path to the docks, our district had remained relatively clear of damage and we had become rather smug about it. And some of our neighbours boasted that they never bothered with the shelter at all. When the Anderson shelters had first been built in our back yards, neighbours had vied with each other in their decorative finishings. Some were even carpeted and the camp beds had candlewick spreads. Tinned food was stored in there and any surplus from our rationed goods. But over the months those stocks were depleted and the shelters became mere humps in the back gardens, over which the women strewed washing to dry. But my mam and I stuck to our shelter. It was cosy in there, with our little thermos of tea which we drank conscientiously whether we wanted it or not, because my mam was convinced that tea was the irrefutable way of British survival. Then, after that terrible night of January the twenty-eighth, we didn't go there any more.

The air raids were getting worse. They were more frequent and more intense, and for the first time we started to worry when my dad had to go out on duty. On the night of the twenty-eighth, the air-raid siren went earlier than usual and we rushed to our shelter, my mam and I, and we sat there in terror, too afraid even to pour out our thermos. We heard the bombers flying overhead and the indignant roar of the anti-aircraft fire. Then for the first time since the war had begun, we heard a bomb explosion that was clearly in our very neighbourhood. And both of us thought of our dad. My mam wanted to run out into the street to call his name and to search for him. I had to restrain her. We could do nothing but sit and listen to the bombs falling and the sound of an astonished crater.

After a while, the guns ceased their firing and there was an appalling silence. But somehow there was no relief in it, for it was a silence we'd never heard before. It was the silence of mourning and we dreaded the all-clear signal that would give us licence to view whom and what we had lost. When the siren wailed, my mam started to cry. She was expecting the worst and was arming herself with the paraphernalia of loss. I put my arm around her and helped her out of the shelter. I knew that the bomb we had heard had fallen very close, and somehow I was convinced that it had detonated in the back lane, thus removing for ever all evidence of interference and revenge. But as we emerged into the garden, it was clear that the back area of the terrace was untouched, and entering the house we knew that the site of the detonation was the street itself. We were hardly through the scullery door before we heard my dad's frantic voice from the front.

'Betty, Betty,' he was screaming. 'Bron, Bronwen.'

It was a long time since I'd heard him call my mam by her name. Usually it was 'Mam' or 'missus'. And, sometimes, plain 'you'. Perhaps, long ago, he had used 'Betty' for loving. Now it was brought out only in emergency and panic.

'Dai, Dai,' she shouted and she ran towards him. I followed her, the 'Bronwen' of his panic, ignoring the dresser crockery on the floor, the upturned lamp and the broken table. For some reason the Bakelite was secure on its stand, ready to give us the latest on the back lane. We embraced together, the three of us, each glad to find the others alive.

'Duw, duw,' my dad kept saying. 'It's terrible, terrible, terrible. Duw, never known a night like it.'

We disentangled ourselves from each other, embarrassed by our embrace. We were not by nature a tactile family and we were ill-equipped to deal with the aftermath of touch.

'What happened?' my mam asked.

'Come and look.' My dad led us out of the front door, and there, obliquely opposite, one half of number forty-five was sheepishly strewn across the street.

'What about the Watkins then?' my mam whispered.

'Talk about luck,' my dad said. 'They were out. Went to the flicks. Not home yet. They'll have a bit of a shock. Duw, it's terrible,' he said again.

'Direct hit was it?' my mam said.

'Nearly.' My dad paused, knowing the implications of what he was going to say. 'It was on the shelter. There's a fire in the back.'

'Well, that's it,' my mam decided. 'Never liked that shelter. We're not going in it again.'

'Got to go somewhere,' I said.

We looked at each other. A single name was passing through all our minds but none of us was able to voice it.

'Better wait for the Watkins to get back,' my mam said, changing a subject that had never been. 'They'll need somewhere to put down for the night.'

The fire engines were turning into the terrace and within seconds their hoses were on the garden of number forty-five and an audience of the whole street turned out to watch them. In the flickering light you could see their faces, triumphant with survival. We waited and watched and dreaded the Watkins' return.

'I'll go down to the corner,' my dad said. 'Wait for them I will. Give them a bit of a warning. Cushion the shock like.'

Then Mr Griffiths passed our door, bent on the same errand. 'Let's go,' he said to my dad. 'Got to tell them before they see it.'

But they were too late. The Watkins had already rounded the corner of the terrace and they stood there, both of them, and Mrs Watkins' mouth was seen to open in a soundless scream. No one moved towards them but we all watched as they clasped each other and moved, as if cruelly propelled, towards the site that had once been their home. Then my mam and me, we turned away and went back into our house, and unbelievers though we were, we gave thanks to God that we were still alive and our broken goods and shattered windows did not matter to us at all. It was thanksgiving time in the terrace, and time for making tea. My dad came in shortly afterwards. 'They've gone to the shelter up the hill,' he said. 'Poor buggers. Must have lost everything.'

'Except their lives,' I said. I felt the need for priorities.

'You're right, luv,' he said. 'Got to count our blessings.' He put his hands on my mam's shoulders. 'Any tea, missus?' he said. We were back to normal.

It was only eight o'clock and we couldn't be too sure that the siren would not go again. My dad said it wasn't worth clearing up and we could all do it in the morning. 'I'm not going in that shelter again,' my mam said. 'I'm going to take all the stock out of there. Didn't save all that tinned food for it to be bombed.'

She didn't seem to regret the passing of her best dinner plates. 'You can't eat china,' she said, so we had tea in chipped cups. 'Let's make a start,' she said.

So we set to work. The rest of the evening was undisturbed and we worked till very late, cardboarding the windows and clearing the debris away. We all overslept the next morning and I was late for school but after the battering the city had taken the night before, punctuality had little priority. There were many absentees. Transport had been disrupted, most tramlines were down, and the main road through the city was blocked. In Assembly we prayed for those who had been killed or injured, then we went back to our classrooms and worked with a survivor's fury. And in a state of faint euphoria. I had forgotten all about the back lane until my dad brought home the *Echo*. Not surprisingly, its front page was devoted to the night's destruction and one had to turn to a news-unworthy page six to discover that the man who had been helping police with their enquiries into the Splott murder had been released without charge. My mam and my dad were very cross indeed.

'Must have done something to take him in in the first place,' my dad said.

'They'll be sorry,' was my mam's contribution.

For my part I was unsurprised, my faith in British justice being confirmed. But I have to confess it was a relief, for I could not have dealt with his being put on trial. I wished the police would stop their investigations. Surely with the air raids and the devastation, they had better things to do.

My dad came home early from the munitions factory that day. Not enough workers had turned up to effect production. We were sitting down for our tea when my mam broached the subject of shelter. 'Will you go and ask her, Dai? Or shall I?'

They still couldn't mention her name.

'Mrs Pugh, you mean?' I said. I felt that if we were going to ask her a favour, she was entitled to some identity, especially if that favour were granted. 'I'll ask her if you like,' I said.

'You won't put a foot in that house, girl,' my dad said.

I laughed. 'How am I going to get down to her cellar if I can't set a foot in her house?'

'None of your cheek, girl,' my dad said, and my mam and dad looked at each other.

I had put the name Pugh on the table, together with the purpose of our request. It was up to them to deal with it. And it would not be easy. For to tell the truth, Mrs Pugh was a terrace unmentionable. In short, she kept a bawdy house. Nobody knew how many girls she put up there for they were rarely seen on the street. Mrs Pugh's business was reliable and secure, as secure as that of an undertaker. Whatever the state of the economy, either in war or peace, there was never a shortage of death or sexual appetite. Moreover, the Americans had recently established a base some five miles out of the city and Mrs Pugh was doing a roaring trade. Part of the terrace's hostility was due to envy, but envy was nothing to boast about. So they cloaked the term in moral rectitude. 'Disgusting' was the common word that dropped in passing Mrs Pugh's house, and the fact that she kept her garden so beautifully designed only served to fuel their indignation. 'Disgusting,' they'd mutter, and made sure their children crossed the road to avoid her frontage.

But Mrs Pugh, apart from her financial advantages, had yet another asset. She owned the large corner house on the terrace, and that house had a cellar. Not an Anderson exposed to the elements and direct hits in the back yard, but a vast underground hideaway, protected by the solid structure of a whole house. In these perilous times, when civilian lives were at stake, Mrs Pugh's solid hole in the ground was pure gold.

'You did her a favour once,' my dad said. 'You're the only one in the street who's ever spoken to her.'

'She'd have forgotten about that,' my mam said.

'What favour, Mam?'

'Your mam sewed her blackout curtains at the beginning of the war. Didn't have to do it. Just offered, your mam did.'

'Well, she couldn't sew, could she,' my mam said.

'Didn't have to do it though.' My dad raised his voice. 'She owes us a favour.'

'I'll go and ask her then,' my mam said.

'I'll come with you, Mam.'

My dad offered to clear the table. He wouldn't go as far as doing the washing-up, but he wanted to see the back of us. He wanted to ensure that we had a safe place to lay our heads when the sirens screamed in the dark.

'I'll go and wash my face,' my mam said.

'Looks clean enough to me.' He knew my mam was playing for time. 'Go on. Get it over and done with.'

We put on our coats and walked arm in arm to the end of the terrace. When we reached the house, my mam looked around her. She did not want to be seen entering a house of sin, and especially with a nubile daughter on her arm. But mercifully there was no one around. In any case, it was getting dark and that was cover enough.

'You ring the bell,' my mam said, as if to do so was an act of heroism requiring courage and nerve. I pressed the bell and the chimes rang out inside. Posh, I thought. In those days, chime bells only rang in large houses with driveways and gardens and carriage lamps each side of the door. We waited and listened to the slippered footsteps inside.

Mrs Pugh herself answered the door. I knew it was Mrs Pugh, although we'd never met. But I'd heard stories of brothels and madams and although I didn't believe them, Mrs Pugh corresponded exactly to the picture of a madam I had imagined. She was, in a word, blowsy. And not only in dress. Her features were blowsy too, from her flabby chin, her loose and bulbous nose, her puffy eyes and shivering chin, to her very ankles, which bulged in a flop over her slippers. She was smiling.

'Why, Mrs Davies,' she said, 'this is a pleasant surprise.' Mrs Pugh was not Welsh. She was from London and though she'd lived most of her life in Cardiff, she was not infected by the Welsh accent or by its tone or syntax. It was the only aspect of Mrs Pugh that the terrace found excusable. At least she wasn't Welsh, and thus, with her sullied profession, she could not touch national pride. But English though she was, she was still beneath their contempt and not worth speaking to. This probably explained the singular welcome she gave to my mam and she asked us quickly indoors, sensitive to our fear of being spotted on her doorstep.

Inside, the house was a red wonderland. I stood in the hall and marvelled at it, at the red-flocked wallpaper and gold lamps on the wall. There was a scent too, vaguely familiar, then I connected it to the Evening in Paris perfume that my mam bought in Woolworth's and sometimes dabbed behind her ears. I suddenly saw my mam in a new light, and also in a new kind of loving. I followed them both into a fairyland parlour and it was difficult to accept that this house was in the same terrace as our own, and I prayed to God that it would be spared the bombs.

The parlour was wall-to-wall silk-carpeted. Well, it looked like silk. It shone like a lilac sun, and I automatically took off my shoes before entering. Mrs Pugh smiled. 'It's nice with bare feet,' she said. 'My girls never wear shoes.' She was quite open about her calling. Proud of it even, as well she might be I thought, since it had furnished her with silk carpets and flocked wallpaper. We sat on the pink sofa and she offered us a cup of tea, and a biscuit.

'Oh, no,' my mam said quickly, feeling she'd already been offered welcome enough, but I said, 'That would be very nice, Mrs Pugh,' because I didn't want her to feel we were too picky to eat or drink in her house.

She smiled at me again and rang a little gold bell on the table beside her. Very shortly a young girl came in. She was barefooted too, and wrapped in a silk kimono. I wanted to grow up to be like her, but then I realised that she was already no older than I. I wondered whether she was on her way to bed or whether she had just got up. Whatever, she smelt of sheer depravity, and I envied her.

'This is Petal,' Mrs Pugh was saying.

My mam nodded a reluctant greeting. Viewing my pleasure at the girl, she was clearly sorry she had brought me along.

'Could we have some tea, dear?' Mrs Pugh said. Petal smiled and left the room, and as she did so, she winked at me and I wanted to be her best friend.

'That was a terrible bomb last night,' Mrs Pugh was saying. 'We're all lucky to be alive.'

That was a cue, I thought, for my mam's request. But she didn't pick it up. Perhaps after viewing Petal, she'd had second thoughts. And how many more Petals were there? she must have wondered.

'The Watkins lost their home,' was all she said.

'Poor dears. But they weren't hurt,' Mrs Pugh said. 'And that's all that matters.'

There was a photograph album on one of the tables. Mrs Pugh caught me eyeing it.

'Look at it, dear, if you like,' she said. 'It's got pictures of all my girls.'

She clearly assumed that I knew what she was talking about and I saw my mam pale as I picked it up.

'They're only photos, Mam,' I said.

'And very pretty ones too.' Mrs Pugh defended her goods. 'And all of them Welsh,' she added pointedly, so that we could think again about the purity of our race. 'They come from the Valleys.'

There were two girls to each page and each photo had a name. Primrose, Lily, Petunia, Iris, Marigold, Daffodil, Snowdrop, Orchid. Hardly names from the Welsh mining valleys. Mrs Pugh had rebaptised them all and her house was a veritable Kew Gardens. I had never seen any of the girls in the terrace and I wondered if they all lived in Mrs Pugh's house and gathered together on bad nights in the cellar.

Soon Petal returned with the tea tray. The cups and saucers were spattered with roses and there was a rose plate of biscuits too, their clear provenance the American PX at the camp. Chocolate biscuits they were, the like of which we had not seen for many years. I longed for Mrs Pugh to take me in as one of her girls, to give me a kimono and a new flower name. I fancied myself as Hyacinth. Petal poured the tea and then withdrew, giving me another wink as she left. But it was a different wink this time, and something more than friendship, for I felt a strange tingling in my stomach. I hoped I would see Petal again soon.

'Did you want to see me about something special?' Mrs Pugh said as she passed the biscuits around.

'It's a favour I'm asking,' my mam began.

'Ask ahead.' Mrs Pugh took a biscuit herself and settled down to listen.

'You know last night,' my mam said, 'there was a direct hit on the Anderson in the Watkins' garden. Well, that's all we've got you see, an Anderson, and after last night, well . . . I don't trust it any more and I was wondering . . .'

'You'd like to use my cellar.' Mrs Pugh finished it off for her.

'I know it's a big favour I'm asking,' my mam said meekly.

'I haven't forgotten those blackout curtains you made for me,' Mrs Pugh said, 'and one good turn deserves another. You're welcome in my cellar, Mrs Davies, whenever the siren goes. Both of you. And Mr Davies too,' she laughed. 'If he's got enough courage.'

I laughed too. The thought of my dad in the midst of all those blossoms was quite ridiculous. He wouldn't have known where to put his eyes or his hands.

And so it was arranged. I prayed all evening for a siren but the night was clear and I went to bed and dreamed of Petal.

For a whole month after that, the Germans gave Cardiff a wide berth. And as a result people were less on the alert. Shelter stocks were rifled in the illusion that they would not be needed again. People went out in the blackout and torches' eyes spotted the streets. There were even small queues at cinemas. The picture house was what my mam and dad missed the most. Before the war, they would go every Saturday night to the Empire in Queen Street. My mam liked the organ best, that leviathan that rose from the pit in a halo of coloured lights. She would tremble in its boom of music that seemed to be made of melodic thunder. Sometimes the audience would sing along with the tunes until the lights faded and the organ sank into the bowels of the earth. That was the part that my mam liked best of all and she was always slightly disappointed when there was nothing more to do than watch the film. But she did like *The March of Time* and that usually came after the organ and gave the latest war news in sonorous tones and graphic pictures. After that she would perhaps doze a little and pick up only bits and pieces of the film, and wait until she got home when my dad would tell her the whole story.

It was during this lull in night raids that my dad suggested an outing to the pictures. It was a Saturday and we could go in the afternoon and come home for our supper. Then the pub, he said. My dad had clearly decided peace had been declared, and that life was back to normal. So we went out that afternoon, the three of us, and we didn't even bother to take our gas masks.

In those days, films were continuous. There was never any interval and it did not seem to disturb anyone to arrive in the middle of the main feature. One simply stayed in one's seat until its second time around, when the point of departure coincided with the point of arrival. Such a method required attentiveness and the exercise of memory, since the plot line of the film was interrupted by the organ and *The March of Time*. But my dad, who dozed through the organ and the news, was able to hold the story intact and retell it with clarity on our way home.

I don't remember the film very clearly, but I think it was called *Dangerous Moonlight*. When we arrived, about halfway through, we noticed that many in the audience were crying. You could hear the sniffling along the rows. For our part, we had nothing yet to cry for, but we got our hankies ready for the sadness we anticipated with such joy. And when, in the fullness of time, we reached the point in the story where we had come in, we opted to stay till the end and get our full tears' moneyworth.

It was dark when we left the picture house and we walked arm in arm to the tram stop. On our way, the air-raid siren wailed over the town. We stopped, the three of us, and listened. It had been so long since we had heard that noise that it took a few seconds to connect the sound with its possible consequences. As we stood there, we heard the drone of aeroplanes overhead. The siren was clearly very late and gave no time for to seek shelter. At that moment a tram trundled down the street, and I ran ahead of my mam and dad for to stop it and keep it waiting for them. At the time they were passing a hardware shop and I was irritated by their dawdling. As the tram approached I heard the bang and the shattering of glass. I looked back to where they had been and on that spot I saw two figures lying on the ground. My knees trembled.

'Hop on, girl, now. Be quick,' I could hear the tram conductor shouting. I could not stand firmly, so I crawled to the spot where the figures lay. The ground was covered with glass and bits of wood and brickwork, but I was careless of what injuries they might inflict. Other bodies lay in my path. They could have been dead, or perhaps they were pretending so that the pilots wouldn't think it was worth having another go at them. When I reached my mam and dad, they lay in that same stillness, and I prayed that they were feigning too.

'Mam,' I shouted. 'Dad.' I looked at them and I felt my nostril twitching. Their positions astonished me. My dad was lying on top of my mam and his overcoat was covered with splinters of glass. My mam lay beneath him, trembling. Not long ago, though it seemed like yesterday, I had been in exactly that position, but on my body was no gesture of protection. Rather one that was bent on my ruin. I bent over them as the blood flowed from my nostrils on to my dad's coat. 'They've gone,' I whispered.

My dad shifted. 'You all right, luv?' he said, lifting my mam to her feet.

'Your nose is bleeding,' my mam said, ascribing it to the air raid, but by now I knew the provenance of my blood, but it was convenient to have an air raid to blame.

'Knocked my nose,' I said, and she was satisfied with that and we huddled together for a moment in thanks for our survival.

'The buggers,' my dad said. 'There won't be any more trams. We'll have to walk.'

We heard the fire engines and the ambulances screeching.

Suddenly swarms of people were on the streets, rushing for shelter. We followed them to the crypt of a nearby church where an air-raid warden stood and ushered us inside.

'I should be on duty,' my dad said.

We huddled in the crypt. 'I hope your Auntie Annie's all right,' my mam said, fixing the kinship on me. She was our only relative and our only concern. For me, any thought of Auntie Annie came with the carving knife and in no way would my nose-bleeding abate. My mam had returned it over Christmas when my auntie came home a week before she intended. As I had prophesied, she had quarrelled with her daughter over the pudding course and she had caught a rare Boxing Day train from Abertillery. Next Christmas she would spend with us and bring the knife with her.

'Better listen to the news when we get home,' my dad said.

It was not long before the all-clear sounded and we heard the trams running once more.

'Hope the house is still there,' my mam said as we took the short cut down the back lane. For my part I would have taken the long way around, but there was no logical reason to suggest it. From the back of it, the terrace looked as we had left it. And so was the front but for the shreds of the Watkins' leavings still scattered across the road. The local news reported yet another raid on the docks and assured us that there was no injury or loss of life. The bombs had missed their targets and fallen into the water.

'We'll have our tea then,' my mam said, satisfied that my Auntie Annie was still with us. 'I'll pop over and see her tomorrow,' she said.

My nose had stopped bleeding by then, as if scores had been settled, though I knew that that was an illusion and that, for the rest of my life, my nose would pick its moments to remind me of an event that would never need a reminder.

My mam and dad were in a sudden good mood.

'Touch wood, we were lucky,' my dad said.

Any reference to our good fortune usually elicited from my mam a reminder of the terrible Mildred and her orphaned progeny.

'Must go and see Annie tomorrow,' she said. She was acknowledging that my Auntie Annie was her sister, and I think she must have forgotten Mildred's name.

They sipped their cocoa happily, but I could not share their content, for I was aware that I had missed my chance of being with Petal, and all those exotic blossoms in Mrs Pugh's cellar.

CHAPTER FOUR

But the news reporter was wrong. There *were* casualties and my Auntie Annie was one of them. Not exactly a bomb casualty, but the injuries she had sustained were no doubt due to the war. She had apparently been in her bedroom when the siren wailed and in her rush to get down to the shelter, she had fallen down the stairs and knocked herself out on the stone floor. All this information we received from a neighbour who, having failed to get a reply at Auntie Annie's door, looked through the letter box and saw my auntie spreadeagled on the floor, a clotted smudge of blood on her nightie.

'Took her to the Royal Infirmary they did,' the neighbour said.

We thanked her for her trouble, then got on the tram which took us back where we came from, for the hospital was but a stone's throw from our terrace. We found Auntie Annie in a ground-floor ward. She was sitting up in bed with a bandage around her head, with a bewildered look on her face as to her whereabouts. The sight of my mam and me confused her still further. She managed a smile but she was clearly in pain. I rushed over to her bed and took her hand.

'What happened to me?' she said.

My mam took her other hand and recounted the neighbour's tale.

'Did I have my knickers on?' she asked. Her modesty was her only concern.

'I'm sure you did,' my mam said, knowing the importance of knickers seeing as how she always wore them in bed herself.

'That's all right then,' Auntie Annie said, and she relaxed into the pillows as if, now that the knicker question was settled, she could get on with the business of getting better.

We sat and talked for a while, holding her hands. We told her about our visit to the pictures and about the poor Watkins' half-house. My mam confessed her loss of faith in the Anderson shelter but she made no mention of Mrs Pugh and she gave me a look that signalled that the house of blossoms was not to be part of our conversation.

Then my Auntie Annie said she was tired, and we kissed her goodbye and wished her better.

On our way out of the ward, my mam had a word with the Sister who told us that apart from a slight head wound, her patient was suffering from shock and that they would keep her in for the rest of the week. Once outside the hospital, my mam sat on a bench and, without any warning, she started to cry. 'What's the matter, Mam?' I said, though I knew the matter very well. My mam loved her elder sister, but only occasionally was she aware of it.

'Nothing's the matter,' she said, and rather roughly, because she had been caught red-handed with her feelings. 'I'm just relieved she's all right,' she said. 'Now we'll have our dinner, and you'd better get to school.'

I'd missed the morning with no compunction. Auntie Annie was more important than school. In those days, despite the coming exams, absenteeism was rife, especially after an air raid, and nobody questioned the reasons. My mam made me a dried egg omelette for my dinner and a cup of tea with broken biscuits.

'I'll make a cake for your Auntie Annie,' she said. 'I'll take it to her tomorrow.'

There were no more raids that week, and at the end of it, we took Auntie Annie back to her house. She refused to come and stay with us for a while. Wanted her own bed for a change, she said. So we let her be, and she promised she would visit us during the week.

The following Sunday, I went to tea with my best friend, Molly Smith. When I say 'best', that's what I mean, but she wasn't 'best' enough for me to tell her about the back lane. Nobody could ever be best enough for that. In any case, of late, I hadn't thought too much about it, until on my way home, and passing Mrs Pugh's house, I saw two policemen at her door. The sight of the Law was an obvious connection with my crime, but that was but a tenuous connection with Mrs Pugh. I knew that brothels were illegal and that it would be quite natural to find the Law on her doorstep. But I had heard that the police often viewed such an enterprise with a blind eye, in return for favours which were usually in kind. But if the Law had come for its pay-off, it would hardly be wearing its uniform. I dawdled as inconspicuously as I was able, and then Mrs Pugh answered the door, her blowsiness filling its frame. I caught her smile and then I was forced to walk on and to speculate on the matter of their investigation. As soon as I got home I reported the event to my mam, who I knew would pass it on to my dad, and between them they would make it their business to find out why the police, who surely had better things to do in war-time, would pay a uniformed visit to the house above the cellar on the corner. I longed for an air raid and a cellar conversation which might explain the visit. I don't know why I was so curious about it. After all, it was none of my business. Yet somehow I felt connected to it, or rather to the back lane of it. I had a crawling feeling in my stomach that that visit had something to do with me, and when my nostril began to tremble, I knew that the connection was well and truly founded. My appetite for an air raid waned considerably and when the siren shrilled that evening, I was reluctant to go to the cellar. But my mam insisted. She was curious about the Law's visit and I began to regret that I'd reported it.

We reached the corner house before the siren had wailed to a stop. We rang the bell and the door was answered immediately as if Mrs Pugh was waiting behind it. Which she was, but not necessarily for us, but it was there, behind the front door, that she was wont to take her stand to usher and count her flock into the cellar below. And we were guided into the queue of blossoms as they descended the cellar steps.

Shortly we were all settled below. There were benches around the cellar, but no blossom took a seat. They were waiting for the descent of their madam. She stood at the top of the cellar stairs, looked below and made a quick head-count, then she shut the door behind her and descended. Once she had seated herself, the blossoms took their places. She motioned to my mam and me for to sit by her side. For a while there was a silence in the cellar. It seemed that madam had to speak first before the girls could loosen their tongues. I looked around for Petal. All the girls were wearing identical kimonos, and in such uniform, they tended sadly to look the same. But one of them smiled at me, which was how I knew she was Petal.

'Now quietly, girls.' Mrs Pugh broke the silence. 'Talk in whispers. We mustn't miss what's going on outside.'

The girls started off with a few giggles and then they settled into whispered conversation, and I felt very much an outsider.

'I saw you today,' Mrs Pugh said to me. 'You were passing my house when I had that visit.'

'What visit?' my mam asked innocently, and I was grateful to her that she hadn't shopped me.

'I had the police today,' Mrs Pugh whispered.

I was surprised that she seemed to have no wish to keep the visit quiet, and my mam was glad of it because it saved her the trouble of undercover investigation.

'What did they want?' my mam whispered back.

'They came about that murder in the lane. They said a witness had come forward, and given them cause to believe that the victim had made a visit to my house shortly before he was murdered.'

I looked at her. Her brow was furrowed. She seemed to be thinking of what to say next. It was as if she was parroting the police terminology: 'a witness had come forward'; 'they had cause to believe'. She was mindlessly reproducing their official words.

'I asked them in,' she said, slipping back into her own vernacular. 'After all, I couldn't keep them talking on the doorstep. I gave them a cup of tea. I don't know why. I didn't feel guilty or anything. *Why* should I be nice to them? They showed me a sheaf of pictures of the dead man. And I remembered him. I recognised him from the photos. I remembered him very well in fact, and for a very special reason. He didn't have enough money to pay. He told me he was on leave. He gave me some sob story about being in the jungle and I said, What jungle?, but he didn't seem to know what jungle he'd been in. I told him that if he didn't have enough money, he would have to go, jungle or no jungle. He argued for a while, but in the end he left. I remember he kicked the door as he went out. And there he was, on the photograph they showed me. Then they asked me what day he had visited and what time. Well, I have people coming through my door all hours of the day and I couldn't be expected to remember the exact time of his visit. They tried to get me to confess to it being on the twenty-third, but I was not going to do them any favours. I couldn't remember the date and I wasn't going to bear false witness.'

Again she was back in the Law's vernacular.

'The cheek of it,' my mam said. 'Would you believe it?'

My nostril twitched, but it didn't worry me. I knew there would be no blood. I was getting to know my nose pretty well and I knew that it would prickle only at a gentle reminder of my crime. It would wait for a direct and traumatic association with the back lane before it would bleed its protest.

'I helped them as much as I could,' Mrs Pugh was saying. 'I couldn't do any more. I just hope they won't come here again. It's not good for my business.'

I looked across at Petal but she was talking to the blossom beside her. There were about six of them in all, and I could only guess at their names, for they all looked the same, dressed as they were in their working kimono clothes. I'd never seen any of them coming or going in the street so I presumed they were all full-time givers of pleasure, and that they lived in the house and shared their rooms and secrets. I imagined they giggled a lot, and I envied them, and the thought crossed my mind that after my exams I would send in an application to join Mrs Pugh's seraglio. Though I would have a bit of explaining to do to my mam and dad.

When the all-clear went, shortly after Mrs Pugh's recital, we went back home, and in my room, I went over the matter of Mrs Pugh's story. I had to recognise that it contained a certain and terrible logic. That it was quite rational that a man who'd been turned away from a pleasure house, humiliated by his poverty, yet with his sexual appetite still raging, and no doubt fuelled by his rage, it seemed logical that he should vent his spleen and his sperm on the first available target. Perhaps that was me. For his appetite and his intent, I was in the right place at the right time. I could have been any woman, and from any place. My nostril itched again at this speculation.

I was in a bad mood and Mrs Pugh's revelations had not pleased me, and Petal had not even smiled in my direction. I would make an early night, I thought, and escape into sleep, aided and abetted by a few paragraphs of *Middlemarch*. I was alone in the house. My mam had slipped over to the Infirmary to deliver a home-made cake to Auntie Annie, and my dad was out on duty. I had done all my weekend revision and there was nothing to stop me going to bed, but much as I wanted to escape into sleep, I knew that Mrs Pugh's report would over-come even *Middlemarch*. The enquiries into the back lane murder were too close to home. If my surmise was correct, it was easy to establish the victim's motive, but that gave no clue as to the motive of his assassin. There had been no evidence of attempted rape in the back lane, and it was unlikely that such a possibility had crossed the Law's mind. I talked myself into believing that they wouldn't visit Mrs Pugh again. But the fol-lowing day, on my way home from school, I saw the shadow of two of them in Mrs Pugh's wonderland parlour. We would have to wait for another siren before receiving Mrs Pugh's lat-est bulletin.

But the nights were quiet, and on one of them my mam and dad went down to the pub. They would not risk the cinema again. It was too far from home. Shortly after they had left, the front door bell rang. I wondered who it might be and I had a vague hope it might be Petal. But it was a caller very far from Petal. Mr Griffiths stood at the door and in his chief warden uniform, and for some disturbing reason, my nostril began to twitch. I had come to think of my nose as a reliable barometer of my feelings. Its twitch was a warning, like any air-raid siren. There may or may not be a bomb, as there may or may not be blood. I couldn't fathom any connection between my nose and Mr Griffiths. He must have known my dad was out. My dad had to report to him before he went any-where, so that his whereabouts were known. I asked him in. I don't know why, but it seemed impolite to keep him standing on the doorstep.

'Just wanted a word with your father,' he said, and my nostril twitched like a jumping flea.

'He's out,' I said. 'Down the pub with my mam. Didn't he tell you?'

'Must have slipped my mind,' he said.

I didn't ask him to sit down. I wanted him to go. If he stayed, there'd be trouble. My nose told me so. But he didn't make to take a chair. Instead he came towards me.

'There's a handsome young woman you're growing up to be,' he said.

Nobody had ever called me woman before, and at my age it had a faintly dubious ring. I giggled and backed away. But he pounced on me, his hand on my frayed gymslip, the corner grocer's playground, and his other hand up my skirt and into my knickers. I wondered whether there was something the matter with me that I invited such behaviour. But I would not allow myself to think in that way for I knew it would lead to ruination. I was shivering with rage, and I kicked him with fury, his ankles, his legs. My kicking was wild, random. I did not deliberately aim for his groin. It just happened to get in the way of one of my high kicks. He groaned and doubled up in pain, and I kicked him again and again and again, and slowly with infinite pleasure.

'Get out,' I shouted at him. I wasn't afraid. I knew he was in no condition to attack me. I pushed his groaning body towards the front door and I opened it wide.

'I'll tell my mam on you,' I shouted. 'And my dad too.'

He struggled to his feet. He was terrified that passers-by would hear. I watched him stumble across the road. 'Why don't you go to Mrs Pugh's on the corner?' I shouted after him. And then, as an afterthought, 'I'll tell Mrs Griffiths on you too,' I said.

I slammed the door after him and noticed that my nose had stopped twitching. But I was trembling and I had to sit down to calm myself. I was suddenly overcome by a pall of depression, that I seemed to be an obvious target for man's assault. I tried to comfort myself with the thought of Mr Griffiths' terror of being discovered. Of the gossip in the neighbourhood and even perhaps, as a result, the loss of his precious chieftainship of the regions' wardens. But these thoughts did little to lift my depression. I had threatened that I would tell my mam and dad on him. And even Mrs Griffiths herself. But I hadn't meant that latter threat. I just wanted to frighten him a little bit more. I wondered now how serious were my other threats. I was wary of telling my dad. He would not believe it. In his heart he might, and he would seethe with impotent fury. But he would choose not to believe it because he couldn't afford to. Mr Griffiths was his superior, and if he wholly believed in my accusation, it would behove him to react, and that reaction might inflame animosity in the whole terrace. Mr Griffiths would deny it, of course, then my dad would be faced with the possibility that his daughter was a liar. Or worse. If she was not lying, she had simply asked for it, and the good and pious and superior Mr Griffiths had weakened. It was this latter possibility that troubled me most. I had no doubt that my dad loved me, but not perhaps to the point of betraying his own gender. So I would *not* tell my dad, I decided, but I would most certainly tell my mam. She would have no problem with believing my story. She thought all men were after the same thing. I'd often heard her say it, and always in a joke, but that was only to cover her earnest opinion. Yes, she would believe me all right and she would possibly tell my dad, and make him believe it too. Then together we would have to deal with the problem and I could assume the status of the injured party and innocent victim, which I truly was.

It was only nine o'clock. It would be at least two hours before they would come home, and I desperately needed to get my story off my chest. I would go down to the pub, I decided.

I was under age so I wouldn't be allowed to go inside, but I could nip in quietly and unseen and call my mam outside. I put on my coat and took my torch. The terrace was quiet. It was only a few minutes' walk to the pub, but I took my time, rehearsing my story on the way. But it struck me that if I felt the need for rehearsal, I might indeed be lying and there was a terrible moment when I thought I had imagined it all. So I started to run, not easy in a blackout, and despite my speed, it took a little time to cover the three road junctions between the terrace and the public house. I stopped outside it to catch my breath, then I opened the door a chink, and peeped inside. My mam and my dad were standing at the bar, and between them stood the unexpected. Mr Griffiths, raising his glass in a belated alibi. I was incensed and I screamed, 'Mam!' across the room. My cry was greeted with a sudden silence and a turning of many eyes towards my trembling person. Amongst them, the frightened stare of Mr Griffiths. Nonplussed. Terrified. Then my mam rushed towards me. I noticed that my dad made to follow her, but Mr Griffiths held him back with a restraining arm, and at that moment, I decided to tell my dad after all.

My mam closed the saloon door behind her. 'What's the matter, girl?' she said. 'What's happened?'

'It's all right,' I said. 'I'm all right. I wasn't hurt.'

'Who hurt you, luv?' she said, holding me.

I started to cry with the relief of her consolation. Then, between sobs, the whole story drained out of me.

'The bugger,' she almost screamed when I had done. 'Stay here. I'll go and get your dad.'

I wanted to peep through the door once more to view yet again Mr Griffiths' vain restraint, but my weakness overcame my curiosity. For I felt spent and feeble. My lethargy held me on the spot where my mam had left me. Shortly my dad appeared in my mam's tow.

'Tell him,' she said to me. 'Tell your dad what you told me.'

But I couldn't. It wasn't that I feared his disbelief. I was simply embarrassed. It was women's talk I had to speak, and my dad would be as embarrassed by it as I.

'Then I'll tell him,' my mam said.

I moved away a little and turned my back. I didn't want to see or hear his reaction. But after a while, I heard it. Couldn't help it, for he was shouting like a madman.

'I'll kill him,' he said.

I wanted to rush to him and to hug him for his faith. But that was women's ways and would have embarrassed him too. My mam came and hugged me and we watched my dad as he tore back into the pub and we waited for the clap of thunder. But rage, especially in one like my dad, could be silent too, and shortly he stepped out of the pub with Mr Griffiths at his side. My dad had made no show at the bar. He had simply asked Mr Griffiths to accompany him outside with that policeman's euphemism that heralded a brutal attack.

'The missus and I would like a word with you,' he said softly. 'Go home, luv,' he said to me. 'We won't be long.'

I was glad to be given leave. I didn't want to view Mr Griffiths' righteous indignation, or to hear his furious denials. For I had no doubt as to the manner of his reaction. By now I was crying my heart out, but out of my rage, I found enough strength to turn round and shout, 'And I'm going to tell Mrs Griffiths too.' And moreover I meant it. I would call in at her house on my way home and tell it plain on her doorstep. And I would tell other neighbours too, though not Mr Thomas perhaps. I might even tell Mrs Pugh. All that would be as good as putting it in the *Echo*. But these thoughts did not console me and I was sobbing still, as I rang Mrs Griffiths' bell, with no notion of what I was going to say but with an overwhelming need to pour it into her astonished ear.

She opened the door gingerly. Her hair was tousled, and I noted her dressing gown. I had clearly got her out of bed. No bad thing, since she would need all her wits about her to stomach her husband's homecoming.

'What d'you want, girl, this time of night?' she said crossly. 'And what are you crying about?'

'I just wanted to tell you,' I said, and I was astonished at the calm in my voice. 'I wanted to tell you,' I said again, 'that your husband came to our house this evening and he tried to interfere with me.' My nose twitched at the phrase, but it didn't faze me. I needed to make myself quite clear to Mrs Griffiths, who stood there, mouth agape, without the strength to strike me. 'He grabbed me,' I hurried on, 'and he put his hand up my knickers. I kicked him in a terrible place and I threw him out of the house.'

She stared at me and began to tremble.

'That's all,' I said, and I turned away. I had reached her gate before she found her voice.

'You dirty little slut,' she shouted. 'You filthy little liar.'

I heard the tears in her voice which told me that she had believed every word I had said. I let myself into our house, and slammed the door to shut out the echo of her broken fury, and I sat down at the kitchen table and I wept my relief away. And shortly I felt better and I went to put the kettle on so that the tea would be ready for my mam and dad. From the kitchen I heard their key in the lock and suddenly I didn't want to see them. All that I was aware of was that I had got them both into deep trouble and perhaps it would have been better if I'd kept my mouth shut. I expected them to be cross with me. But my mam came into the kitchen straight away and put her arms around me. 'He'll never do it again, I promise you,' she said.

But that was not what I wanted to hear. It had been *done* and what was she going to do about that?

'I'm going to bed,' my dad shouted from the hall.

I forgave him. He was too embarrassed to face me. He had done all he could in his fashion. He had been brave beyond all my expectations.

'What did he say?' I asked.

'Said he didn't do it,' my mam said. 'Said you'd made it all up. "Better watch that girl of yours," he said. Then your dad, bless him, because he didn't have any words, just punched him in the face. Not once but twice, so he got a bloody nose and a black eye as well. Looked a treat he did. Don't know what he's going to tell Mrs Griffiths.'

'She knows,' I said. 'I told her.'

'When?'

'On my way home.'

My mam didn't quite know how to take this new development, but she was clearly disturbed by it.

'Well, he won't have to explain then, will he,' was all she could say.

'What will happen now?' I dared to ask.

'Nothing,' my mam said. 'It'll get around, I suppose. There were people outside the pub watching. Some from the terrace. They heard it all. I don't know how he's going to show his face. Still, we don't have to worry about that.' She paused, loosening her grasp on my shoulder. 'Bronwen, luv,' she said, and I could sense what was troubling her, 'he didn't . . . well . . . he didn't put his thing in, did he?'

'No, Mam,' I said. 'I kicked him before he could do anything.'

'Well, that's a blessing then,' she said.

She would hardly have called it a blessing; a miracle, rather, had she had an inkling of my history. How what with the corner grocer, the back lane, and now Mr Griffiths, my nether quarters had been so rudely interfered with. Nor could she know how staunchly I had repelled each man's invasion, and one to his deathly cost. But I was still a virgin, and that was my triumph, and I longed to share it with her. But such a sharing was impossible.

When I went to school the next morning, I was obliged to take the short cut through the back lane. I could not risk the front of the terrace with the possibility of running into Mr or Mrs Griffiths. And then it occurred to me that they were possibly doing exactly the same on their sorties, taking their own back lane for cover, and I decided I would come home via the terrace and bugger them. After all, I was not the guilty party.

I was anxious to know why the Law had made a second visit to Mrs Pugh's house, and I decided to tell my mam about what I had seen behind Mrs Pugh's parlour curtains. When I got home, I found her wrapping a small sponge cake, a twin to the one she'd made for my Auntie Annie.

'Had some of the mixture left,' she explained. 'Thought I'd give it to Mrs Pugh. Kind of thank you, like.'

'I'll come with you,' I said. I knew my mam was always glad of company and it would give me an opportunity to relate my window viewing. On our way to the end of the terrace, I told her.

'What d'you think they were doing there? I said.

'Mrs Pugh'll tell us, I'm sure,' my mam said. 'She's always very forthcoming.'

She gave us a blowsy welcome and was overjoyed with the cake. 'Haven't tasted a real English sponge for years,' she said. 'I'll cut it now with our tea. It's brewed already. Daisy,' she called, I was sorely disappointed. Petal was clearly off duty. The kiminoed Daisy came into the room, smiling.

'Could you bring two more cups, dear?' Mrs Pugh said. 'And two plates. We're about to have a great treat. And if you're a good girl,' she laughed, 'we'll leave some for you. Had visitors again,' Mrs Pugh said as she started pouring. She needed no prodding. She waited for Daisy to return with the cups, and when she left, 'The same two policemen who came before,' she went on.

'What a nuisance,' my mam said, donating a sympathetic ear in the hope of returns. 'What did they want this time?'

'Same as last,' Mrs Pugh said. 'I don't know why they connect this house with that murder.'

I could have told her why, and with infinite logic, and I experienced a fleeting sense of power.

'They wanted to know exactly who had been here that night. So I described my regulars. It was a fair bet that some of them were here. Only descriptions because naturally I don't ask for names. I had the impression that it was routine, that the poor devils didn't have a clue where to look next. Whoever killed him's probably left the country by now.'

'There's nowhere much to go,' my mam said. 'Not during a war, at any rate.'

'It'll be one of those unsolved mysteries,' Mrs Pugh said. 'In time they'll forget all about it.'

'Duw, his poor wife,' my mam said. She was Mildreding again.

'Finding the murderer's not going to bring him back,' I said, my nostril twitching.

'Must give some satisfaction though. Like to see him hung myself,' my mam said.

I could not help but wince at her grammar. The past participle of 'hang' was 'hanged', and I was a grammar prig, even if it came to the gallows.

'I don't believe in the death sentence myself,' Mrs Pugh said. 'There can always be some terrible mistake.'

I prayed that no terrible mistake would be made on my behalf, though I would have weathered that too if called upon, rather than give myself up.

I clung to my mam's arm on our way back to our house. I was sorry she believed in capital punishment, and I was confident I would never give her a personal reason to change her mind. We were halfway to our house when Mr Griffiths came out of his. And was about to cross the road. But as his foot left the kerb, he recognised the enemy terrain on the other side. Rather than turn back in obvious retreat, he chose the no man's land of the road between. He stared straight in front of him as he walked. As we levelled, my mam spat into the kerb, and though he didn't see it, he must have heard it and been mortified. I'd never seen my mam spit before. There was nothing vulgar about it. It was merely her declaration of a war of attrition.

CHAPTER FIVE

Within two weeks, the whole terrace was spitting. Poor Mr Griffiths could well have used a brolly. For word of his 'interference' had spread; had first been disbelieved, and then, with gossip and rumour, and finally out of their need for salivating scandal, the whole of the street accepted it as truth. He still remained chief air raid warden and the other men in the street, with the exception of my dad, that is, obeyed his orders, despite their better halves' disapproval. For the men, it was gender loyalty. If they couldn't stick together on the battlefield, an arena for which they were too old to gain admittance, then they would do it in the street. But as the weeks passed, the women lost interest in the story, and their disgust and scorn faded, to the extent that they began to question the whole tale and by the time I broke up for my Easter holidays, it was as if it had never happened. For none of them believed one word of it.

Except for my mam and dad. They kept faith with it, and my mam never let up on her spitting.

Since that last policemen's visit to Mrs Pugh, there had been no further bulletins on the back lane. It was as if they'd given up their investigation and the Splott murder would enter the files of 'Crimes Unsolved'. And that was all right by

me, because I would never lift a finger in helping them solve
it.

In the like manner of the Christmas lull in manoeuvres, the
Easter holiday marked an unspoken truce and me and my
mam and dad took our hamper and went for a picnic on
Caerphilly mountain. And it was like it was normal, without
any war or back lane or anything. I think my mam had forgotten Mildred's name, and my nostril hadn't twitched for
weeks. So I was pretty well clobbered to come home and find
two policemen waiting on our doorstep, and in full view of the
terrace too, with a chink in all the net curtains and the watchful eyes waiting for us to come home. And my nose sirened.

'What can they want, for God's sake?' my mam said.

I could have told her. Yet I couldn't understand it. There
was no reason at all, apart from architecture, to link our house
with the back lane. And on a Good Friday too. You'd think
they'd have more respect.

'What is it?' my dad said as he reached for his keys.

'Mr and Mrs Davies?' one of the policemen said.

'That's right.' My mam's voice was trembling.

'Can we come inside?'

My dad was glad to get them out of public view. We stood
awkwardly in the hall.

'We've come about Annie Dixon, your sister.'

My mam started to cry.

'What is it?' my dad said.

'Now she's all right. She's going to be all right. She was run
over. A bicycle, would you believe, in City Road. We had to
take her to hospital. The Infirmary. She's all right, mind. Bit
of a shock. And a broken leg. She told us to tell you.'

'But she's all right?' my mam whispered.

'You can go and see for yourself. Bertram Ward. On the
ground floor.'

I could have kissed them. Both of them. I was in the clear

and my nostril was serene. I wanted to run out into the street and tell them our house was innocent and see those net curtains drop with disappointment.

'Better go now then,' my mam said.

So we didn't take off our coats. We wrapped up the cake and biscuits left in the hamper and we gave the Law time to get out of the terrace, then the three of us left the house, bold as brass, because we had nothing to hide.

My accident-prone Auntie Annie was lying in her bed, propped up by pillows. Part of the covering sheet was folded back to reveal her plastered limb and her bare bunioned toes stuck out as living-flesh proof that the leg was still there. She looked sad, pale, and slightly ashamed of herself.

'What mischief have you been up to then?' my dad said, trying to make a joke of it all.

She gave a crooked smile. 'My fault it was. Wasn't looking,' she said. 'Still, could have been worse. Got to stay here for a week, the doctor says. And the plaster for six weeks. Don't know how I'm going to manage.'

'Don't worry about that,' my mam said. 'Want us to tell your Blodwen? We could write to her tonight.'

Auntie Annie didn't answer immediately. The subject of her daughter was mined territory. 'There won't be any post over Easter,' she said, in an attempt to use the Royal Mail to excuse her indecision.

'I think she ought to know,' my mam said.

'I'm not dying yet.'

Only four little words, but they spoke volumes of the pain of her daughter's neglect.

'Of course you're not.' My dad put his hand on the plaster – it was easier than touching her flesh, and it carried as much affection – 'but she ought to be told.'

'We're not friendly. You know that. She'd think it was blackmail.'

My mam was angry. 'But it's not. You've got the plaster to prove it.'

I saw tears gather on Auntie Annie's eyelids. 'I'd like to see her,' she managed to say.

'We'll arrange all that,' my dad said.

From the hospital, we went straight to the police station. They had telephones there, and policemen in Abertillery. They could go to Blodwen's house as easily as they had come to ours. Blodwen could be with her mam in the morning.

'She's never going to manage on her own in that house. With all those stairs and her on crutches,' my dad said. 'Have to come and live with us.'

'She'd be better off with Blodwen in Abertillery,' my mam said. 'No bombs up there.'

But I knew that my Auntie Annie would gladly risk the bombs sooner than stay in Blodwen's house with her drunken husband and unruly kids. And the rift between her and Blodwen would never mend, not as long as she stayed with that Gareth anyway. My auntie had told her, years ago, when she was getting married. 'You're making a big mistake, Blod my girl,' she had said. And so had my Uncle Gwyn. He was alive then. But Blodwen didn't listen and over the years she realised her mam had been right and it was that that she could never forgive her for. Though my Auntie Annie, give her her due, she'd never said, 'I told you so.' She just tried to make the best of things. She wasn't angry with Blodwen. She was just sorry for her and her miserable life, and at those times she missed my Uncle Gwyn most of all because she had to shoulder the burden of sorrow alone.

'You'll come and live with us,' my dad said again. 'No argument.'

I loved my Auntie Annie and I would have been happy for her to live with us. For ever even. But at that moment, I wondered how she could negotiate the steps to Mrs Pugh's cellar.

We would have to go back to the Anderson again, and there would never be an opportunity to see Petal. I often wondered about Petal. I couldn't understand the nature of my attraction towards her. I dared to think that it was her profession that excited me. I was certain that she didn't like men. Indeed she probably hated them. She saw them only as a means of making a living. Somehow or other, I saw myself in that role and I wondered if I could play it and still remain a virgin. For after the back lane, that was my life's ambition. After the struggle I had put up to keep myself intact, it would have been a pity to waste that triumph. But I thought that in Petal's job I would have to succumb. Perhaps I could be a madam, I thought. Like Mrs Pugh. You could be a madam and still remain intact. And still be rich at the expense of men. And still have Petal around for one's own enjoyment. Yes. That was what I would be when I grew up. A madam, with a large house on a windy corner. Having decided what course my life should take, I didn't mind settling for the time being for the Anderson shelter. 'Yes, of course,' I said. 'You've got to come and stay with us, Auntie Annie.'

'We'll make up a bed in the parlour,' my dad said.

'You're a perfect daughter,' Auntie Annie said to me. 'The best of them.' I didn't take that as much of a compliment, seeing as how her standard of comparison was much wanting. 'And always will be,' she went on, and I wondered if I could still be a good daughter and a madam at the same time.

We left her much cheered and we went straight to the police station to make the Abertillery arrangement.

'I hope we're doing the right thing,' my mam said. 'There's something about that Blodwen that doesn't make you feel any better.'

'She's her daughter,' my dad insisted. 'Who knows? A hospital's a good place to mend quarrels.'

Funny man, my dad. Sometimes he said things you never

expected of him. My mam was a bit like that too. Full of surprises. Both of them.

We all kept clear of the hospital the next day, not wanting to witness their fraught and perilous encounter. Yet we were itching to know what had happened. 'Maybe she'll come over from the hospital,' my mam said, and she made an extra rissole for supper in case Blodwen decided on a visit. So we were prepared. When the front door bell rang, we were just sitting down to eat. I didn't know my cousin very well. She was much older than me and I didn't see her often. My attitude towards her was coloured by my Auntie Annie's sorrow. And therefore prejudiced. My mam told me to answer the door.

I didn't expect to find her so pretty. Or to be looking so well and content. From my Auntie Annie's stories, I'd imagined a battered wife and a downtrodden, helpless mother. But she was far from either of those. The first thing I noticed was her nylon stockings which spoke of an American base in the region of Abertillery. And of many other things too. Her clothing was smart, a London look, I thought, though I'd never been there, but I'd heard about the metropolitan chic. I felt very shabby beside her.

'Aren't you going to ask me in then?' she said.

I must have been staring at her for quite a while. 'Hullo, Blodwen,' I said. 'Come in and nice to see you.'

'There's big you've grown,' she said, eyeing the small sandhills on my chest.

I turned away and led her down the hall. 'Blodwen's here,' I shouted.

My mam made every effort to welcome her, for she too had been influenced by her sister's stories.

'How's your mam then?' was all my dad could say.

'We had a very nice visit,' Blodwen said, and pointedly, 'Very friendly. I've asked her to come and live with me in

Abertillery.' She declared it as if she thought that only with such a promise could she earn her supper.

'There's nice,' my dad said. 'Come and sit down, luv.'

My mam didn't know whether Abertillery was good or bad news. She was confused and she decided to let it pass. She put a plate of food at Blodwen's place. 'Eat it while it's hot,' she said.

Blodwen searched in her handbag. 'I've brought you something for pudding,' she said. She placed two Hershey chocolate bars on the table.

If my mam and dad hadn't yet noticed the nylons, there was no mistaking the provenance of the chocolate bars. And both of them silently drew the same conclusion. Blodwen Dixon had gone a-whoring. And brazen about it too.

But I warmed towards her. Partly because, like my parents, I suspected she was in the same business as Petal. And in any case, what with a drunken husband and uncontrollable kids, she was entitled to some pleasure on the side. If you could call it pleasure, that is. But she still had the bonus of chocolate and nylons to show for it. I wondered what present she had brought my Auntie Annie.

'Did your mam think that was a good idea?' my dad asked.

'She doesn't want to come,' Blodwen said, and the relief in her voice was unmistakable. 'I begged her,' she said, 'but she said no, she wouldn't. She was glad I'd asked her though.'

'She'll come and live with us,' my dad said. After his sight of the Hershey bars, he didn't think that Blodwen's way of life would sit well with his sister-in-law, and she'd be back in Cardiff, and on crutches, within the week.

'When are you going back?' my mam asked.

'Last bus tonight.' Blodwen said. 'But I'll be down again in the week. Bring the girls perhaps. They're off school now, and she'd like to see them.'

So would I, I thought, and wondered whether they would be wearing nylons too.

'I took my mam a food parcel,' Blodwen said, 'so she won't be wanting.'

'A food parcel?' my mam said. 'What's that when the cows come home?'

'Some cakes, biscuits, fruit and chocolate. Nice things.'

'Must have cost you some coupons, that lot,' my dad said.

'There are ways of getting stuff if you want it. You don't need coupons.' Blodwen was not even smiling. There was no wink in her voice. It was flat and matter-of-fact. 'There's a war on,' she said. 'We all have to do our bit. Like Churchill says.'

I was sure that Mr Churchill did not have Blodwen's sense of 'bit' in mind when he called for blood, sweat and tears. But her 'bit' had provided her mam with a food parcel and Auntie Annie would not question where it came from because she wouldn't want to know.

I was just about to clear the table when the siren screamed. Blodwen was terrified. She'd never heard such a noise in Abertillery. 'What do we do? What do we *do*?' she panicked.

'Well, I'm going on duty,' my dad said, then added pointedly, 'We all have to do our bit.'

Poor Blodwen feared for her life, but for my part, I was delighted. I would see Petal again.

'Come on, let's go,' my mam said.

'Where, for God's sake?' Blodwen was rooted to her chair in terror.

'Down the street to the cellar,' I said.

'Out?' Blodwen was incredulous.

I dragged her to her feet. We pulled on our coats and rushed to the corner. My mam rang the door bell.

'Door's open,' Mrs Pugh's blowsy voice rang out from inside. We pushed our way into the hall and shut the door after us. Mrs Pugh stood there marshalling her blossoms underground. After the last of the girls, three soldiers in American uniform descended.

'We'd better be on our way,' one of them said.

'Oh no, you'd better not.' Mrs Pugh was firm. 'Down you go with the rest of them,' she said and sheepishly they obeyed her and followed the girls below.

I looked at Blodwen's face. It clearly could not believe what it was seeing. And half believing, she was appalled.

'What are we doing in a place like this?' she whispered to my mam.

'It's got a cellar. That's why.' My mam was a bit short with her, then she turned to Mrs Pugh. 'Got a visitor. My niece,' she said. 'Hope you don't mind.'

'Standing room only,' Mrs Pugh laughed and ushered us downstairs.

It was indeed standing room and one of the blossoms offered my mam her part of the bench. I was glad no one offered a seat to me. I did not want their respect. I did not want them to think I was any better or even different from themselves. But Blodwen was disappointed to be ignored seat-wise because, despite her nylon stockings and Hershey bars, she felt infinitely superior. She leaned against the whitewashed wall, disgusted.

It was quiet in the cellar, without even an echo of anti-aircraft fire.

'False alarm,' one of the girls said.

Just then there was a loud burst of cracking gunshot.

'I hope Dai's all right,' my mam whispered.

'It's the docks again, poor buggers,' Mrs Pugh said. 'Not many people down there any more. No children anyway. They've all been evacuated.'

'We've got some evacuees in Abertillery,' Blodwen donated. She was insistent on doing her 'bit', even vicariously. 'Come from Cardiff, some of them.'

I don't know whether she expected us to say thank you, but she seemed put out by the lack of response to her claim.

'We thought of sending our Bronwen,' my mam said. 'Some

classes in her school have gone to Tonypandy. But she didn't
want to go, did you, luv?'

'Some of them go and then they come back,' Mrs Pugh
said. 'They get homesick, you see.'

'I think the Welsh are some people,' one of the soldiers
drawled with admiration, and the whole cellar basked in this
foreigner's praise and modestly held their tongues.

The anti-aircraft fire continued and it sounded as if it would
be a long night.

'They'll be worried about me back home,' Blodwen said.
'Have to get back first bus in the morning.'

So Blodwen would sleep with us that night, or what would
be left of it. And that would give her ample time for her
offended post-mortem on Mrs Pugh's safety arrangements.

But the night dragged on, with the occasional lull and inter-
mittent fire. It was still quiet in the cellar. I think that the
presence of the American soldiers, those golden geese from
across the ocean, was a restraint on the girls' usual giggles and
whisperings. Petal crouched in a corner. She was smiling but
without much mirth. The smile was part and parcel of her job,
as fixed as her kimono. I realised then, and with some sadness,
that she had never really smiled at me as at someone in particular. It was her standard and rather sad greeting to the
world in general.

When the all-clear went, it was almost morning.

'No point in going to bed now,' Blodwen said. 'Sleep on the
bus I will.'

But my mam insisted she get some breakfast down her
before she left, so we sat around the kitchen table, the three of
us – my dad hadn't yet come home – and Blodwen started on
Mrs Pugh's establishment.

'Disgusting, I thought,' she said. 'And in your own back
yard too.' She stared at me as if it were my fault. 'And brazen
with it as well,' she added.

'They're only doing their bit,' my mam said. 'Like every-body else.'

But Blodwen wasn't going to have her 'bit' tainted by theirs. 'But they do it for *money*,' she said.

For my part I saw little difference between money and nylons, but Blodwen clearly did. She was exploding with dis-gust and it seemed to me that perhaps she did see a connection between the blossoms and herself and it frightened her.

'I'll be glad to get home to Gareth,' she said. For in spite of her drunken lout of a husband, she felt safe with him, even though she was two-timing him with Hershey bars. He was her anchor, however unstable, and for a moment I think she might even have loved him.

'I'll be off then,' she said, finishing her tea. 'I'll be down again in the week. Bring Gareth I will, if he'll come.'

My mam must have hoped he wouldn't. Gareth would do little to assist her sister's recuperation.

As we let Blodwen out of the front door, we saw my dad coming down the terrace. We were always glad to see him after a tour of duty. He always came back with news. On his rounds he gathered details of the night's raid, the location and the damage.

'The docks again,' he said, taking off his coat, 'and I think Riverside copped it a bit. The railway's damaged anyway. Won't be any trains today.'

'Well, we're not going anywhere,' my mam said. 'Neither are you, Dai. You're going to have your breakfast and you're going straight to bed. Your shift starts at four o'clock. I'll wake you at three.'

He was glad to do as he was told. He worked hard, did my dad, and what with the munitions and his warden duties. He even had an allotment a couple of miles from our terrace, and he'd go there sometimes on his bike and work at it and bring back a cabbage or some potatoes. He did his bit all right. He loved his King and country. He had loved the Prince of Wales once, but then he'd turned against him what with that Wallace woman. My dad thought that he should have put his country before everything else.

'Wales deserves better,' my Auntie Annie had said. She had felt a personal let-down. My Uncle Gwyn had died shortly afterwards and my Auntie Annie blamed his death on the abdication. Anyway, like I was saying, my dad certainly did his bit and he deserved the rest my mam insisted on.

'Tomorrow I'll get the bed ready for Annie,' he said. 'I don't want you two to go shifting things.'

'There's good you are, Dai,' my mam said.

My dad was very fond of my Auntie Annie and my mam appreciated it. He didn't have any brothers or sisters of his own, and his parents were gone like my mam's, and my Auntie Annie was his only family. He would be happy to look after her.

'We'll go over this afternoon and see her,' my mam said.

'Good night then,' my dad shouted from the top of the stairs. 'Or good morning or whatever it is.'

I cleared the breakfast table. I had just over a week left from my Easter holidays, and I had a lot of revision to do. In the summer, I would have to sit for my Higher Certificate examination and it would be my last term in school. I somehow convinced myself that once my schooldays were over, so was all my schoolgirl mischief. And that included the back lane. At the back of my mind I knew it was folly, but I had to cling to that conviction at least until after my exams were over. I was determined to do well, and to go to university, and to travel even, if by then the war would be over. So I set to work with my revisions and took down *Middlemarch* for the hundredth time. I was determined to finish it before term began. I told my mam that I would be staying at home to revise and that she could go to the Infirmary on her own. In such a good cause, she was happy to oblige.

The house was quiet. Our PGs were probably asleep. They worked the same shift as my dad. At four o'clock, they would walk in a threesome down the terrace, and catch the factory bus. I never knew the nature of my dad's work. He never talked about it. I don't think he liked it very much. He excused it as being his 'bit', but I sensed it was a bit he preferred not to play. I settled down to work and by some miracle I was able to concentrate. Before the end of the day I had ploughed through three-quarters of *Middlemarch*, and still without any pleasure. The book was a chore. Perhaps had I read it later in my life, free from the duress of examination, I might have enjoyed it. But I confess I have not given it another chance.

My mam brought home a good report of Auntie Annie's progress and she reckoned she could move into the parlour at the end of the week. We had our supper together, then she settled down to knit another of her balaclavas. Knitting was my mam's 'bit' for the war effort. She enjoyed it. The wool kept her fingers warm, and it was easy for her to imagine the comfort they would bring to our boys, as she called them, on cold foreign fields.

The rest of the week passed peacefully. There were no air raids and I worked solidly on my revision. Blodwen came and disturbed the calm for a while with her talk of Mrs Pugh and the disgusting life her blossoms were leading. My mam and I were glad to see the back of her. And then, on the weekend, we brought Auntie Annie home.

She was on crutches, and for her age – she was older than my mam – she seemed to manage them very well. After a few days' practice, she could negotiate the few steps down to the Anderson in case there was a raid during her stay. But from the beginning she was anxious to get back to her own home. My mam, though, loved having her there. What with my dad at work and me at my revision her sister was company, and I often heard them rattling away in the kitchen talking about their childhood together. And their laughter, and I wished then that I had a sister or a brother just for company in my old age, and for someone with whom I could have shared the back lane which had, in the fullness of time, become unsolved history. I knew then that my old age would be spent in talking to myself, telling myself a tale that I refused to believe, yet telling it over and over again, until it was meaningless. But even then I would tell it to myself, because it would itch me forever like a burr.

At the start of the term I went back to school, armed with *Middlemarch* wisdom, and taking the back lane route as my daily fix. Each day I looked forward to coming home and finding my mam and my Auntie Annie in the kitchen giggling their reminiscences away. Auntie Annie had two more weeks to suffer her plaster of Paris and then the support of a strong elastic bandage would give her her ticket home.

'Don't know why she doesn't sell that big house of hers,' my dad said, 'and come and live with us.'

I think he fancied himself being a two-sister man.

'Who's going to buy a house in war-time?' my mam asked, and my dad had to agree that the business of real estate was temporarily in abeyance. Over the weeks, my Auntie Annie had never seemed an extra in the house. It was as if she had always been a natural part of it and my dad was going to miss her as much as my mam and when the time came for her to be fitted with the bandage, he tried to persuade her that she was not ready to lose her crutches and that at least another month was required to get used to doing without them. After that, no doubt, he would have found another reason for her to stay. But Auntie Annie itched for her own fireplace and for her own aloneness. Above all she longed for the absence of witness.

When bandage day arrived, my mam took her back to the Infirmary. Blodwen had promised to come during the day to help settle her mother back home but my mam wouldn't rely on it, and she would insist that her sister would remain until the day that Blodwen saw fit to arrive.

I was in school that day, so it wasn't until I came home that I saw that Auntie Annie was still in residence. She had been given a walking stick and she was practising her steps around the kitchen.

'Who says I'm not fit to go home?' she said to me crossly.

'If you want to go home, Auntie Annie,' I said, 'I'll take you.'

'There you are, Betty,' she said to my mam, 'our Bronwen knows I can go.'

'You'll stay till Blodwen comes,' my mam said with some authority, and Auntie Annie backed down, resigned to a losing battle.

It was another week before Blodwen put in an appearance, armed with Hersheys, tinned fruit and boxes of assorted biscuits which for some reason she called cookies. And none of them were broken. Blodwen had clearly been doing her 'bit' way beyond the call of even her dubious duty. None of us questioned their provenance. We all knew how, why and where they came from and we didn't want it known that we knew. Despite Blodwen's presence and her do-gooding intentions, Auntie Annie was excited at the prospect of going home. Blodwen had even ordered a car to take them. I had the impression that she was anxious to get her good deed over and done with as quickly as possible, then get home to Abertillery and to the joys that the war had brought her.

My dad was at work at the time, so when the car came, we were spared his last-minute persuasions. I was sorry to see Auntie Annie go, and my mam had a little weep in the kitchen.

'She only lives a twopenny tram ride away,' I said. 'She hasn't gone to Australia.' In those days, Australia was a place of no return and it still retained its penal aroma.

'I don't know how she's going to manage on her own,' she said.

'She'll manage because she knows she'll have to,' I told her, and my mam, for comfort, resorted to the warmth of her balaclavas.

It was a Friday. I had the whole weekend for some final revision, for my exams were due to start the following week. In a way I was looking forward to them, and would have gladly forged ahead were it not for a letter that came in the post on the Saturday morning. We didn't get much post in our house. We didn't have any friends or relations who lived outside Cardiff. And the only letters that came through our door were bills and all kinds of notices. But this letter that came on Saturday was no ordinary letter. It had the stamp of the Cardiff County Court on the envelope. And it was addressed to my mam. Mrs Betty Davies, it said, loud and clear. We were sitting round the table having breakfast. My dad didn't work on a Saturday and he was still in his pyjamas.

'Open it then,' he said.

'Don't like to.' My mam was still holding the letter in her hand and her hand was trembling. The authority on the envelope clearly frightened her.

'Cardiff County Court,' she read. 'Is it a summons or something?'

'You haven't done anything wrong,' my dad said, a little impatient now. 'Shall I open it for you?'

'No. I'll do it,' she said. 'In a minute. Have my tea first.' She laid it beside her and took a sip of tea, but she didn't take her eyes off the envelope. We both stared at her, waiting. Then, when the tea was finished, she had no more excuse for delay and she picked up the envelope again, turning it over to its benign blank side.

'Use a knife,' my dad said, passing one over.

A proper letter was so rare, it had to be treated with respect,

envelope and all. My mam was glad of the knife for it offered
a chance of further delay. She slit the envelope very carefully,
taking her time, then, with a trembling hand, she withdrew the
letter. It was doubly folded and she spread it out but she did
not lay it on the table. She held it in front of her so that my
dad and I couldn't see what was written, so we had to watch
her face for signs of its message. And slowly a smile burgeoned
around her moving lips and we knew that whatever she had
feared, she was not guilty of.

'What is it then?' my dad said. 'Come on now, what is it?'

'Just a minute. I haven't finished reading it yet.'

I hoped she'd be quick because I knew my dad could get
very angry if he felt left out of things.

'Come on, Mam,' I said, on my dad's side.

'Well, listen,' she said at last. 'Mrs Betty Davies,' she read.
'Two, Column Terrace, Splott, Cardiff. May the fourteenth,
nineteen forty-four. That's just the beginning,' she said.

'Well, go on then.' My dad could hardly contain himself.

'Dear Mrs Davies,' she obeyed. 'This letter gives notice that
you will prepare yourself for jury service between the dates of
June the twentieth and the twenty-seventh. Attendance is compulsory. Absence is permitted only in the case of illness for
which a doctor's certificate must be presented. If for this reason you are unable to attend, or if you need further
information, please write to the Chief Clerk at the above
address. We will inform you further of the date and time of
your required attendance. Yours truly, Emlyn Hughes. That's
in handwriting,' she said. 'Then Emlyn Hughes is printed
underneath, with Chief Clerk in brackets. Well,' she said,
putting the letter on the table, 'what d'you think of that,
then?' She was clearly delighted with the invitation. It gave her
a sense of great importance. 'Well, we haven't paid our rates
all these years for nothing,' she said. 'We're entitled to a say in
things.'

'Well, I'm glad it's not me,' my dad said, but he wasn't glad at all. 'Couldn't afford to lose my pay.'

'What shall I wear then?' my mam said.

'It's not a fashion show, woman,' Dad said. He was getting crosser and crosser.

'More tea, Dad?' I said to calm him down. I topped up his cup whether he wanted it or not. Drinking it would give him something to do with his hands which I could see were twitching in his lap.

My mam sensed his envy and she folded the letter away. 'It's not important,' she said. It was her way of telling him she loved him.

We were silent then around the table. I knew it would take my dad a little while to come to terms with his wife's sudden and public recognition. My mam tried to hide her pleasure.

For my part, I was uneasy. I don't know why. And suddenly, on the white tablecloth in front of me, I saw a drop of silent blood. I looked at my mam.

'Happened again, girl,' she said, handing me a hanky. 'Have to see a doctor about that nose of yours. Lie on your back now.'

I went to the sofa and did as I was told, holding the hanky to my nose. There had been no itching nostril, no warning, no notice of the flood. Sometimes we could hear the planes overhead and the bombs dropping even before the siren had wailed. And sometimes it didn't even wail at all. That was the nature of my present nosebleed, and what worried me most was that my nostril was no longer reliable.

CHAPTER SIX

The following week I sat my first exam. It was the English literature paper, and on the whole my revision had paid off. There was a question on *Middlemarch* and it was so general, I could have answered it without having read one word of the book. It struck me that whoever set the question hadn't read it either. I had a three-day break until my next paper. It was a quiet period at home, broken only by the hum of my mam's sewing machine as she refashioned her clothes for her court appearances. She had given up on her balaclavas, deciding that for the moment the dispense of justice was more important than the warmth and camouflage of our jungle boys. There were no air raids or warnings. The name of Mildred had not dropped from my mam's lips for weeks and the whole back lane episode seemed to have been forgotten, or had been relegated to that file of 'Crimes Unsolved'. We didn't even buy the *Echo* any more. We picked up whatever news was available from our neighbours in the terrace, but they too had lost interest in the lane, and had little to offer. When my dad was on the night shift, he often came home with the *Western Mail* that you could pick up for free at the gates of the munitions factory, and one morning, during this quiet time, he dropped it on the breakfast table, still pristine and folded and there for anyone's reading. I picked it up for want of anything else to do. I remember my dad was washing his hands in the scullery and my mam was brewing tea at the time, and I caught sight of a headline in the middle of the front page. 'Man arrested on murder charge,' I read. My nostril twitched and I was grateful that my early-warning system was once more in operation. I hid the headline with my hand, as if my sweating palm would blot it into invisibility, then I quickly took it into the parlour for to read it without anyone's eye-droppings.

I read: 'A man was arrested late last night in connection with the Splott murder on December 23rd' and he was at present helping police with their enquiries. I was confident that during the day he would be released without charge. I tried to think no more about it until that evening when my mam went out to buy the *Echo*. Ever since her summons to jury service, she had taken a profound interest in matters of law and its procedure, and she would nightly turn to the court column like an addict to his fix.

'They've got him,' she said suddenly.

'Who?'

'Him. You know. The Splott man. The murderer.'

My nose twitched but thankfully there was no blood. 'How d'you know they've got him?' I said.

'Read it for yourself, girl. It's in the paper.'

I picked it up and tried to steady my holding hand. And there, at the top of the front page, the headline read, 'Man charged with Splott murder'. I wanted to tear the paper in pieces and indeed to shred every copy of the edition in the vain hope that news pulped was no news at all. I forced myself to read on.

'Hugh Elwyn Baker,' I read, 'a builder of Splott, Cardiff, was this afternoon charged with the murder of Peter Roger Thorne of London, on the 23rd December of last year. He was cautioned and taken into custody. He will appear in court tomorrow morning.'

I was forced to sit down. My knees were trembling so. I wondered what grounds they had for charging him, and since I could imagine none at all, I could only surmise that overnight they had beaten a confession out of him. I wanted to run to the police station and tell them they were making a terrible mistake, but I was not prepared to tell them why I was so sure. I was deeply disturbed by it all, and worried that my examination work would suffer as a consequence. I had an exam in the morning, my French paper, otherwise I would have attended the court and held my astonished tongue. I thought I might persuade my mam to go. 'Do you good,' I said. 'Be a kind of dress rehearsal. Bet you've never seen the inside of a court,' I teased.

She didn't take much persuasion. 'You're right, luv,' she said. 'I should go for practice.'

My dad suggested that she might have better things to do, but it was only because he was a little jealous.

'I'll tell you all about it, Dai,' she said. 'First hand.' And he had to be satisfied with that promise.

My mam was up and dressed and looking very smart by the time I left for school that morning. I managed to put the court proceedings out of my mind and I was able to acquit myself well with the French paper. I was free in the afternoon, free to revise for my history the following day, so I went home for dinner excited for, but fearful of my mam's report. She had the dinner laid ready on the table. Just the two of us. My dad wouldn't be home till four o'clock and then she'd heat it up again.

'Well, what happened?' I said.

'Let me serve first.' My mam was anxious to set the scene for she had a tale to tell. I waited until she'd served my rissole and mashed potatoes and put the same on her own plate.

'Go on,' I said. 'What happened? Were there lots of people there?' I wanted to ease her into the scene.

'Crowded it was,' she said. 'Had to queue. Needn't have dressed up. There was one woman there in her apron, would you believe.'

I wasn't interested in the fashion details. 'What happened when you got inside?'

'It was all over in about five minutes. Bit disappointed I was.'

'But what was it that took five minutes?' I tried not to sound impatient.

'Well, the judges came in, three of them there were, and they sat facing us on a bench in front of a long table. Then two policemen brought in the culprit. I took one look at him, and I said to myself, Betty Davies, I said, I swear on my mam's soul that that man is guilty. No doubt about it. None at all.'

I wondered whether all jury members were like my mam and whether, as a result, the whole jury system was unreliable. 'Well, you don't know, do you,' I said. 'Not until you've proved it.'

'Could read it in his face I could,' she insisted.

'What happened then?' I said. 'When they brought him in?'

'He stood there between the two policemen, and one of the judges said, "Hugh Elwyn Baker," out loud he said it,' and my mam's voice took on a legal ring, ' "you are charged with the murder of Peter Roger Thorne on the twenty-third of December of last year. How plead you? Guilty or not guilty?" "Not guilty," he said, and brazen with it.'

'And then?'

'The judge said, "You will be committed to trial at the County Assizes on the twentieth day of June. Until that time you will be remanded in custody." ' My mam knew the jargon by heart.

The date of his trial rang a bell and my nose began to twitch. I got up quickly from the table. 'I've got to go to the toilet,' I said. I knew that this time my nose was going to do more than twitch, and I wanted the flood private. I rushed to the bathroom to stem the flow with toilet paper and to accept that the date of the man's trial had rung a very cracked bell indeed. Because it was exactly the date of my mam's jury summons and she had already found him guilty without having heard one syllable of evidence. I feared that between now and the trial, I would lose enough blood to warrant a transfusion. I didn't want to go downstairs again until the bleeding had stopped. I feared my mam would note its timing and connect it with the back lane. You never knew with my mam. She could be quite clever sometimes.

She called me from downstairs. 'Your rice pudding's on the table,' she said.

'Coming,' I shouted. The bleeding seemed to have stopped and I washed my nose clear of all traces. I ate my pudding and did the washing-up, then went straight to my room and my history notebooks. At four o'clock, I heard my dad come home, but I didn't go downstairs because I didn't want to hear an encore of the court proceedings which I had no doubt my mam was retelling, and without any expression or elaboration, so that it would sound dull and boring for my dad's benefit. But she would still insist on her 'guilty' decision and my dad, having seen and heard even less than she had, would probably agree with her. I dared not think of the consequences of their judgement.

In two weeks' time my exams would be over, and after that, school would be a mere routine until the end of term. But the trial would have started before then, and with luck might even be over, and with any justice, poor guilty-looking Mr Baker would be freed. And the Law would have learned once and for all that they were never going to find the murderer, and they might as well give up their search.

There was no harm in day-dreaming, and as I mused on such a felicitous outcome, I heard the front door bell ring. I went to the landing and looked over the banister into the hall. My mam answered the door, which was just as well, because my dad would have lost his wordless voice had he found Mrs Pugh on the doorstep. 'Can I come in for a minute, luv?' I heard her say.

I came down the stairs with a casual tread. 'Finished my work,' I said, and then in the same breath, 'Hello, Mrs Pugh.'

She greeted me as my mam led her into the kitchen. My dad got up from his chair when Mrs Pugh came in. Not because she was a madam — for that reason alone he might have stayed seated — but because she was a woman, and moreover one who offered shelter to his family. And quickly he excused himself saying he had work to do, though neither my mam nor I, and certainly not my dad, had any idea of the nature of that work. I supposed he expected women's talk, and thought it best to absent himself.

'Don't let me disturb you,' Mrs Pugh said, but he was gone and my mam didn't try to stop him.

'Go and put the kettle on, Bron,' she said to me.

I went into the scullery. There was no door between that and the kitchen so I could hear their whole conversation. I was very curious to know why Mrs Pugh had paid her first visit to our house. I left the whistle off the kettle, for I wanted no disturbance, and I put out our best cups and saucers on the tray.

'I hope you don't mind my coming, Mrs Davies,' Mrs Pugh was saying. 'I don't know what to do, and I've got to talk to somebody.'

'Call me Betty,' my mam said, thus giving her neighbour a licence to tell her anything on earth, and in confidence too.

'I've had visitors again,' Mrs Pugh said. Or rather whispered.

'Who?' my mam whispered back, entering the conspiracy.

I moved silently near the arch between the rooms.

'The police,' Mrs Pugh hissed.

I saw the kettle boil. 'Tea's coming,' I shouted, because I didn't want to miss another word. I heard them suspend their conversation and I took in the tray for starters and put it on the table. Then, assured of their continued silence, I went to the scullery and brewed the tea. They were still silent when I returned with the pot.

'I'll pour,' my mam said. 'You go up to your room now, Bron.' She must have spotted the three cups and saucers on the tray.

'Let her stay,' Mrs Pugh said. 'I don't mind. I'm sure she can keep her mouth shut.'

She didn't know what a master clam I was, nor the terrible imperative to be so. But I could have kissed her. I felt so flattered that she'd invited me into her conspiracy, for I knew from her whispering tone that conspiracy it truly was.

'There were three of them this time,' Mrs Pugh went on, and still in a whisper.

'What did they want?' my mam whispered back.

'The same old thing. They wanted me to talk about the man who'd come from the jungle, you remember, the one who didn't have enough money. They wanted to know the time he was here. What time. That was all that seemed to matter to them. The time. Well, I couldn't for the life of me remember, and I told them so. I knew it was pretty dark outside, but that could have been any time. Then one of them said, "Were you listening to the news? D'you think it might have been six o'clock?" I told them I never listened to the news. Then one of them said, "We think it was about six o'clock. We have reason to believe it was six o'clock." They were driving me mad with their six o'clock. And I smelled a rat. I sensed they were trying to force me to say it was six o'clock, because that time would have fitted into their theories. Whatever they were. So

I said straight out. "I don't know what time it was. All I know was it was dark." Then one of them said, "Mrs Pugh," he said, and I didn't like the way he used my name. "Mrs Pugh," he said, sort of confidential, "you don't want to lose your establishment, do you?" Then I could see what he was getting at, and I looked at him and I said, "Yes, it must have been six o'clock. I heard the pips on the news." "That's a good girl," the other one said. "You'll say that under oath, won't you?" Then I realised I'd have to say it in court. Oh, Betty,' she said, laying her hand on my mam's arm, 'I don't like myself at all. I'm an honest woman. Always have been. All my life. I just don't think I can get up in court and say six o'clock if I'm not sure. I just don't know what to do.'

'You've got your living to make,' my mam said, then turning to me, 'You're not to breathe a word of this. D'you hear me?' she said. I shook my head. But I was shattered. It seemed to me that they had built up a solid case against poor Mr Baker even if it had required a small twisting of the truth to prove it.

'I won't say a word,' my mam said. She did not mention that she might well be on the jury in the case, but I was sure that if she were, she would, out of respect for Mrs Pugh, privately take her testimony with a pinch of salt.

'But supposing it wasn't six o'clock,' Mrs Pugh insisted. 'Supposing it *had* to be six o'clock in order to find him guilty. I should never in my life forgive myself.'

Suddenly I felt very sorry for her.

'It *was* about six o'clock,' I said. 'I saw him myself.'

'What are you saying, girl?' my mam almost shouted at me.

'D'you remember when I was coming back from Auntie Annie's with the carving knife for the turkey?' I spoke the words without flinching. 'It was the same day, wasn't it? December the twenty-third. Well, I saw a man coming up the lane. It might have been him, I didn't see his face, but he was like the man they said in the paper the next day. Red hair and such.'

'Yes, that's right.' Mrs Pugh was excited. 'I remember now. He had red hair. Always puts me off, red hair.'

'I know it was six o'clock,' I went on, 'because I could hear the news from the back lane.'

'Could have been him,' my mam said.

'Must have been,' I said.

My offer seemed to satisfy Mrs Pugh. 'Maybe the police were right then,' she said. 'Six o'clock was it? You sure?'

'Well, I heard the news,' I insisted.

'Well, there you are then,' my mam said. 'Just as well you didn't come back later, girl. You might have seen the murder.'

She shivered, and so did I. But for different reasons. She trembled at what might have been, and I at what was.

'I'll do it then,' Mrs Pugh said. 'I'll say it. Six o'clock.'

'You're not to mention Bronwen's name though. I don't want her brought into it,' my mam said sternly.

'I wouldn't dream of it, Betty,' Mrs Pugh said.

'Now that's settled, you can have some more tea.' My mam topped up her cup.

'I don't mind if you tell Mr Davies,' Mrs Pugh said. 'I wouldn't expect you to keep secrets from your husband.'

'My Dai's got a mouth like a clam,' my mam laughed. 'I won't tell him anyway. And neither will you, girl.' She turned to me again.

I shook my head in promise. My dad wouldn't have believed it anyway. He had absolute faith in the police force. In his eyes they were incorruptible.

'You don't have to wait for the bombs to come and see me, you know,' Mrs Pugh said. 'I don't get many visitors, personal ones that is.'

Then my mam felt that she ought to tell her about her jury summons and the possibility that she might be called to serve at the trial. 'So it would be awkward, like, if I was to call on a witness,' she said. 'Afterwards, of course, I could, when it's all over.'

Mrs Pugh understood and was satisfied. She finished her tea and, much relieved and grateful, she took her leave and my dad reappeared the moment she had gone.

'What did she want then, when the cows come home?' he said.

'Nothing. Women's talk.' My mam knew that would silence him and she left it at that. Shortly afterwards he went out on duty and she had me on her own. She was clearly disturbed about my near miss with murder. 'Of course you were in the lane that night,' she said. 'Never struck me though. Must have happened just after you came in. We can thank God for that at least,' she said. She was not given to thanking God at any time, so her relief at my early return from Auntie Annie's must have been sublime. I thought I might mention it but I didn't want to push my luck too far and I hoped that in the still and sleepless hours of her nights, she would not make the dire connection.

Over the next two weeks, I managed each of my exams without disturbance, and I marvelled at myself that I could so detach from my mind that which my mind could not in any case accommodate. In the fullness of time, my mam received her jury summons, and not surprisingly, it was for the twentieth of June. Her excitement was boundless and gave vent to itself only when my dad was out. When he came home she was her sober self, but still at her sewing machine in respect of her court appearances.

'It's not a mannequin parade,' my dad said one evening, when the burr of the machine was getting on his nerves.

'Got to show respect,' my mam said.

Although my exams were finished, the school term did not end until mid-July, by which time I supposed the trial would be over. And it would be impossible for me to take time off from school unless I truanted and that would not look good on my leaving report. In a way, I was relieved that I had an excuse not to attend. I would have found it hard to hold my tongue on the prosecution. I would have to rely on my mam and her daily bulletins, but I was not too assured of their reliability.

On the twentieth of June, a Monday it was, my mam was up early, dressed and ready to see that justice would be done. I wished her luck, not knowing what I meant, and then I went to school. But bereft of exams and confronted only with the dull and daily grind of school routine, I could not concentrate. My mind was in the courtroom and my eye on the poor and innocent Mr Baker in the dock.

There was no one in the house when I got home from school. My dad was on the day shift and my mam was still dispensing justice. I was impatient for her to come home. I washed up the breakfast things that were still on the table, and tidied up a bit, so that she would have nothing to do when she came home except to tell me about the day's proceedings. I even put the kettle on and prepared the tray, so that she need not lose any time. I heard her key in the door, and I shouted, 'Mam, what happened?' before she could even take her coat off. I regretted showing my curiosity so plainly and I was unsettled by her reply. She came into the kitchen and told me to put the kettle on. By this time it had boiled, and the tea was shortly on the table. I poured it for her, but I was careful not to question her again, though my curiosity was killing me. She took a large sip of her tea.

'That's nice,' she said. 'Terrible tea in that court canteen. Don't have to pay at least.'

Then I couldn't help myself. 'What happened, Mam?' I asked.

'We're not supposed to talk about it,' she said.

'Why not? It'll all be in the *Echo* anyway.'

'Not what the jury say to each other there won't,' she said.

'I don't want to know that,' I said. 'I just want to save buying the *Echo*.'

On that basis she was prepared to deliver a bulletin. 'Nothing much,' she said, 'but then it's only the first day. We didn't get started till about twelve. I don't know what they were doing, the judges and the clerks, but it was nearly dinner time before they let the people in. Crowded it was. No one I knew, though.'

That didn't surprise me. My mam didn't know many people and most of them lived in the terrace.

'No one from our street?' I asked.

'Not that I saw,' she said.

'Then what?'

'Well, then they empanelled the jury.'

'They what?'

'That means we had to give our names and occupations and then the lawyers could object if they wanted to.'

I marvelled at my mam's new-found vocabulary. I feared that by the end of the trial, my dad would view her as a stranger.

'Then we had to be sworn in,' she went on. 'And then they brought him in.'

'Who?'

'The murderer, of course. Who else?'

'Mam,' I said patiently, 'he may be innocent.'

'There's no smoke without fire,' she said. 'There were two policemen one on each side of him. They were all standing. Then the clerk said, "Hugh Elwyn Baker, you are charged with the murder of Peter Roger Thorne on the twenty-third of December last. Do you plead guilty or not guilty?" And then, bold as brass, he said, "Not guilty, sir." '

'Well, what else could he say?' I said.

'Well, anyway, that's what he said.'

My mam clearly hoped for a more appreciative audience. She poured herself some more tea.

'What happened then?' I said.

'It'll be in the *Echo*,' she sulked.

'Come on, Mam,' I persuaded her.

She took her time with her tea. 'Well, then the clerk turned to us on the jury and he repeated more or less what the prisoner had said. He told us that after having heard the evidence, we had to decide whether he was guilty or not. Then we were supposed to have the opening speech for the prosecution, but by then it was dinner time so the judge adjourned till after.'

My mam's mouth was full of new and wondrous words and she obviously savoured them, for she took another sip of tea as if to relish them and wash them down.

'Where did you have dinner?' I said.

'We've got a special room. Most of us brought our sandwiches, but you can get tea in the canteen.'

'Who are the others?' I asked.

'Some posh ones there are,' my mam said. 'You could see from their clothes. Live in Cyncoed they do.'

In those days, Cyncoed spelt arrival. It was an almost rural area, dotted with large detached houses with driveways and gardens. Only on a jury could my mam have brushed shoulders with them.

'Did you talk to anyone?' I asked.

'There's one woman lives in Canton. Gwyneth Williams is her name. She's very nice. Not married. Lives with her mam. She's like me. She thinks he's guilty too.'

'But Mam,' I almost shouted at her. 'You haven't heard any evidence.'

'You've only got to look at him,' my mam said. 'Then after dinner,' she went on quickly, avoiding any further interruption, 'we all went back and sat in the same places. Then the counsel for the Crown, that's what they call the man who's accusing the murderer, he got up and made his opening speech. The case for the prosecution, the judge called it. He went on and on and on. He repeated himself a lot. I dozed a bit. It was so stuffy in there, but I heard most of what he was saying.'

'You must get them to open a window,' I said, alarmed that at least one of the jury was missing out on possibly vital clues.

'What did he say?' I asked. I was pretty desperate to know what case the Crown could possibly have against poor Mr Baker.

'That Mildred,' my mam said.

I hadn't heard that name in quite a while, but it had lost none of its jarring rattle.

'Mildred?'

'All her fault,' my mam said.

I was relieved that at last Mildred had fallen from grace, and was no longer pity-worthy. But I was intrigued to know why. 'What's Mildred got to do with it?'

'She went off with someone else, it appears. He came home on leave. He was never near a jungle, whatever he said. Anyway, when he got home, the house was empty, and he found a note. She'd gone off with another man and taken the kids with her.'

I was happy that old Mildred could bear some of the guilt but I wasn't convinced as to the reason.

My mam sipped her tea slowly. She knew that I would be her only audience. That when my dad came home, he would bring the *Echo* with him, and read it for himself with his lips moving. She was going to milk my ear dry.

'Well, it stands to reason, doesn't it?' she said at last. 'Getting a note like that. Coming home on leave. Well, it seems he rang up his friend from a phone box, this murderer – he's a builder, see, so he's got a phone – and he asked if he could come and stay. He used to live in Cardiff, see, before he

went to London, not far from here, round by the pub where
we go. And his friend said, course he could come. Sorry for
him he was. Well, when he arrived from London, his friend
was out on a job. But his wife was there. I suppose she must
have comforted him a bit and well – you know, one thing leads
to another, and when the friend came back, he caught them at
it.' My mam assumed that I would know what the 'it' was.

'And so he threw him out.' My mam could see that I was
shocked so she felt free to give herself an interval. She topped
up her teacup.

I waited. 'Good heavens,' I said, in polite appreciation of her
narrative. My mam was not a woman of many words, and such
a speech earned some acknowledgement.

'Well, as you can imagine,' my mam went on, tea-fortified,
'he was furious. He had a drink or two, a bit drunk I suppose
he was, and he went straight to the pub, *our* pub, mind, it
used to be their pub, him and his friend, well, that used to be
his friend, and he thought he'd find him there. There were
witnesses who saw him drinking and getting drunker and
drunker and about a quarter to six he left, and one of them left
at the same time. They were going the same way, so he followed him, keeping an eye on him, like, because he didn't look
too steady on his feet. Well, he followed him to the corner of
the terrace, our terrace, not far, mind, and the murderer
stopped and leaned against the wall. The witness asked him if
he was all right, and he said yes, so the witness went on
home. Now listen to this, girl,' my mam said. 'A man answering the description of the victim came out of the house on the
corner of our terrace, and that was just about six o'clock – the
judge said there were witnesses to all that – and the next
thing we know he's dead in the back lane only a few seconds'
walk from the corner house. Well, that looks like guilty to me,'
my mam said. 'Open and shut case. It all fits, doesn't it?'

It didn't exactly fit for me. 'What about the knife?' I said.

'Well, that's it.' My mam took another gulp of tea. 'When the police went to his house, they found a carving knife in the kitchen that exactly, mind you, *exactly* fitted the dead man's wounds.'

'But lots of people have got carving knives,' I said, as if counsel for the defence.

'Yes,' my mam agreed. 'But this one had motive, see. *Motive.*'

My mam's legal vocabulary burgeoned with each sentence.

'He had a weapon, and he had a motive. No doubt about it in my mind,' she said.

I was worried. It was a plausible enough case. A few holes perhaps, which prosecution witnesses would no doubt fill. I was glad I couldn't attend the court. I might have disgraced myself with confession.

'What else?' I asked.

'Well, that was all for the day,' my mam said. 'It was such a long speech. After it, the court was adjourned and we go back tomorrow for witnesses for the prosecution. Wish I'd been a lawyer,' she said suddenly.

Well, she certainly had the vocabulary, if not the judgement. 'You could have been anything, mam,' I said.

Later on my dad came home, armed, as I expected, with the *Echo*. 'I've read it,' he said, even before he took off his coat. 'Read it on the bus.'

Thus my mam was deprived of encore, but she took no offence.

'Well, what d'you think then?' she asked.

'Sounds pretty guilty to me,' my dad said.

I was glad that he was not with her on the jury and I prayed that the others were not of such like and sudden mind.

'Will Mrs Pugh be on tomorrow?' I asked.

'I'm not sure,' my mam said. 'They've got lots of wit-nesses.'

That night we went to bed early, except for my dad who was on fire-watching duty. I was glad to be on my own and to concentrate on getting my mind off my mind.

When I came home from school the following day, my mam was already there and I feared it was all over with and the innocent man condemned. 'You're home early,' I said.

'Adjourned,' she said. She'd grown fond of the word, and she spread it over four or five syllables. 'I think the judge was tired,' she said.

'What went on today?' I asked.

She already had the tea on the table and there would be no time lost for the delivery of her daily bulletin.

'Well, first there was the publican. You know, old Harry from behind the bar. He said he saw the murderer come into the pub at about twenty to six. And he said he was already drunk and he had two more pints of beer. There were other witnesses who were in the pub and they all said the same. And the man who followed him. He was in the witness box a long time, and he just told what we already knew from the opening speech for the prosecution. All that bit about leaving him at the end of the terrace. It went on and on and on. And there was cross-examination from the defence, but I don't think they did any good. I don't think they'll have any case at all.'

'No Mrs Pugh?' I asked.

'She's tomorrow, I suppose,' my mam said.

The prosecution case seemed to be building itself to a point beyond destruction. I couldn't imagine what the defence could say in poor Mr Baker's favour. It seemed to me that through a series of very unfortunate and ill-timed coincidences, the innocent man could well be found guilty. When my dad brought home the *Echo* that night, I read it myself, in the hope that my mam had got it all wrong, or left bits out, but it turned out that her report was accurate to the last detail.

'It's not going to go on much longer,' my mam said. 'The

prosecution will probably end tomorrow. Then I'll put on a new frock for the defence.'

A man's life is at stake, I thought, and my mam is concerned with her wardrobe.

'The Cyncoed lot wear something different every day,' she was saying. 'But I'll wait till the prosecution's finished.'

My mam was right. It did finish that day when Mrs Pugh made her court appearance. According to my mam, she was very soberly dressed. There was no sense of blowsiness about her. She wore a grey suit with no trimmings. She took the oath, my mam said. She said where she lived, but not what she did there, then she repeated exactly what the police had told her to say. It didn't really matter, my mam said, because other people had talked about six o'clock before. She wasn't the only one. She wasn't nervous, my mam said, and I assumed that my and others' confirmation of the time had given her confidence. The defence counsel had nagged her about the time, trying to put her off her guard, but she had stood her ground. Her feet were planted firmly on six o'clock, and she did not waver. She left the witness box, her corner business secure.

She was the last witness for the prosecution, so the counsel said, and the court was then adjourned. Till the next day and my mam's change of wardrobe.

Every night the case was minutely reported in the *Echo* and my dad read it slowly and faithfully. I think he both hoped and dreaded to see my mam's name in the papers. The night that the prosecution rested its case, there was an air raid. When the siren sounded, my mam insisted I go down to Mrs Pugh's cellar. That night she would use the Anderson, she said. It was not proper, she thought, that in the middle of the trial she should be seen to consort – another new word – with one of its witnesses. I didn't argue. It was a long time since I'd been down the cellar, and I felt blossom-deprived. Mrs Pugh opened the door to me, blowsed once more, and ushered me down the cellar steps. She didn't ask where my mam was. She must have understood her absence. All the blossoms were there in their kimonos, except one, who was dressed in blowsy fashion, a miniature clone of Mrs Pugh herself. She smiled at me and slowly I recognised her as Petal. I presumed that in Mrs Pugh's absence in pursuit of justice, she had taken over the management for the day. Mrs Pugh settled herself by my side, as the air-raid siren faded.

We heard the bombs almost immediately. They seemed so close, I worried for my mam and dad.

'Did my bit today,' Mrs Pugh shouted in my ear.

'I read it in the paper,' I lied. I didn't want to let her know my mam talked about it.

'I'm glad it's over with,' she said. 'Well, for me, anyway. Not for him though. Poor devil.'

'What will happen, d'you think?' I asked.

'Well, so far he sounds guilty to me, but we haven't heard his defence yet.'

It was a relief to find someone with an open mind.

Another bomb fell, a little more distant this time. I had a vague illusion that it might have fallen on the prison so that poor Mr Baker might die in any case of natural causes, and through no fault of mine. But I didn't want him to die, naturally or otherwise, and there was no way I could save him. I thought of my mam sitting alone in the Anderson, listening to the neighbourhood bombing and probably worrying about me. Then I thought of my dad and considered him a hero, out in the open like he must be, fighting the fires. I thought of my Auntie Annie, but I didn't worry too much about her. She lived in a neighbourhood where a bomb had never been dropped, and short of last minute off-loading, she was not in danger. But that night, I wanted the all-clear to go. I wanted to be with my mam. It seemed to me to be wrong for families in peril to be separated.

We could still hear the anti-aircraft fire, and slowly it stuttered into silence.

'It'll be the all-clear soon,' Mrs Pugh said, and no sooner had she said it, than we heard its wailing. I rushed up the cellar steps and out of the door and into the street and slowly all the torch-lit neighbours dribbled on to the doorsteps.

'Bomb in the back lane,' I heard one of them say, and I prayed that my mam hadn't gone into the Anderson. I ran towards the house, and there she was, torch-bearing on the step. She put her arms round me, a rare gesture from my mam, but her relief overwhelmed her. 'There's a bomb in the lane,' she said. The shelter's all right, but I wasn't in it.'

'Let's go and see,' I said.

We held hands and went through the house and into the garden. At the end of it, there was no back door. It had splintered on to the garden path. And the lane was choked with steaming rubble. It would take some weeks to clear, and my back lane fix would be long denied. But that didn't worry me. There was something more. The back lane bomb was rudely ill-timed. Had it happened the night of the carving knife, it would have obliterated all evidence of the crime, body and all. But that it should have happened now, on the eve of poor Mr Baker's defence, occurred to me as a frightful omen, as if Mr Baker's innocence no longer had any proof.

CHAPTER SEVEN

My dad was burned that night. Not badly, but bad enough to keep him off work and duties for a while. His hands it was. An incendiary had dropped in someone's back garden and the shed was ablaze. My dad had gone too close. I wished it had been Mr Griffiths. But he was supervisor, and they were rarely in the line of fire. Both my dad's hands were bandaged and he was in pain a lot of the time, and what with my mam out all day and me at school, he had no one to complain to. My mam suggested he come to the court, but for whatever reason, he refused. So most of the day, he read the paper and listened to the wireless and though he had difficulty holding a glass, it didn't keep him from the pub. When he was there, I suppose he was regarded as a bit of a hero, and he might have felt an equal status with my mam, who was being important elsewhere. But on the way home, he always bought the *Echo* for to read the proceedings himself. He was often out when my mam came back from the court, so there was only me to report to. She didn't seem to mind. She understood. My mam was good at that sort of thing.

She came back that evening with the opening speech for the case of the defence. It was short in comparison with that of the prosecution and its lack of length seemed to infer a lack of matter, that there was not too much to be said on Mr Baker's behalf. But my mam gave me the gist of it.

He'd said that much of what the prosecution had said was true. That indeed his client had been enraged by his friend's behaviour, that he had indeed thrown him out of his house, and that he had taken a lot to drink. And in that drunken stupor he had had thoughts of dire revenge. What man wouldn't have such thoughts? So he had taken the carving knife from the kitchen and gone after him. All that, his client would readily confess to. But his thoughts of revenge were only thoughts, and drunken ones at that. He had gone to the pub, it was true, because that was where he and his friend used to drink. He'd also had two pints of beer and then he'd staggered home. It was true that the witness had seen him on the corner of the terrace, and it was also true that he had rested there. That spot was on his way home, and it was possible he rested because he wanted to sober up before he went back to his house. Which was exactly what he did, ladies and gentlemen of the jury, he said. Straight back to his house, in time to hear half the news bulletin. And there was absolutely no witness who could prove that he did otherwise.

'That's more or less what he said,' my mam said. 'He was a good-looking man, I'll say that for him, much better than the prosecution one.'

For a moment I hoped my mam and the rest of the jury would be swayed by the defence counsel's good looks, but there were men on the jury as well, and men on the whole are not well-disposed to those of their gender more handsome than themselves.

'Then what?' I asked my mam.

'Then came the witnesses for the defence. There were only two of them, and they were both about the murderer's character. Nothing to do with what went on that night in the back lane. First there was his doctor and then there was his foreman at his work. You'd think the defence could have put up something better than two character witnesses. Duw, poor bugger didn't have a chance.'

My mam had clearly not wavered in her verdict since her first day in court, and even before that, when Mr Baker's arrest had first been announced.

'What did they say?' I pleaded, though all hope had drained out of me.

'The doctor said he was a friend of the family, and that the accused was a good husband and father to his children.'

'He's got children?' I was more concerned with Mr Baker's children than with Mr Thorne's. And more with Mr Baker's wife than the insufferable Mildred.

'He has three children,' my mam said, 'and none of them yet in school. He should have known better.'

'Why isn't he in the army?'

'The doctor said he's got chronic asthma.'

'Poor devil,' I said.

'Not such a poor devil as the man he killed.'

'You don't know, Mam,' I pleaded. 'It hasn't been proved.'

'Oh, it'll be proved all right. Another few days and it'll all be over.'

It would be over for my mam too, I thought, saddled as she would be with a new and altered wardrobe and without a catwalk for display. And having tasted a small fame, she would find herself in the wilderness of mundane routine. And balaclavas. But at least my dad would perk up a bit, and he wouldn't have to buy the *Echo* every evening. I wanted to ask her outright what she thought the verdict would be, but I was fearful of her reply.

'When will it be over then?' I dared to ask.

'Well, tomorrow they'll start with the summing-up for the defence. The way things have been going, that shouldn't take very long. Then after that it'll be the same for the prosecution. Then the judge will give his final speech and then we'll be sent out to make a decision. Duw, I'll be glad when it's all over. And I won't in a way. Be funny having nothing much to do all day. I'll miss it.'

'Who's the foreman of the jury?' I asked.

'A Mr Hughes from Cathays. Now he's a sensible man. No question. What he thinks will be very important.'

'And what does he think?' I asked.

'Same as me,' she said. 'Same as most of us, I think.'

For the next few days I went to school and immersed myself in end-of-term activities. Each day when I got home, I didn't ask my mam for any report, but she gave it to me anyway. It had become a habit with her and I was her only audience. But one day she was already home when I came back from school. Before I had time to take off my coat, she said, 'It'll be all over tomorrow.'

My nostril twitched, but I didn't fear the bleeding. That would come tomorrow, I thought. And in a deluge.

'Don't know what to wear,' she was saying.

Her wardrobe had taken precedence over justice.

'I shall wear the suit,' she said. 'Sober it is and respectable. Shall need to be that in view of the verdict. And duw, I know what that verdict's going to be.'

'What's that, Mam?'

'Guilty, of course. No question. That's what we all think anyway.'

My nose twitched again. That night I couldn't sleep. I tossed and I turned. I wanted desperately to go to court for the last day of the trial and I wanted equally desperately to hear no more about it. Ever again in my life, and I was prepared to pay for that ignorance with an eternal nosebleed. I dozed off finally and when I woke in the morning, a decision had been made. I don't know that I ever made it. It had rather come upon me, more in the form of a command than a choice. I would play truant from school, and go to the final hearing.

I put on my uniform because I had to. My mam always saw me off before I left so I had to keep up appearances. My dad was still in bed, so we two were alone at breakfast, me in my gymslip, and my mam in her sober, justice-dispensing suit. I wished her luck, again not knowing what I meant, and I waved to her as she stood at the door. I had to take the front way because the back lane was blocked. I dawdled a few blocks away, then I waited to give her time to leave. Then I crept back into the house, hoping my dad was still asleep. I changed quickly into a skirt and jumper, and I was ready before my dad could turn over. Then I went to my hanky drawer – no such thing as tissues then, and toilet paper was rough and hard to come by – and I took out what was there, even the embroidered ones, because I feared there might be quite a bit of mopping-up to do.

The courthouse was only ten minutes' walk away, but I took my time. I had to make a few detours because the bomb damage had closed a number of streets, and when I reached the corner of the court, I could see there was a sizeable queue in waiting. I joined it at the end, clinging to the wall, in case any teacher from the school had chosen to attend. I eavesdropped on the conversation in front of me, that was salivating for a guilty verdict and expected it with absolute certainty. I fiddled with the lump of hankies in my pocket, and as the queue moved slowly forward, my knees trembled, and I had it in mind to run from there and to hide with my hankies until it was all over. But I knew that I had no choice, and my legs propelled me forward. The queue moved in an orderly and steady fashion. It wore a subdued expression plainly assumed as proper for its surroundings. I sat myself at the back of the court although there were a few places with a better view of the proceedings, but I did not want to be conspicuous, in case my mam caught sight of me. But I could see her, loud and clear, for despite the sober suit she wore, she outshone the rest of the jury, for her look was radiant with decision. There were sundry people milling around the well of the court, and I knew they were important because they wore wigs and strutted with authority. Then somebody banged a gavel and asked the court to rise. Which everybody did in respect of the judge, who entered and took his seat, a signal for us all to settle once again.

'This court is now in session,' he said. 'Let the prisoner be brought to the dock.'

His accent was very English. His trip to Wales was purely professional. This fact depressed me, for the victim was an Englishman at the time of his death, and the accused undeniably Welsh. The judge, impartial though he might try to be, could not deny a national prejudice.

My nostril was surprisingly still as I awaited the arrival of Mr Baker, but I clutched at my hankies as if they were a life raft.

I heard the banging of a door and heavy steps on a stairway. I saw the top of his head first, level with those of the two policemen on either side of him. Then his whole face. I noticed that his black hair was parted in the middle, a fashion that couldn't have brought out the best in him, for it was a woman's style that usually promoted a fringe. But Mr Baker had no fringe, but a very low and bare forehead which the middle parting did nothing to disguise. I wished I'd had an opportunity to advise him. His suit did very little for him either. It was brown pinstripe with very large lapels, and though I couldn't see his shoes, I knew they had to be winkle-pickers. My mam had not been unfair in her first impression. In all Mr Baker's features, in his bridgeless nose, his over-neighbouring eyes, and his sunken chin, there was not a single trace of innocence. But I believed in him. With absolute and certain faith, and I was probably the only one in the court who did so.

He gripped the rail of the dock with his two terrified hands. Then he looked directly at me. Right into my face. I could have sworn that were so, as if he was begging me to come clean. At least that's what I thought, until I noticed a woman sitting directly in front of me who was raising her hand in a little finger-wave of encouragement. I deduced that she was Mrs Baker and I wondered who was looking after her three children.

There was a terrible silence in the court. The judge shuffled his papers, but even that movement was silent. At length he turned to face the jury and they, in their turn, faced him, like ranks of obedient schoolchildren. I knew from their faces that they had already come to a decision and the judge might as well have been talking to a wall. His address to the jury was a formality.

'Members of the jury,' he said. 'The accused man, Hugh Elwyn Baker, is charged before you with the offence of murder.'

The woman in front of me shivered visibly, and her companion, sitting alongside, laid a hand on her arm. I wondered whether Mrs Baker thought in her heart that her husband was guilty.

'The charge against him,' the judge continued, 'is that on the twenty-third of December last year, he murdered the man named Peter Roger Thorne.' More shivers from the woman in front of me, and I doubted whether she could stay the long and gruelling course. The judge went on about the need to establish guilt beyond all reasonable doubt. As he outlined the case for the defence and the prosecution, I kept my eyes on the jury. I could have sworn that few of them were listening. They had heard it all before and their minds were already made up. My mam was staring at the judge but her thoughts were elsewhere. She was probably wondering to what further use she could put her wardrobe. She might even have been toying with the idea of taking a job. There was plenty of part-time work around for women in the war industry, though I couldn't see her packing shells or parachutes. But she could perhaps do voluntary work, looking after the welfare of families of servicemen. That would take her out a bit, and help air her wardrobe. Or perhaps she was thinking of my dad and of how relieved he would be that it was all over, and she could once again take her rightful place in the home.

There was much shifting in the court, the shift of boredom. I wondered if Mrs Baker was bored, and perhaps even her husband, despite the fact that the judge's speech was all about him. I looked at his face but it was devoid of any expression. He looked like a foreigner who was waiting patiently for some translation.

The judge was clearly coming to the end of his speech. I heard an unmistakable finality in his tone. 'If you are satisfied,' he was saying, 'that the accused killed Peter Roger Thorne, that he had the motive and that he had the weapon, it would be your duty, whether or not you regarded it as an unhappy one, to return a verdict of guilty. Members of the jury,' he concluded, 'you will retire to consider your verdict.'

Mrs Baker was now in full flow. Her face was buried in her companion's fur coat-collar. The jury stood up as one, and filed out after their leader. When they had retired, members of the public rose and made their way to the exit doors. Mrs Baker was in no condition to move, despite a suggestion of a cup of tea which I eavesdropped from her companion. I decided to stay where I was for fear of being seen. But also because I was not inclined to overhear the verdict of the man and woman in the street. 'Shouldn't be long,' I heard one of them say as he left, and I didn't know whether such a prophecy was good or bad. I watched the prisoner as he was turned by his guards. After a few steps, only his head was visible, and that dreadful giveaway of a middle parting. The court was now mostly empty. Even the important-looking wig-heads had disappeared. But some of the lawyers sat around and chatted to each other, even those from opposite sides, and they appeared to be the closest of friends. I was now the sole occupant of the back row of the court and I feared that in my isolation, I might be conspicuous. I thought it better to mix with the crowd in the waiting hall outside. I slithered to the exit. The hall was crowded and it would be easy to lose myself in its mass.

Through a crack in the crowd, I saw a familiar face. It took me a while to place it, and then I suddenly connected it with a newspaper photograph of the dreaded Mildred, grieving widow of the murdered man. She was surrounded by comforters, one of whom was surely the man she'd gone off with. I didn't wonder who was looking after *her* children. It was all her fault. I imagined her dead husband coming home to find her note, and in his raging hate of all women on earth, he had gone on a rampage of coital punishment. And even in that, he had been thwarted. First by being caught by Mr Baker, then by Mrs Pugh for his poverty, and finally by me for his interference. Poor bugger, I thought, and for the first time since the back lane, I felt sorry for him. I looked daggers at Mildred. I wondered she had the nerve to put in an appearance.

I leaned against the skirting of the crowd and a voice from nowhere announced that the jury were about to return. They had been out for barely half an hour, and I wondered whether it took an equal length of time to find a man guilty or innocent. The crowd surged towards the court doors. Once again I wondered whether or not I should go home and once again I was propelled in the direction of the verdict.

I took my seat at the back of the court. The silence that fell, fell by degrees, and when it was settled it was as if ordered by a ghost. It was a silence that smothered even the ascending footsteps of the prisoner and the entrance of the judge. Only when the jury returned was the silence broken. Solemnly they took their seats, aware that they were kings of court, and now the focus of all our attention. Then the clerk of the court rose and said, 'Members of the jury. Are you agreed upon your verdict?'

The foreman rose. He was about to celebrate a few seconds of fame. Never again in his life would he sense that frisson of absolute power.

'We are,' he said. His voice broke a little with stage fright. Then it was the clerk's turn once more. 'Do you find the prisoner, Hugh Elwyn Baker, guilty or not guilty of the murder of Peter Roger Thorne?'

The foreman waited for the echo of the victim's name to die away around the court. He wanted no residual echo. His verdict would be declared into a crater of silence. 'Guilty,' he said. Mrs Baker screamed and once more her companion offered her fur collar for comfort and soft-pedalling.

The clerk spoke again. 'You find him guilty of murder and that is the verdict of you all?'

'That is so,' the foreman said.

I looked at Mr Baker. His eyes were closed. Perhaps he was praying. Or he might even have gone to sleep, so devoid was his face of any expression. Mrs Baker's sobs, now muted by fur, were still audible. People in her row shifted themselves out of her proximity as if in fear of contamination. There was a murmuring in the courtroom so that the judge once again had cause to use his gavel.

'Prisoner at the bar,' the clerk turned to address Mr Baker. 'You stand convicted of murder. Have you anything to say why the court should not give you judgement of death, according to the law?'

My confession was on the tip of my hot and fiery tongue, and I prayed it would never, never give voice. But I said it to myself, in a whisper, over and over again.

We were all waiting for some words from the prisoner. If

for nothing else than the fact that he was sorry. He opened his mouth for to speak. I saw it form a few words, but there was no sound.

'I ask again,' the clerk said. 'Have you anything to say?'

This time the sound obliged. 'I am innocent,' he said. Gently and softly, and suddenly Mr Baker had achieved such dignity and decorum that it is possible that each member of the jury wondered if they had made a terrible mistake.

The judge rose. He slipped his hand into his pocket, where he had been hiding the props of the verdict. He placed the black cap on his head. Then he spoke.

Since that time I suppose I have learned the words by heart, but I remember them now as if it were yesterday. 'Hugh Elwyn Baker,' the judge said, 'you have been found guilty of murder. The sentence of the court upon you is that you be taken from this place to a lawful prison, and thence to a place of execution and that you be there hanged by the neck until you be dead. And that your body be afterwards buried within the precincts of the prison in which you shall have been confined before your execution. And may the Lord have mercy on your soul.'

I felt the tears run down my cheeks. But there was no blood. Tears were worse, I thought. A worse life sentence, for they demanded specific explanation, whereas a nosebleed seemed to a viewer to be purely physical and could be medically explained away. Constant tears would be viewed with more suspicion than sympathy. I used one of my hankies, and then I joined the crowd which was moving towards the exit. I left Mrs Baker and her companion and I felt a measure of relief as I moved out of her orbit. Outside the court, I recognised some of the jury members, and I decided to wait for my mam. I didn't care any more if my truancy was discovered. It seemed to me to be such a trivial offence. She saw me and called my name.

'What's the matter, luv?' she said, coming towards me and seeing my tears.

'I'm sorry for him,' I said.

'He deserves it though,' my mam said, though I noticed there was less conviction in her voice than before. 'What are you doing out of school?'

'Playing truant. I wanted to see you in action.'

That pleased her a little. 'I'll write you a note,' she said. 'Say you're ill. Now stop crying,' she said. 'There's nothing you can do about it.'

But I knew there was much I could do about it. Three words in a policeman's ear, 'I did it', and Mr Baker could be back with his wife and family.

'Let's go home and have a nice cup of tea,' my mam said. 'Have to take off this suit first though,' she said. 'Don't think I'll ever wear it again. Duw, I don't want to think about it.'

We walked home in silence and my tears slowly dried. Dad was waiting for us in the kitchen and there was no *Echo* in his hand.

'Heard it on the wireless,' he said, forestalling my mam's final bulletin. 'Guilty he was. Doesn't surprise me. When's the hanging then?'

'There'll be an appeal,' my mam said. 'Bound to. There always is. I'll get the tea.' She was anxious to change the subject.

'I'll get it, Mam,' I said. 'You go and take off your suit.'

She went upstairs.

'How's your hands, Dad?' I said.

'Bandages off tomorrow. I shall be able to hold a glass of beer proper,' he said. 'What's your mam going to do tomorrow then?'

'Why don't you ask her yourself?' I said.

I went into the scullery to make the tea. I put out some broken biscuits. I thought my mam deserved a treat of sorts. She was downstairs by the time the tea was brewed and dressed in an old everyday frock with an overhead apron. Her drab and dull clothing signalled her return to housewifely life. I put my arms around her. 'You did very well, Mam,' I said.

It was what my dad should have said, and she would have wanted it from him. But she had to settle for me. And as she poured the tea, my dad said, 'Bron's right, you know. You should do it every day.'

So my mam was satisfied.

I went back to school the next day, armed with a note. And my mam took my dad to the hospital for to have his bandages removed. I'd noticed she'd put on one of her jury dresses and I was glad she'd taken the trouble to look smart for my dad.

We'd listened to the wireless while we were having our breakfast and it was on the news. And not the Welsh one either, but the national, and my dad was very proud. Only the last item of news it was, but at least it was on the national agenda. Made my dad feel part of the universe it did.

There was only one week left of school and then I would be done with it for ever. My exam results would come at the end of August and then I would know if I could go to university. I thought of Mr Baker, but I didn't give up hope. There would be an appeal. Quite often they succeeded and the sentence would be commuted to life imprisonment. And if that happened, I would find a way of visiting him. And talk him out of his middle parting. And bit by bit, I would tell him. I'd tell him the truth and I'd get it off my chest once and for all.

We had a school concert at the end of term and my mam and dad came. My dad had gone back to work, but he took time off special, and he wore his suit too. And my mam wore a jury frock and I was very proud of both of them. Most of the concert was singing but there were recitations and the orchestra too. Miss Hardcastle, our headmistress, gave a speech, and though she was English, she was very pleasant and not uppity at all. She said that the sixth form had done very well and that she was optimistic about its results, and my mam looked at me and smiled. I smiled back, but I wasn't happy. I kept thinking of Mr Baker sitting in his cell and feeling the rope around his neck. And I felt it around my neck too, where it was more justly deserved. But I kept smiling to fend off the tears.

The day after we broke up, my mam took out her sewing machine once more, and turned my gymslip into a very smart skirt. She took the badges off my blazer and removed the red binding. 'Wear it to university you will,' she said.

Every day we listened to the wireless and from it we learned that an appeal had been lodged on behalf of Hugh Elwyn Baker. The Home Secretary, the wireless said, was giving full consideration to the case. The word 'full' lifted my hopes a little. At least his consideration would not be half-hearted.

'How long will that take?' my dad asked.

'Well, he'll have to go through all the papers, won't he,' my mam said. 'Shouldn't take long though.'

My mam was the authority on the law in the house, by virtue of her experience, so we took her word for it. But we listened to the news every bulletin. We didn't bother any more with the Welsh service. We had become much too grand for that. Day after day we waited. We listened to the eight o'clock news in the morning, the one o'clock, the six and the nine. And all the war bulletins in between. For a whole week we were well versed in the progress of the war on all fronts. The flying bombs had hit London, and the Red Army was within reach of Warsaw. We knew all that, but we were waiting for news about Cardiff.

'Taking his time he is,' my dad said at the end of the week. 'You'd think he would have made up his mind by now.'

'I'm sure he's got lots of other things to do,' my mam said, though I could see no reason why she should leap to the defence of the Home Secretary.

It was the following evening that the news came through. It was on the six o'clock bulletin and my mam was pouring the tea at the time. We'd listened to all the war news when Alvar Liddell said, 'Finally,' as a means of introducing his last report. 'Finally,' he said, 'the Home Secretary has considered the case of Hugh Elwyn Baker, sentenced to death for the murder of Peter Roger Thorne, and he sees no reason why the sentence of death should not be carried out. The appeal is denied. The execution will take place at Cardiff Prison at eight o'clock tomorrow morning.'

And my nose, without warning, started to bleed.

'Poor bugger,' my dad said.

'His poor wife and children,' was my mam's contribution. At least it was a change from boring old Mildred. But for my part, I couldn't find any words at all.

And still with no words, at least none that would spill out, except perhaps in the nightmare I couldn't recall, I rose early in the morning and made my way towards the prison. As I reached the end of the terrace, I heard the clock strike the half-hour. I wondered what Mr Baker was thinking, and whether the last thirty minutes of his life would cruelly crawl, or graciously gallop towards its unjust end. By the time I reached the prison gates, Hugh Elwyn Baker had but ten minutes to make his peace with the sheer unfairness of this world and to picture if he could, for the last time, his wife and children.

There were many people at the gates, come to gloat or mourn. But all were silent. Some knelt on the harsh ground in prayer. Some wept, some shifted with a survivor's shuffle, as we waited there for the eight o'clock passing bell. When it tolled, there was a sigh which hovered like a sad breeze, a sigh shrouded in despair. Inconsolable. The worshippers remained on their knees, their prayers louder now with the urgency of abandoned hope. Then one of their number began to sing, and the soft and gentle hymn of 'Abide with Me' pealed over the prison square in final abdication. But no sound came from my lips, choked as I was with my shame. At last, the white notice was pinned on the prison gates. As the warder withdrew, the crowd surged forward. But I stood motionless where I was.

And bled.

PART TWO

CHAPTER EIGHT

My name is Bronwen Davies. I have to keep telling myself that. That was my name when I killed a man. After more than fifty years, I wonder whether I am still called Bronwen, whether I am still that person who killed a man because he tried to . . . well, you know what he tried to do. But yes, I am that Bronwen still, and when I think about it now, over fifty years later, it still seems like yesterday.

It was a year after that day when I couldn't sing 'Abide with Me' that the war was over. And we won. It had never crossed our minds that we would lose, even in the worst of times. We just didn't think that way. All of us were very happy of course, except perhaps Blodwen from Abertillery who had had to bid a fond farewell to her Hershey source. There was still rationing and coupons, but there were more tinned goods in the shops, and I didn't have to oblige the corner grocer with my gymslip any more. In any case I wasn't wearing it. It was a skirt now, like I said before, and I wore it to university. I got a scholarship there, and my mam and dad were very proud of me. My dad went back to his pre-war job as a gas-fitter with the Welsh Gas Board and my mam busied herself with new lodgers. When the war ended, Mr Travers and Mr Philips went back where they'd come from. We were neither glad nor sorry to see them go. In their four years of attic residence and bathroom sharing, neither had made much of an impression. So my mam gave up on paying guests and took in students instead. Now that I was a student the term was respectable enough and she was obliged to replace the Travers/Philips income. In the terrace, the one half of the Watkins' estate that the Germans had overlooked was demolished and the Watkins were never seen again. Perhaps they were ashamed. Of all the houses in the terrace, only theirs had been chosen and it looked like a personal punishment for some gross misdemeanour. But the Watkins neighbour, each on either side, now enjoyed a new status, that of semi-detached, though they had to endure the constant traffic of bikes and pedestrians who used the space as a short cut to the back lane. The houses shed their blackout curtains and the criss-cross tape on each window, and the terrace was bright again. Overnight Mr Griffiths had become a nobody, stripped of his uniform and his authority and he was rarely seen outdoors because no one had to respect him any more. I saw him once, clinging to Mrs Griffiths' arm, and for a moment, which I am glad to confess did not last long, I felt sorry for him. Mr Thomas came out of his mourning shell and was often seen at work on his small patch of front garden, while, on the windy corner, despite GI repatriation, Mrs Pugh and her blossoms flourished.

And so did we, in that we got ourselves a telephone. We didn't use it much because it was quite expensive but it was nice to come home and see it stuck on the wall in the hallway. A pay-phone it was, because of the lodgers. You put your money in the slot and dialled the number. If somebody answered you pressed button 'A' and if there was no reply you pressed button 'B' and you got your money back. It was the practice to press button 'B' anyway, even after a long conversation. There was no harm in trying. Our number was one eight eight nine, or one double eight nine, as my mam used to say, tripping it off her tongue like she'd had a telephone all her life.

Despite my problems with *Middlemarch*, I had done well in my English paper at school, gaining a distinction in fact, and it was because of that mark that I was granted a scholarship. So I thought I was more or less duty-bound to read English at university. For some reason I felt I owed it to the authorities. We were like that in our family. We had that tiresome talent for gratitude. My mam was like that. And my dad. Do one small favour for either of them and they were indebted for life. Well, like I said, I went to university, and I still took the tram but this time it was up Queen Street and into the centre of town. The Civic Centre it was called because the City Hall was there, and the National Museum of Wales and all kinds of white important buildings that had to do with government. It was the pride of Cardiff, that Civic Centre, and I used to walk past it every day and wish I had a foreigner at my side to show it off to.

It was all very different from school. There was no such thing as truancy from a university. If you didn't feel like going, nobody bothered you. And you didn't have to wear uniform either. But the biggest difference was the presence of boys. Or men, as they called themselves. But I hadn't known many boys in my life, and I wasn't ready yet to call them men. I felt I was entitled to a 'boy' period before I could take them as seriously as they took themselves. Perhaps they felt the same about us girls who thought we were supposed to be women, so for the first year, at least, the two genders collided in confused expectation and many hearts were given and broken in error. But not mine. After a few initial encounters, I gave the boys a wide berth. They were all like my mam and Auntie Annie had said they were. Dirty creatures and only after one thing. To start with, I liked a few of them. Gwylim especially. But even he turned out like the rest. But at least he gave himself a few weeks before touching me. And then it was just kissing in the park. I liked that. I'd never been kissed before, well, you know, not properly, and I didn't mind it at all. It gave me tingling feelings and at night in bed when I thought about Gwylim's kisses, I felt the tingling all over again. But then he started touching me, and like my mam and Auntie Annie said, he was like the rest of them. But I had lots of girlfriends, and some of them went out with boys and were even going steady as they called it, and I knew that going steady meant more than just kissing, and I began to wonder if there was something the matter with me. But we never talked about that sort of thing, so I stuffed it into the back of my mind where it joined that other unmentionable and that other unthinkable. And all I understood was that they were chaotically akin. I knew I couldn't ever deal with it, so I didn't even try. Somebody else had made my bed and I was obliged to lie on it. But I didn't feel myself unfairly done by. Had I complained about my lot, it would have smacked of a lack of remorse.

I will not dwell on my years at university. Since I was not inclined to avail myself to any event, those years were uneventful. I managed to achieve a reasonable degree together with a Certificate of Education which qualified me to work as a high school teacher. And, as always, my mam and dad were very proud of me. Throughout those years, my nostril prickled from time to time, but there was rarely any blood, and I began to think that my nose, having so repeatedly and so ably called the unthinkable to mind, was now prepared to settle for its natural functions of breathing and smelling. I do not dwell on those years, for in truth I do not remember them well. Perhaps it was because they were so unremarkable. Now when I think of them, it is only Gwylim whom I remember. And his kisses. He must be married now, and a grandfather even. Or perhaps he is dead, but I shall be forever grateful for his tingling legacy.

While I had been at university, my mam had suffered a

rapid turnover of lodgers. She herself had asked them to leave. They were noisy and spent too long in the bathroom. She was happy to give up on the income they afforded when I was able to replace it with part of my teacher's wages.

I got a job in a girls' high school, a ten-minute bus ride from the terrace. I was twenty-two years old, and in those days it was certainly old enough to be thinking of marriage. And if you were not thinking about it, or, as in my case, you dared not, you could be sure that your mam and dad were thinking about it for you. Especially when Molly Smith, your best friend, though not best enough for the back lane, walked down the aisle in her illegitimate white.

My mam and dad never talked about it. At least not directly. Their references were oblique. And visible. My dad had taken up with the *Echo* again, which he had dropped as superfluous after 'Abide with Me'. And now my mam pored nightly over the engagement and marriage columns, reading them out loud, and emphasising the brides' ages when they were given, especially when they were younger than mine. There would come a time, I supposed, when my mam would read the death columns. But these she would read without envy. More perhaps with a survivor's relish. But now she was too young for that. It was engagements that concerned her, and above all, my own.

Her concern, oblique as it was, disturbed me. I loved my mam and dad and I wanted to please them, but I feared that as far as marriage was concerned, I would be a great disappointment. I wasn't against marriage in principle. Indeed I would have loved to settle with a partner and be as happy together as my mam and dad. And I would have liked, too, to have children, if for no other reason than that my mam wanted to be a granny. But all that was in principle. I knew that in practice, I could not fulfil that wish. My nose told me so and I knew better than to argue with it.

I saw quite a lot of Molly in those days. Molly Jenkins, as she had turned out to be. She was anxious to show off her new house and furniture. She was more attached to her material possessions than to the man who had provided them, together with the bun in the oven that had propelled her, white-insistent, to the altar. When the baby would be born, she would declare it premature and thus merit sympathy rather than shame. Molly's husband, Alun, had a twin brother called Dewi whom he was deeply anxious to marry off. Dewi was suffering from his sudden undeniable bachelorhood. Alone, he felt unanchored, and he missed that familiar who for so long had been at his side. Whenever I called upon Molly, and always at her invitation, Dewi just happened to be there. It did not take me long to cotton on to Molly's intention, but there was no way I could oblige her. There was nothing wrong with Dewi except that he was like all of them and only after one thing. But my mam thought, and so did my Auntie Annie, who had joined her in the *Echo* readings, in spirit anyway because my Auntie Annie never bought the *Echo*, both of them thought that 'only one thing' was a small price to pay for a roof over one's head and a lifetime's protection. And again, in principle, I might have agreed with them. But how could I explain to them why, in practice, it was impossible? I hoped that in time they would give up their struggle and accept their long-felt suspicions that there was something very wrong with me.

I suspected that my mam used to confide her daughter problem to Mrs Pugh. We no longer needed her cellar, but my mam had become quite fond of her, and often they took tea together when my dad was out at work, and sometimes I found them chatting in the kitchen when I came home from school. I knew they'd been talking about me, because they seemed suddenly to have run out of conversation as I entered the room.

'Found me a husband yet, Mrs Pugh?' I laughed. I thought it best to make a joke of the whole affair.

'I'm sure you can find one for yourself,' Mrs Pugh said.

'I'm not looking,' I laughed again and I put my hand on my mam's shoulder. I wanted to tell her that I was a good daughter and could be an even better one if I didn't marry. I felt easier being with my dad. He never mentioned marriage or gave any indication of his concern. Though I was sure it worried him. He just left the arguments to my mam. My Uncle Gwyn was like that throughout the Blodwen trouble. He left all the arguments to my Auntie Annie. But in the end, and even to this day, it was my Auntie Annie who took all Blodwen's blame and all my auntie had been was my Uncle Gwyn's patsy. But however my dad was using my mam, I would never blame either of them. They both had my good at heart, but it was impossible for me to be kind to myself.

As I grew older, and still in my single state, my mam's concern intensified. She couldn't understand it at all. I was pretty, I had a good figure, and I'd had a good education. My mam thought I was a blessing for anybody. She simply couldn't understand it. Then one day it occurred to her that my continuing spinsterhood was in some way connected with my nose-bleeding. She was right, of course, but I knew the bleeding was only a symptom, whereas my mam convinced herself it was the cause. Over the years since the back lane, the bleeding had become less frequent, but I could assuredly rely on the Christmas dinner flood. And it was the last Christmas that my mam connected it with the turkey, again the symptom and not the cause, and she decided that I was allergic to turkey meat and thereafter I would be served a Christmas chicken. My poor mam.

I was pushing twenty-seven, still pretty, still slim, still well educated and still a blessing, when she broached the nose subject while we were chatting in the kitchen.

'Are you ashamed of it, luv?' she said.

Then before I could give an answer, even if I'd had one, she said, 'Nothing to be ashamed of. Part of your nature it is, girl. No man is going to take exception. Shy of it you are,' she said, 'and there's absolutely no need.'

She was shouting at me now, and I heard it as the crescendo of her pain. And I was so moved by her sadness that I decided there and then that whatever the cost, I would marry the first available man I would meet. And within the week, he made his appearance.

David Parsons was his name. He was handsome, slim, well educated and a catch. I rehearsed my future. Bronwen Parsons. It would do. The only drawback as far as my family was concerned was that he was English, but at my age, they couldn't afford to be picky. Even Auntie Annie overcame her prejudice and found some compensation in the fact that at least he had a Welsh forename and she decided she would call him Dai.

My meeting with David Parsons was accidental. At least that's how my mam read it. But in truth it was a pick-up and it was I who did the picking. It was on the day that my school broke up for half-term. It was only three o'clock and I dawdled my way home. There was a tea shoppe on the corner of the school building. It was newly opened, a novelty in those days. It symbolised a post-war optimism. I had never been inside, though I passed it every day, and through the windows I could see that it was usually crowded. On that day, relieved perhaps that a whole week's holiday was in store, and already in a holiday mood, I had the courage to enter. It was pretty crowded and my nerve began to fail. There was one table in the corner at which a lone man sat, the man later to be known as David Parsons. It was clearly a table for two. I resented the fact that he had not taken full advantage of the accommodation. I resented it on behalf of the management and their subsequent loss of profit. And it was with the purpose of making up that loss that I made a resolute move towards the table and without even asking his permission, I sat down opposite him. Looking back on it now, I probably made that move for the sake of my mam, and the café's profit or loss had nothing to do with it. I did not look at the man's face, but I saw a pot of tea in front of him, and a half-eaten sponge cake on a plate. I watched his hand pick up the cake fork, and the hand impressed me. It was smooth-skinned with long and tapering fingers. I thought he might be a musician.

'Is it nice, that cake?' I asked without looking at him.

'It looks better than it tastes,' he said.

I found no fault with his answer, so I looked at him and was astonished at his rough and worldly good looks. He smiled at me and I experienced a moment of happiness I had not felt in a long while.

'You can finish it if you like,' he said, passing the plate towards me.

It was a gesture that a brother might have made, or a father who was watching his weight. Or perhaps even a long-standing husband who still indulged his weak-willed wife.

'D'you come here often?' he said.

'This is my first time.'

'Mine too.'

Just then the waitress hovered at my shoulder. I asked for a coffee. It seemed perverse to order a coffee in a tea shoppe, but I was feeling perverse and behaving in a way quite contrary to my nature. The waitress was in no way put out. She simply repeated my order and made her way to the tea-urned kitchen. We looked at each other. Another smile. One of us had to say something. I scratched in my mind for some topic that had nothing to do with either of us. I was not curious as to his person or his profession. Or any aspect of his character. I simply wanted to marry him to please my mam. And for that I didn't need to know anything about him. But I was prepared to tell him about myself should he show any interest. After all, if he was going to be my husband, he was entitled to some details about his intended. Although the choice was mine, I was cunning enough to disguise it as his own decision. He lost no time in investigating what he was letting himself in for. 'What do you do?' he asked.

'I'm a teacher. English. I work at the school up the road.' At that point I should have asked him what he did for a living. But I honestly didn't care. He offered his credentials never-theless, and without any encouragement on my part.

'I'm a teacher too,' he said. 'I lecture at the university. Chemistry.'

My mam would be over the moon with that, I thought. In her terms, just to go to university was sure arrival. To teach there was a triumph beyond compare. I totted up the approx-imate sum of our total earnings. We could live well enough on that income and I could still give some of it to my mam.

'What's your name?' he asked.

I gave it to him and he volunteered his own.

'David. David Parsons,' he said.

I considered he was very forthcoming. I could spend a life-time with him with my mouth firmly shut. And in my silence even my nostril might go about its own breathing and smelling business and leave the back lane alone. I smiled at him again and with genuine pleasure. I thought I would be very happy with him. And with this thought, I took my share of the questioning.

'Where d'you come from?' I said. 'You're not Welsh, are you?' I may well have put that question on behalf of my Auntie Annie, but I too was interested in his provenance.

'I'm from London,' he said.

'Were you in the army?' It was a way of finding out his age.

'Navy,' he said. 'HMS *Chatham*. Not far from home. And never moved from there. It was a training ship, but the war was over before I could see any service. I was lucky,' he said.

It was then that the waitress brought my coffee. David asked for another tea and I was glad he wanted to spend more time with me.

'Are your parents still in London?' I asked, and as I watched him pale I deeply regretted the question. And then I did something that was totally against my nature. I touched him, I put my hand on his. It was my gesture of apology. He did not look at me, but he put his other hand on mine.

'Killed in the Blitz,' he said. 'Both of them. At least they were together.'

'I'm sorry,' was all I could say.

'If they'd stayed at home they would have been all right. Our house was untouched. But they were visiting and they were caught on the way home. It was in the City. At a bus shelter.'

'I'm sorry,' I said again. 'It must have been terrible for you.'

He took his hand away and lifted his cup. I did likewise and we were silent until the waitress came back with his tea.

'D'you have any brothers or sisters?' I asked.

'No. I'm an only. I was pretty lost after the war, I can tell you. But I got a grant to go to university. I'd done my Higher Certificate before the war and I wanted to go on with chemistry. And I wanted to get out of London. I was given a place here so I sold the family house and bought one in Cardiff. After my degree I was offered a lectureship. End of story.'

Well, he was certainly handsome, he was certainly slim, he was certainly well educated. And even more certain than any of these was that he was a catch.

He finished his tea and called for the bill, and as I reached for my handbag, he motioned it aside. I thanked him and noted that he left a generous tip. On our way out of the shoppe, he told me that he had a meeting to attend but he asked if he might see me again. I gave him our telephone number. 'One double eight nine,' I said, as my mam would have told him, and he wrote it down together with 'Bronwen' in a little notebook.

'I'll call you tomorrow,' he said.

So began our courtship. Or, as my mam put it to Auntie Annie, 'Bron and Dai are going up the mountain.' And we did exactly that for one whole month before he touched me. And then it was to kiss me as Gwylim used to do, but there was no Gwylim aftertaste. And when I lay in bed at night, it was Gwylim I had to think of to feel the tingle. But that didn't worry me. In truth I was relieved. There was about David's kisses a sense of arrival, a feeling that they had landed and had no intention of going any further. And my nostril confirmed it, for it did not move one prickle.

I was happy in those days. David was a wonderful companion. We saw each other every day and each meeting's end was sealed with an arrival kiss. I could in all senses accommodate him. And happily. After about a month of our courting, I decided to take him home for supper. My mam wanted notice, at least a week she said, for to shop and to prepare the meal.

'D'you like him, girl?' my mam asked.

'I do,' I said, unconsciously rehearsing my nuptial vows.

'Well, that's all right then. Shall we have your Auntie Annie?'

'Of course,' I said. 'I want him to meet the family.'

'Well, you won't be meeting his family, will you. Poor soul,' my mam said.

I hoped she wasn't going to make a Mildred of David's blitzed parentage, and I asked her not to mention them.

'I wouldn't dream of it,' she said. 'Poor boy.'

'He's all of thirty, Mam,' I told her.

'Nothing like a mature man,' she said and I knew she didn't have the slightest idea and certainly not the experience of what she meant. 'What's his house like then?' she asked for the umpteenth time.

'I told you.'

'I want to hear it again.'

She knew it by heart. So did my dad to whom she had relayed it and no doubt with her own embroidery. And so did my Auntie Annie.

'Well,' I started again on my real estate recital and I sounded like a house agent lauding a property hard to shift, 'it's in Cyncoed.' In many ways, its location said it all and my mam would have been satisfied with just that. But I went on to describe the kitchen and what we would have called the parlour. But there was a dining room as well, with flocked wallpaper that called Mrs Pugh to mind. I couldn't describe the upstairs of the house because I'd never been beyond the ground floor and my mam was very pleased with that because it showed that David Parsons had respect for me. But not only had I not seen the upstairs of David's house, I didn't want to think about it in case it reminded my nose. Armed with hankies, I would deal with that storey after the wedding.

Not that David had proposed to me. And I did not expect it. I considered that move to be mine. But the night before he was due to have supper at our house, he gave me an arrival kiss at the beginning of the evening and I knew that something of moment was about to occur. After the kiss had landed, he continued to hold me in his arms.

'Bronwen,' he said, 'will you marry me?'

He's stolen my line, I thought, but it did not displease me, for now I knew that whatever would happen in our marriage, either for good or bad, he would have asked for it. But I was very happy. I answered straight away and with great joy because apart from making my mam happy, I considered that a marriage with David would make me very happy too. We sealed our vows with yet another arrival kiss, and after that we stayed together only a short while, for we each needed to be by ourselves. And I was glad to get home early for I was excited to break the news to my mam and dad.

They were having a cup of tea at the table when I got home. And a cake, too, for the broken biscuit days were over. When I told them, they sat and stared at me and then my mam started to cry. For years she had been saving those tears of joy which often during that time had threatened to curdle into sorrow. My dad was dry-eyed. He'd been schooled not to cry and certainly not in front of the ladies. But I knew that once he was alone, and assured that no one was looking, he would allow a few tears to fall.

My dad had bought some brandy to drink after tomorrow's supper, and he insisted on opening it there and then, so that we could drink a toast to my future happiness. Theirs too. And that's what we did. Just a small drop each, so that there would be plenty left for the next evening's celebrations.

'The house looks lovely, Mam,' I said. I could smell the polish, both of furniture and silver.

'We want to make a decent impression, girl,' my dad said. 'Especially now you'll be moving to Cyncoed. What a story for the terrace. Put it in the *Echo* we will.'

We lingered for a while over our brandy. I knew we all wanted to go to our beds. There were things we wanted to think and talk about, even to ourselves. I was the first to say good night and I kissed them both and both responded awkwardly.

'Can't wait to tell your Auntie Annie,' my mam said to cover her embarrassment. 'Pity she isn't on the phone.'

That night, before going to bed, I took off all my clothes and looked at my body. I don't think I had ever done that before. I had had no occasion to examine it and I was not vain. But that night, I felt I should look at David's entitlement, though I was going to make damned sure that he was never going to see it. For myself, I found it pleasing enough. Its shape was comely, and there was not an inch of spare flesh.

For a moment I regretted that no one else would ever see it. My nostril would forbid such an exposure. So I would have to be content with viewing it myself from time to time, and never, never to put it to any pleasurable use, and to be satisfied with arrival kisses.

It took me some while to get to sleep that night. I thought of David and over and over again I rehearsed my married name. Bronwen Parsons, Bronwen Parsons. As a mantra. And still I could not sleep. I covered the ground floor of David's house, inch by carpeted inch. I viewed the bareness of it and its crying out for a woman's hand. But that thought only served to keep me awake. And then at last, I went a-tingling with Gwylim. And sleep overcame me.

My mam was up early the next morning, and I heard her tinkering in the kitchen. She was singing too and I knew that she was happy. It was a Saturday and my dad would be having a lie-in, and I decided to get up and take him a cup of tea. But my mam thought it better to let him sleep.

'Don't want him under my feet today,' she said. 'There's lots to do.'

'Like what, Mam?' I said, since she had told me last night that everything was ready.

'I've got to lay the table for a start,' she said.

'I'll do that.'

'You have your breakfast first, then you can go to the corner and get me some cream.'

I didn't mind the errand, even though it was the same old groceryman who knew my gymslip by heart. But the old man had aged beyond appetite, and in any case, he no longer recognised me in my adult clothes.

'What we having, Mam?' I asked, though I knew the menu by heart. She had gone through it often enough since the invitation had been issued. But I knew my mam liked to itemise it as testimony to her good housekeeping.

'Well, we're starting off with tomato soup,' she said, though such a course hardly proved good management. There was the parsley garnish of course, but that would scarcely rate an entry into the *Good Food Guide*. 'Then there's salmon,' she said. 'Real salmon, not the tinned stuff. And all the trimmings. Salmon's cooked, and the potatoes are peeled. It'll just be the salads, and I'll do those later.'

'And afterwards?'

'Tinned peaches and cream,' she said with a flourish in her voice. 'We want to make a good impression, don't we, girl?'

'What are you going to wear, Mam?'

It had been almost ten years since the back lane, and my mam's wardrobe still consisted of her jury attire. She had bought nothing new since. Not so much for economy's sake, but that she wished occasionally to relive her moments of celebrity. My dad never made the connection, so it did not bother him.

'I'll wear my green,' she said. 'The one with flowers.'

She had no other green dress, but she wished to spotlight it, for she wore it on her first appearance on the opening day of the trial.

'And what are you wearing, luv?' she asked, though she must have known because I only had one best dress, a red shirtwaister with a black belt.

'My best,' I said.

'You'll look lovely you will. Your auntie Annie has bought a new frock. Went to Howells' she did. First time she's bought a frock in twenty years. You'll say she looks nice, won't you?'

'She probably will,' I said. I'd only ever seen her in one dress. A black one on which she varied brooches. I wondered whether I'd get yet another brooch for my wedding present.

'Our house is a bit different from Cyncoed,' my mam said nervously.

'David's marrying me. Not our house,' I said. 'Anyway, he

knows about our house. I've told him. He said he didn't care if I lived in a tent.'

'Well, we're a bit better than that,' my mam said. 'Still, he'll have to take us as he finds us.'

We heard my dad coming down the stairs. 'All ready then?' he shouted. He was in a good mood. He came into the kitchen still in his pyjamas, a white shirt folded over his arm.

'Iron it for me, luv,' he said to me. 'Want to look smart. Don't want to let you down.'

'You won't, whatever you wear, Dad,' I said.

I wondered if all daughters loved their parents as I did mine. My mam always said I never gave her any trouble, but that was only because she never gave any trouble to me. Nor my dad. They just loved me and left me alone. I wondered whether I could do the same for my children. But for me, children were only a fantasy. I knew that I would never have any, for I could not submit to the act that would produce them. Somehow or other I would have to explain that to David, with careful omissions of the back lane, but I would postpone dealing with that until I'd come to terms with the first carpeted storey of his Cyncoed home.

My Auntie Annie arrived early, shortly after her dinner, and she insisted on sitting down all the time so that she would not dirty her frock. She conducted the conversation from her chair, and to that chair we addressed the menu which she already knew by heart, and once again the layout of the Cyncoed home in which I would dwell as Mrs Bronwen Parsons.

'I like your dress, Auntie Annie,' I said once I had done with my real estate recital.

'Stand up,' my mam said, 'so's we can see it proper.'

My auntie stood up and with such care as if she were wearing glass. She smoothed herself down, though there were no creases, for the material was silk.

'Well, what d'you think then?' she said. She blushed a little, knowing that she looked more than presentable.

'It's beautiful, Auntie Annie,' I said. 'I've never seen you in
a colour before.'

'Makes a change from black, I'll say that for you,' my mam
said. But she clearly did not imagine that her sister would have
gone as far as wearing red. Red was a colour my mam associated with Mrs Pugh, and it took some adjustment to relate it
to her older and sober sister. She hoped David Parsons would
not be taking away a misleading impression.

'Two reds we'll be,' Auntie Annie said, 'and a green and
what with your dad, a brown.'

It was known to be the only suit my dad owned and he
brought it out every Christmas along with his phrase 'I am
replete', as if both hung on the same hanger.

'Come and see the table,' my mam said.

So Auntie Annie had to get up again and glass-tread to the
parlour. I followed them. My mam had gone to town on the
table, what with flowers and white paper serviettes. She'd
even taken down the dust-laden Christmas decorations and put
them by for the next turkey-carving. But even as that red-light
thought crossed my mind, my nostril was still and I began to
hope that the advent of David Parsons had erased my past.

'I think I'll go and have my bath,' I said. There was nothing more I could say about Auntie Annie's new dress or the
table settings, and I wanted to be alone for a while.

'Leave the water in for me,' my mam said. Her sense of
economy never left her, and the ending of the war and its pro-
scribed water-saving had made no difference. Neither had it
seen the removal of the black band around the bathtub and
from habit, I would not overlap it. I decided I would lie in the
bath and think of David and my future. It was a deliberate
decision, for I knew such thoughts would not arise of their
own accord. I ran the water to its allotted span, undressed, and

laid myself fully stretched on the cold enamel. It was not a
bath to wallow in nor comfortable enough to indulge in any
thought at all, leave alone the perilous ones of my future. So
I quickly washed myself and dried, and put on a dressing
gown. I would postpone my thoughts until my bedroom. But
sitting there on my bed, with no discomfort to disturb me, I
could in no way envisage my future, and therefore I could not
dwell on it. Neither could I think of my past. That was nostril country, and best avoided. So I thought of the present and
the celebration supper to come. And I wondered what David
would wear. I had never seen him in anything but corduroys,
both jackets and trousers. His shirts were varied but never for-
mal. I imagined he would arrive in a suit with a tie instead of
his usual silk cravat. I was excited. I was happy, and I would
allow no thoughts of past, present or future to unhinge my
mood.

I dressed myself and was pleased with the outcome. I heard
my mam come out of the bathroom. She was probably shivering from the remains of my already tepid bathwater. I gave her
time to get dressed, and then I went to her bedroom when she
was ready to be admired. She'd dressed up her jury frock a little. She'd attached a lace collar to the neckline. I didn't think
it was any improvement and my face must have betrayed my
disapproval.

'You're right, luv,' she said, and she took off the dress and
quickly unpicked the collar. Then she re-dressed herself.

'That's better,' I said. 'You look lovely. Is Dad ready?'

'He's downstairs, in a chair like your Auntie Annie. Keeping
themselves clean.'

We went downstairs and joined them in the parlour in time
for the six o'clock news. There was still an hour to go before
David was expected. There was nothing to do in the kitchen, so
we sat still and listened carefully to every item of the half-hour
bulletin, keeping our frocks clean. From half past six till seven

o'clock, we sat and stared at each other. I was about to break this silence with an enquiry after Blodwen, which was indeed scraping the bottom of the barrel, when mercifully the door bell rang. Nobody stirred. My father shrank further into his seat to declare his immovability. My Auntie Annie relaxed, knowing that she was not in the running for answering the door.

'You go, missus, it's your place,' my dad said from the trenches. My mam started to giggle. She was trembling with nerves.

'I'll go,' I said. 'I'll bring him in here.'

Then the three of them stood up in position of greeting.

I rushed to the door. I could see his blurred outline through the stained-glass window, the only window in the house that had survived the bombing. I hesitated before opening. I had caught my mam's nervousness. She was still giggling. I could hear the echo of it in the hall and I hoped that it would have subsided before we entered the parlour. At last, I opened the door. At first I couldn't see his face. It was masked by an enormous bunch of flowers and I thought, we only have one vase and it won't be nearly big enough. He lowered the bunch as I called him inside.

'For your mother,' he said. He kissed me on my cheek.

'And I thought they were for me,' I laughed.

'I've something special for you,' he said. 'I'll give it to you later.'

I took his free hand and led him into the parlour.

'This is David,' I said, and I introduced them one by one. All were speechless. The remnant of my mam's giggling was the only sound to break the silence.

'These are for you,' David said, handing the flowers to my mam.

The enormity of the bunch overwhelmed her. 'Duw, thank you,' she said. 'Thank you ever so much. They're lovely, aren't they, Dai?' She turned to my dad for help.

'Very lovely they are,' he said. 'Aren't they, Annie?' He passed the buck in his turn.

'Better get them in some water then,' Auntie Annie said, having no one to pass the buck to.

'I'll do it,' my mam said. 'Got to go to the kitchen anyway. Now sit down all of you, and Dai Davies, you can pour the sherry.'

My dad was glad to be given something to do, and my mam was glad to be out of it for a while. Her nervous gigglings embarrassed her and no doubt she was at that moment giving them full rein in the kitchen to be rid of them once and for all.

I ushered David to a seat while my dad poured the sherry. I noticed that his hand was shaking. My mam giggled, and my dad shook, and in my eyes it was a declaration of their care and love for me, and hopes for my happiness. Only my Auntie Annie sat serene, concerned still with keeping her frock crease-less and clean. My mam returned in time to take her sherry and she sat and stared at the floor. It was my Auntie Annie who initiated the conversation. 'How d'you like Cardiff then, Mr Parsons?' she said.

'Call me David,' he smiled, 'and yes, I like it very much.'

'Bit different from London,' my dad offered. He'd never been to London, but a small sip of sherry must have fired his imagination. I relaxed because I sensed that the initial stiffness had slackened.

'Yes, it's very different,' David said. 'But I prefer Cardiff. It's quieter and more friendly.'

'The Welsh are different,' Auntie Annie said. 'A very hospitable people they are. Quite different from the English.'

I hoped my Auntie Annie was not going to get on the nationalist wagon, for she would be unstoppable.

'Let's leave politics alone. This is a celebration,' my dad said, as if one were antithetical to the other.

'Better sense of family, the Welsh,' my auntie persisted.

She may have been right, but family was not a safe topic in David's presence. But he rose to Auntie Annie's assumption.

'I wouldn't know,' he said. 'I don't have a family any more.'

Serves you right Auntie Annie, I thought. But she did not take it amiss.

'Sorry I was to hear about your mam and dad,' she said.

'We were a happy family though, before the war. A bit like yours really,' David said, addressing himself to my mam. 'We did everything together.'

'What did your dad do for a living then?' This from Auntie Annie.

My mam and dad thought that was a rude question but they were glad it had been asked. They'd been too shy to ask it of me, or indeed any question relating to David's personal life. Perhaps they feared flaws, and they wanted no impediment to our marriage.

'He was a doctor,' David said.

There was no doubt that that made an impression for it was greeted with awed silence.

'A family doctor,' David added.

'A tragedy,' my mam said, and I recognised the Mildred tone, for though Mildred had fallen from grace, my mam's sympathies were readily transferable.

'Well, it's all in the past now,' David said, and I wished that I could find my own past so ably accommodated.

'Shall we have supper then?' my mam said.

As she stood up, David stood automatically and his good manners were noted around the parlour.

'Sit down at the table,' my mam said, and she went to the kitchen leaving my dad to arrange our places. But I could see that he was at a loss so I took over, and placed David between my mam and Auntie Annie. And I sat myself next to my dad to look after him.

The conversation eased over supper. David was as curious

as to my background as my mam and dad were about his. And though he'd heard much of it from me, he was happy to hear it again and from its original source. And so my mam and Auntie Annie, fortified as they were by the white wine they had sipped full of manners, shared their childhood in Tonypandy with their coal-mining fathers and uncles. They giggled their reminiscences together, holding nothing back, and it was as if David was already part of the family.

'No stopping those two when they get going,' my dad said when he could get a word in. It was his sole contribution to the conversation, but he was happy to listen from the sidelines.

So we listened to their stories of the tin baths in front of the roaring coal fires, the back-scrubbing and the accidents in the pit, the neglect of the mine-owners, and the final coughing silicosis and burial. But they giggled about these too, concentrating on the wakes and the mournings full of beer.

I could see that David was impressed and as I looked around the table, I resolved to remember that at that evening, and in that gathering, I had felt very happy. Somehow I knew that I would need that reminder for the rest of my life.

When the peaches and cream were eaten, my dad brought out the brandy and special glasses.

'We need a toast,' he said. He had no intention of proposing one. He simply wanted to set the scene. He filled our glasses and we raised them to a silence. At last Auntie Annie found the words to do the honours.

'Here's to our Bronwen and Dai,' she said, and with that new baptism she declared his full membership of the family.

So we sipped, embarrassed, and sat down once again.

'This is the moment, I think,' David said.

He took a small box from his inside pocket and handed it to me. I knew what was inside it, and so did everybody else, but we all prepared ourselves to be surprised.

'Open it then, girl,' my dad said.

I did as I was told, and the bright diamond solitaire winked across the table. David took it out of the box and took my left hand. Without a word, he placed it on my fourth finger. I stretched out my hand for all to see around the table. I looked at my mam's smiling face. A university lecturer, a house in Cyncoed, and now, to top it all, a sparkling diamond ring. Her cup of joy was running over.

CHAPTER NINE

We'd made our wedding plans, David and I. It would be a small affair, but I insisted on a church. And white too. He did not argue and the white insistence seemed to please him. We decided on a date in mid-July when the summer term would be over. He asked me where I would like to go for my honeymoon. Years ago when I was a child, long before yesterday and the back lane, we'd gone on a charabanc treat to Porthcawl, my mam, my dad and me, and we'd stopped off for a picnic on the green. Across the road there was a grand hotel. The Sea-bank it was called and you could see by the cars in the drive, and the people who strolled on the lawns, that the Sea-bank was exclusive and represented arrival. I remember my mam saying, 'One day you'll go in there, girl. When you're grown up and rich.' And my dad had laughed at the fantasy.

'I'd like to go to Porthcawl,' I told David, 'and stay at the Sea-bank Hotel.'

'Is that all?' he laughed. 'I thought Paris at least.'

But Porthcawl was my Paris and the Sea-bank Hotel my Georges V. I couldn't wait to get home to tell my mam.

We had just over six weeks to go and my mam and me, and sometimes my dad and Auntie Annie joined in, we made the wedding arrangements. First there was the guest list to compile. We started off by listing most of the terrace. One of the pleasures of getting married was the omission of Mr and Mrs Griffiths from the guest list. My mam and dad had never forgiven him, and they both made sure that they knew they wouldn't be invited. We ticked off most of the inhabitants of the terrace. They had known me since I was a child and they were entitled to see me well and truly married off. We hesitated at the corner house, Mrs Pugh's domain. Or at least my dad did, but with one look, my mam killed that hesitation, and Mrs Pugh's name was added to the list. It was my Auntie Annie who hesitated on Blodwen, or rather Gareth her drunken husband. 'He'll put us all to shame,' she feared. 'I'll keep an eye on him,' my dad volunteered, so Blodwen and her risky family were listed under Mrs Pugh. I added a few names of friends from school, and Molly Smith who was still my best friend but not best enough for the back lane, and we allowed another ten guests for David. They would all be friends because he had no family and that made about forty in all.

'I've got some money put by,' my mam said. 'We'll have caterers.'

'And I'll supply the wine and beer,' my Auntie Annie said. 'It'll be my wedding present.'

I kissed her and thanked her. Her present was worth a thousand brooches. 'I'll see to the invitations,' my dad said. 'Know a printer I do. At the gasworks. Does it in his spare time. Won't cost the earth. Just write it all down, luv,' he said to me, 'exactly what he should put.'

When my mam and I were alone, I broached the subject of the wedding dress.

'I want a white wedding,' I said. In respect of my strenuous virgin defences, no one on earth deserved a whiter wedding than myself.

'I'll buy the material, Mam,' I said. 'Satin, if you'll make it.'

'Of course I will, luv,' my mam said. 'We'll go out and buy a pattern tomorrow.'

Over the next weeks the house hummed with activity and my mam's sewing machine. I had gone to town on the satin, allowing for a very generous train.

'Calls for bridesmaids that train does,' my mam said.

Blodwen's two daughters would have qualified had they not been well known as delinquents, and Molly Smith, now Jenkins, had a son, and I daren't suggest Petal who might have shed a wholly different light on the proceedings. So that satin train would have to sweep the aisle unsupported.

I had chosen a difficult pattern but my mam saw it as a challenge. It called for twenty pearl buttons as a front opening. And not just buttons, but buttonholes to loop them. My mam loved buttonholing. She was an expert with the needle, as her mam and gran before her. I had inherited nothing of that needle talent and I hoped that David could sew on his buttons himself. It was this centre opening of the dress that took the longest time and my mam left it till last, busying herself with the leg-o'-mutton sleeves and the train. I tried it on a number of times during its making, but I wouldn't look at myself. I thought it might bring bad luck. Whatever that meant. So I relied on my mam's judgement throughout its making. It was about a week before the wedding that she started on the buttonholing. I watched her at work as she sang with pure happiness.

'What are you wearing, Mam?' I asked her.

'Never you mind,' she said. 'I've bought something new. *And* a hat. It'll be a surprise.'

I had bought my own veil and head-dress which needed no adjustment, but even that I did not view in a mirror. I intended to keep that viewing until just before I left for the church, when I could appraise the whole outfit entire.

I saw little of David during those hectic days of preparation.

But he phoned me every buttonholing evening. He had ordered the cars and the flowers, and the excitement in his voice matched my own. For a whole week before the wedding, I gave no thought to yesterday but at the same time I was conscious of *not* thinking about it, and I tried to dismiss a nagging sense of betrayal.

In those last few days of my spinsterhood, the whole terrace was busy. When I looked out of the front window, I saw our invitees returning home with large gift-wrapped parcels, and Dotty Williams, the local dressmaker, came out of number forty-two and went straight into number forty-four, going about a roaring trade. The whole terrace was busy with my wedding. Even the Griffiths, who busied themselves hiding behind their net curtains. I was an event in the terrace, as exciting as the murder in the back lane so many years ago.

But I wasn't thinking of yesterday. For the first time since 'Abide with Me' I concentrated on my future, on my days as Mrs Bronwen Parsons. But even in thinking about it, I felt a traitor. For to entertain a future diluted my obsession with yesterday and I was morally forbidden to envisage today, leave alone a tomorrow. I have said that during the days that preceded the wedding, I gave no thought to yesterday. But I hoodwinked myself. My nose, if nothing else, carried yesterday's indestructible banner.

On the morning of the wedding, a messenger boy delivered two corsages for my mam and Auntie Annie, and a little later my own wedding bouquet. My mam, already overwhelmed by David's references, was overcome by this latest sign of his generosity.

'I'll be getting my buttonhole at the church,' my dad said, fearful of being once more upstaged.

'We'll all be looking lovely,' my mam said, the peacemaker.

My mam and dad had had their baths, sharing the same water as was their custom. But this day I was allowed to have my own bath, topping it up with kettles of hot water, well above the Plimsoll line. My Auntie Annie was coming to our house first in order to take advantage of one of the two wedding cars that David had ordered, and she arrived two hours before pick-up time, and she stood in the parlour to avoid creases. My dad poured her a glass of sherry to give her something to do.

'I'll go and dress now,' my mam said, 'then I'll see to you, luv.' She wanted very much to dress me and especially to loop those twenty buttonholes that she had so diligently sewn. I was happy to let her do so. I was her only child and I was not likely to have a second white wedding.

While I was waiting for my mam to dress, I looked out of my bedroom window on to the terrace and I saw a number of net curtains raised, and behind them a sprinkling of spangled dress-made women waiting for the car. For although David had organised two cars, one for the family and one for the bride, my mam thought it was wasteful, and that those coming from the terrace could pile into the bridal car, temporarily stripped of its white ribbons. My dad would go with them, my mam arranged, for to see to the church seating, and then to re-ribbon the car for its journey back to the bride's home. My dad thought it was all very daft.

'Why can't they walk?' he grumbled. 'Or get their own cars?'

But my mam wanted to share David's generosity. 'It's not every day we have a wedding in the family,' she said, her blanket response to any criticism from my dad. From the raised net curtains opposite, it seemed that the terrace was in a state of anticipation and excitement and there was yet an hour to go. When my dad was dressed, he joined my upstanding Auntie Annie in the parlour and they both made a vertical and sherry pair. At last my mam was dressed and more than ready to prepare her only child for the church. My going-away suit, a grey worsted, with red silk lining, hung on a hanger outside the wardrobe. My packed honeymoon case lay on the bed with a bright 'Sea-bank' sticker on its front. And next to it, on the bed, was stretched my wedding dress with its twenty pearl buttons unlooped to facilitate entry. My mam lifted it gently and motioned me to step into its yards of satin skirt. She said nothing, as if silence was a fitting accompaniment to such an auspicious robing. I stepped inside, and slipped my arms into the leg-o'-mutton sleeves. My mam was my mirror and I could see on her face how pleased she was with her work.

'You've done a lovely job, Mam,' I said. 'You could make a good living dressmaking.'

'Couldn't dress strangers,' she said and she started to button. I made no attempt to help her. They were her buttonholes and she was entitled to savour each and every loop. She took her time.

'Beautiful,' she said after each looping.

At last it was done, all twenty of them, and she stood back to view the whole. 'You look lovely, girl,' she said. 'Now sit down and I'll put on the head-dress.'

I was a good deal taller than my mam, and even if I sat down she was still not on my level. So I sat on the bed, which was lower than the chair, to make it easier for her. And in such position she fixed the head-dress and the veil. 'Now stand up,' she said.

I rose and I could see the tears gather on her eyelids and then, in respect to her reticent roots, go back where they came from.

'Now look at yourself, girl,' she managed to say.

I walked over to the full-length mirror of the wardrobe. I felt my way, for my eyes were shut. I was nervous of looking at myself, at my full-length undeniable white commitment. My mam was guiding me and she placed me central to my reflection.

'Open your eyes now,' she said.

But I couldn't. She was standing behind me, out of the mirror's view, so I pretended I could see my full-length and pleasing reflection.

'It's lovely, Mam,' I said, and I turned away, my eyes now open to the undisturbing view of my mam's happiness.

We heard the cars draw up outside the door. And so did the others in the terrace. For their doors were suddenly opened, and the misters and missuses from the odd and even numbers trooped out in their wedding best. And it was a joy to view the Griffiths' firmly shut front door and the offended raised net curtains of their parlour. Then Mrs Pugh, more blowsy than ever before, brought up the rear of the guest list.

There was a knock on my door.

'Can I look at you, luv?' my dad said.

I nodded my permission to my mam and she opened the door. He marvelled at the sight of me, and, not having any words, he trembled.

'You don't look too bad yourself, Dad,' I said.

'Neither does your mam.' He took her arm. 'Too many there are,' he said. 'Some of them will have to walk. 'S not far. We'll take the ladies,' he said. He turned to me again, 'Duw,' he said. 'Beautiful you look, girl.' Then ashamed of himself, he returned to his arrangements. 'I'll be back in fifteen minutes for you. Won't bother taking off the ribbon. Too much trouble and time to put it back on again.'

They left and I was alone. I went to the window to watch the take-off. My dad saw the women into the second car, and when that was full, there was only the family and Mrs Pugh left to accommodate. I watched my dad usher Mrs Pugh into the front seat and she folded her billowing skirts into her lap. And the white ribbons billowed too in unison. Then my mam and dad and my Auntie Annie got in the back and I watched the two cars out of the terrace. And then, all alone, and with no shadows, I felt my way to the wardrobe mirror and opened my eyes and saw myself as a bride for the first time. And as I looked at myself, I actually *saw* my nostril quiver and I knew that this was no false alarm. I watched as a single pellet of blood landed on the fourth pearl button of my mam's fastenings, then on the fifth, the sixth, the seventh and the eighth, in a straight line, but thereafter at cruel random all over the skirt. And I heard a humming from my trembling mouth of 'Abide with Me'.

I started to unbutton, my fingers cramped in a frenzy. I didn't want to tear at the bodice for my mam had worked so hard in its making. As I unbuttoned, I thought of the bleeding Christ in the church where I was supposed to be married and I asked for forgiveness. At length I was able to step out of the dress and lay it on the bed like a shroud. I tore on my going-away suit to which I was no longer entitled, but going away I certainly was, and God knows where, except for certain, despite the shining label on my luggage, I was not going to the Sea-bank Hotel. I took off my engagement ring and laid it on the bloodstained dress. Then I took my bankbook, and with a betraying eye on my dismal future, my Certificate of Education. And I fled.

The terrace was empty. With the exception of the Griffiths, they were all waiting for me at the church. Along with David who would never forgive me. In sad time my mam would see the blood on the dress, my eerie signature, and she would understand, but in truth she would not understand at all.

I ran. I ran for my life. But most of all, I ran for my virginity. To preserve that, and thus to deprive myself of a lifetime of pleasure and fruition was the principal item in the catalogue of my atonement. It was the least I could do for Peter Roger Thorne, for Hugh Elwyn Baker, but most of all, for myself.

I ran. I leapt on a moving tram in Queen Street that

growled and rumbled to the bus station. There was a fleet of buses there, and I looked around for one that was prepared for take-off. I jumped aboard as the driver was warming up the engine. I found a seat at the back in the corner and I huddled there until we reached the open road. Then I dared straighten myself and tried not to think of what I had done.

I looked at my watch. It was eleven thirty. David had been ditched for half an hour, and there would be enough gossip in the terrace to last a lifetime. My mam would be holding back tears and so would my dad, and when they were alone, they would say 'Why?' together. My Auntie Annie would say nothing at all and wonder on what other occasion she could wear her new dress. Mrs Pugh would be full of understanding yet not knowing why she understood. And Blodwen would think me a fool for forgoing such a catch.

I was glad to see the conductor making his ticket-collecting way to the back of the bus. It would give me something else to think about. When he reached my place, he asked if I had a ticket. I shook my head.

'Where does this bus go?' I said.

He looked at me with a certain pity. 'Swindon,' he said.

I'd no idea where Swindon was, but it was a place with a name that was not Cardiff. 'That'll do,' I said. 'How much?'

'Single or return?'

Single. Most certainly. I had no intention of ever going back.

'Four pounds two and sixpence,' he said, and I wondered whether Swindon was in Wales. I didn't know the rate of fares per mile, so I had no idea how long my journey would take. Nor indeed what I would do when I got there. If Swindon were on a bus route, it must be a town of sorts and as such it must have schools. I would get a job there and make some kind of life for myself.

The passengers were dotted singly all over the bus, as if

their destination of Swindon was a sad and single pursuit. Each one of them had no one to talk to, so it was a silent journey which suited me well enough, for though my troubled thoughts would have welcomed disturbance, they would have found it irritating. I was deeply depressed. And frightened too. I had no fear of my future. That, in one way or another, would see itself out. And I hoped it would not be too long doing so. Rather it was the past that I feared. And not only the back lane of yesterday. I feared my recent past, my past of an hour ago when, in one move, I had managed to destroy the hopes and expectations of people whom I loved. My mam, my dad, my Auntie Annie. To say nothing of David. For I did love him, in my totally unacceptable fashion. With these thoughts, I did not like myself very much. But I was not all bad, I told myself. It wasn't my fault that I was in the lane at the wrong time. It wasn't my fault that what happened there managed to destroy me. It wasn't my fault that my nose had replaced my will. Neither was it the fault of Peter Roger Thorne if one took into account his dismal history of rejection. Nor could I blame the dreary Mildred, for who could fault her for her desertion of a sex-crazed lunatic. I had to face the fact that no one was to blame. Not even myself. But there was little point in telling that to my nose. It had a will of its own, and it ruled me with its cruel compulsion. I was sentenced to an existence empty of loving, a vacuum of response and an anguished sterility. And it was for life.

And with my mind in such a turmoil, I longed for sleep and oblivion. The purr of the bus was soothing, and I willed it as a lullaby, and when I woke up, some few hours later, the bus was slowly manoeuvring itself through a town centre. So this was Swindon, I thought. There was nothing particularly attractive about it, but I was in no mood to appreciate anything. All that mattered to me was that it was not Cardiff and that it was at least four hours away from the site of my downfall. The bus came to a stop at a station not unlike the one at Cardiff. I tried to look on the bright side. That was a favourite phrase of my mam's and already I missed her terribly. I had a little money, enough clothes – my Sea-bank wardrobe would have to do for Swindon – and a Certificate of Education which proved I could earn a reasonable living. But first I had to find somewhere to lodge. And a telephone. I had no idea of what I would say to my mam who no doubt, at this moment, was wringing her handkerchief by one double eight nine, but I had to assure her of my safety.

There was a policeman standing at the bus station, and I asked him if there was a youth hostel in the town. I knew we had one in Cardiff and I knew it was plain but cheap. He looked at my going-away suit, and my Sea-bank-labelled luggage and he must have thought I was worthy of something better than a youth hostel.

'There is one,' he said. 'But there are hotels too.'

There was a burr in his voice as if it had been dragged through gorse. But it was kindly.

'I'd prefer a hostel,' I said.

So he directed me to a place not far from the bus station and I managed to secure a single room there and a pay-box telephone in the hall. My depression lifted a little despite the sight of the machine and its reminder of the urgent and difficult call I had to make. It was almost five o'clock, too late in the day to start job-hunting, and I was faced with a night in a strange place, friendless, and with absolutely nothing to do. And I realised for the first time since my departure what chaos I had brought on myself. The thought crossed my mind that I should go straight home and face the mordant music of the terrace. But I was too ashamed and too cowardly to return.

I lay on my bed and wondered what I would say to my mam. I would have rehearsed it had I had the words, but 'sorry, sorry, sorry' was all that surfaced and in remorseful repetition. They would have to do. They were what I meant. They were words that came from my heart and needed no elaboration.

'Sorry, Mam,' I said aloud. 'Sorry. Sorry.'

I suddenly felt very hungry and I realised that apart from a cup of tea when I'd got up that morning, I hadn't eaten all day. Then I thought of all that food that my mam had ordered, all those salmons and salads and trifles, and I wondered if any of the guests had had the gall to eat it. I ruled out my mam and dad and Auntie Annie, but I could see old Blodwen tucking in with her Gareth at the bottle. Blodwen would say her children were hungry and that they'd come all the way from Abertillery. She would omit the fact that the family had stayed the night at Auntie Annie's, and had had a cooked breakfast before they left for the church. Apart from all the heartache, I had cost my mam and dad a lot of money, and I thought that 'sorry', however much repeated, would never be enough. But I had to try it. I had to put their minds at rest, at least to the matter of my safe being.

I collected change from my purse and I went into the hall. There was no one about, which was a blessing, for God knows what an eavesdropper would have made of my litany of 'sorrys'. Without any rehearsal I inserted my coins, and dialled the number, saying it aloud as I did so, for to practise my voice on my sorrow. The phone was answered immediately. And in panic.

'Bronwen? Bron?' My mam's voice, full of worry, full of fear, full of tears.

'Hullo, Mam.'

'It's Bron. It's Bron, Dai. Thank God you're safe. Where are you?'

'I'm in Swindon.'

'Swindon?' my mam repeated.

'Where's that when the cows come home?' I heard my dad whisper.

'I don't know,' I said.

'Are you all right?' my mam said again.

'I'm fine, Mam.'

'What are you going to do then?'

So far, not a word of reprimand. Not a single 'why', and I knew somehow that my mam would never ask it. So I answered it. Not with any reasonable answer, for I had none. At least none that she could fathom. But I had to acknowledge that there most certainly *was* a 'why' and my admiration for her that she had not asked it.

'I couldn't go through with it, Mam. I just couldn't. I'm sorry. I'm sorry.'

'But you're sure you're all right?' she said.

Just then the pips went and signalled the end of my phone time. I scrambled in my bag for more change, and had to dial again. This time my dad answered.

'You're not to worry, luv,' he said. 'You come home when you're ready. As long as you're safe. Nothing to be ashamed of. Your mam says that too.'

I started to cry. I had hurt them both terribly. I had shamed them in the terrace. I had cost them money they could ill afford. With all that, they had an inviolable right to be enraged, to punish me, to banish me from home even. I was crying because I was angry that they were so forgiving.

'I'll write to you, Dad,' I said, and I could see his lips moving as he would read my bewildering letters. Then the pips went again. 'I've no more change,' I said. I managed to tell them I loved them very much before the line went dead.

I felt no better after that call, and hungry as I was, I had lost all appetite. I thought I might go out for air and look a little at the accidental site of my future. Whatever that meant. But I had a feeling that Swindon would raise an eyebrow at a woman who walked alone. But bugger Swindon, I thought. I hated every square inch of it, even those many that I hadn't seen. I hated it because it wasn't Cardiff and because my mam and dad didn't even know where it was.

I went out and walked along the route I knew, and inevitably found myself back at the bus station. It seemed that the service had ceased for the day, for there was a line-up of coaches fitting each parking bay. I looked at the notices of their destinations. London, Manchester, Liverpool, Exeter. And at the end of the line, Cardiff. I went over to that bus of mine and I leaned against its entry door, so that my body-print at least would go back home.

There was a little café at the end of the station. The few people inside were bus drivers and station personnel. I ordered a coffee and a sandwich. People stared at me and whispered together as if I was a foreigner, which indeed I felt in this strange and random stopover. In my mind I tried to list the advantages of such a situation. I was in an unknown place, with perhaps exciting things to discover. But above all, I was a stranger. Not only to myself, but to others around me. I was anonymous. I had shed my birthplace, my parentage and above all, my back lane. All I retained from that time and that place was my nose and its quivering nostril. And that was unsheddable.

It was growing dark and I felt nervous of strange streets. I hurried back to my lodgings and was grateful to be feeling tired, with a fatigue enhanced by my depression. I hoped to fall into a deep sleep, and to awake in the morning with the strength and even the will to seek a new job and a more permanent lodging-place.

It took me just over a week to find a teaching post. The state schools were closed for the summer vacation, but there was an all-year-round college for part-time students. They offered me a job and I was grateful. The pay was slightly more than the official rate. The classes were small and the students eager to learn. I wrote to my mam as soon as the job was settled. I told them I missed them both and that I loved them, but I did not mention the aborted wedding. Neither did my mam in her letters to me. They gave news of my dad, my Auntie Annie and the terrace, and thanked me for the money I was able to send. Once settled in my new post, I looked around for lodgings. The school secretary gave me an address within walking distance of the college. A Mrs Pratt, a widow, who took in the occasional lodger, and she would be glad if I would call. And I did, on a Friday evening after school.

Mrs Pratt was a short woman, with a lack of height that suggested shrinkage. And this was proved to be true, for later on she showed me her wedding photographs and she was then taller than her already tall husband. I wondered whether over the years of their marriage it was he who had shrunk her, or whether she had seen to it herself, as a means of withdrawal from what had turned out to be an error of judgement.

She invited me inside, and I could hear a great squawking coming from the front room. I was nervous of parrots. They knew too much, and it would not have surprised me if, upon my entry, it would have greeted me with a squawk of 'nose', or 'back lane', just to make me feel at home. The parrot was not a good omen, but the hostel was expensive and diminished the weekly amounts I was able to send my mam. Besides, Mrs Pratt's charges included an evening meal. I gritted my teeth and followed Mrs Pratt into the living room. The parrot ceased its squawking as I entered. It needed its own silence to sum me up. It was a pink parrot, and pleasing on the eye, though it was not easy to look at, for it rewarded you with a glassy stare of accusation.

'What's its name?' I asked Mrs Pratt.

'She's a girl,' my possible landlady answered, a little hurt perhaps that I had not immediately recognised its gender.

'Her name is Mildred,' she said.

My nostril twitched. 'Why?' I said and my voice issued a little scream.

'Because she's pink,' Mrs Pratt said.

'But why?' I asked again. I felt close to tears.

'Because pink is a mild red. Mildred,' she said, pleased with her own cleverness.

I did not know that I could live with Mildred, whatever her colour, and I hoped that Mrs Pratt's costs of accommodation would be beyond my means. But they were well within them and allowed my mam a much larger allowance than I already sent her. I had no choice. So I was bound to Mrs Pratt and her parrot whom I would not name, and with luck, I could give a wide berth to Mrs Pratt's parlour.

I stayed in Swindon with Mrs Pratt and her pink unmentionable for six years. I will not dwell on those parrot years for they were uneventful. Or they might well have been otherwise, but as always, I did not avail myself to any event. Neither did it help that one of my first acquaintances in Swindon carried the name of Mildred, so I was unlikely to seek any more. In all of my six years in that benighted town, I made no friends. I was in my mid-thirties, unanchored, and desperately homesick. In all the years I'd been at Mrs Pratt's, I'd been too cowardly to go home. Even for a short visit. And sometimes, I could not remember what my mam looked like. Then one Monday, which was always the day I received her letters, she wrote to tell me that David Parsons had got married and had moved back to London and a new job. It occurred to me that David Parsons' Cardiff had been like my Swindon, a biding time, sad and uneventful. That morning I felt strangely cleansed, and I decided to go home.

CHAPTER TEN

When the bus reached the outskirts of Cardiff, my nostril began to quiver. But not with its quiver of alarm. Rather with a shudder of pleasure, and I felt hopeful that though the back lane was still there, my nose would have had enough of it. Become bored with it even, feeling that it had bled me enough, and it would free me into some kind of future.

My mam was waiting for me at the bus station. I noticed that she had aged considerably. I could have wept for the wrinkles that had gathered on her face during my absence and its bewildering cause. For never in my whole six Swindon years, and in all her weekly letters, did she mention the wedding that never was, the blood on the dress, the bewildered groom, the food and drink paid for but not consumed. Not a single word. And when she greeted me at the station, holding me in her stiff and loving arms, she said, 'It's all forgotten. It's all in the past.'

Well, there's past and past, I thought. Except for the yesterday, and in my heart and in my hands and in my fingers, that was forever present. Still, I had much to look forward to. There was my dad and Auntie Annie and the terrace, and my own room, and now even a television. My mam had written to me about a year ago, announcing the machine that had wrought a radical change in their lives. She had even sent me a little drawing of the screen and sketched in the familiar dresser in the background as proof of a kind of their acquisition.

We took the tram home from the station, and then walked arm in arm towards the terrace.

'Let's go through the lane,' my mam said. 'It's quicker.'

I was fearful of turning that corner of my maidenhood and I knew that the blood would flow. Which indeed it did, waiting until we had reached number thirty-six to spill its niggling reminder.

'Still having them then?' my mam said.

'The first in ages,' I said.

I hated my nose. And with a passion. The optimism that that organ had bred during the bus journey home from Swindon was shattered by that lane-cornering, and I began to wonder whether I should have come home after all. But the mere thought of Swindon curdled my stomach, as would any place that was without my back lane. And I realised for the first time that, hard as it was to live within the site of my sin, it was harder still to live without it. It was not Swindon's fault. It may well have had its numerous back lanes, but none of them would have touched my ever-alert nostril.

When we reached home, my dad was waiting for us at the open front door.

'Fooled you, Dai Davies,' my mam shouted. 'Behind your back we are.'

'For why did you come down the lane?' he said. 'More obvious down the terrace.'

He was making irrelevant conversation because he did not quite know how to deal with my return. He was too happy with it, and worried too that he would give himself away with a kiss or a hug that was so foreign to his nature. So I ran towards him and hugged and kissed him myself.

'Welcome home, girl,' he whispered, and I heard a break in his voice and I knew that he had missed me terribly.

'We've got a television,' he said.

'I know,' I said, and he knew that I knew.

'I'll make you a cup of tea,' he said. He wanted to get off the subject of my return and back to our old routine, as if I'd never been away at all.

'Your Auntie Annie will be here soon,' my mam said. 'She's missed you, girl.'

'I've missed her too. All of you.' And then I started to cry.

They made no move to comfort me. They both knew I needed those tears. They knew that in those tears, there were six years of 'sorrys' and they let me cry them out. Then when I was done my mam proposed her time-honoured remedy.

'We'll all feel better with a cup of tea.'

When my Auntie Annie came, my mam brewed up once more against the possibility that the arrival of my Auntie Annie would urge the tears once more. But I hugged her dry-eyed, and it was my Auntie Annie's turn to weep and to take a cup of tea for to make her feel better.

'Well, let me look at you, girl, then,' she said.

I put myself on display.

'Lost a bit of weight you have,' she said. 'That's what comes without your mam's cooking.' It was her only reference to my having left home. They knew that I would never leave again, for a threatened marriage would not force me. They accepted the fact that marriage was beyond me, and always had been.

It took me a little time to recover from Swindon and my mam urged me to take it easy for a while, to get about a bit and to see old friends. My dad had had a rise at the gasworks, and what with her savings, she told me she could do without my support for a while.

It was the beginning of summer and I promised to find

myself a post for the winter term. The first friend I contacted was my best. Molly Smith who had for a few years been Molly Jenkins, but now had rid herself of her provider's name, but had managed to keep the house and the chattels he had provided. Despite her fraying marriage, Molly had managed another child, a girl this time, and she muddled through on her alimony and her memories.

Molly had no scruples in referring to my aborted wedding, and I was comfortable enough to tell her the whole story, all, that is, except for the blood.

'I just couldn't go through with it,' I told her.

It was Molly who told me what had happened. She told it with infinite sadness and without a trace of blame. And in a monotone too, a fitting pitch for recollection.

'Well, your dad had gone for over an hour, and there we were, all waiting. Then your dad came back into the church and went and spoke with your mam. Poor old David. They had to tell him, whatever it was, because none of us knew. We could only guess. I saw David go white, then he went to the vicar, and the vicar it was who said you'd disappeared. Duw. Then your mam had a word with the vicar and he said there was a buffet and that it would take place as planned. So we all left the church, silent like. I thought everybody would go home but they didn't, so we followed them to the Carlton Rooms. But your mam and dad went home and so did your Auntie Annie with them. But Blodwen went to the party with her Gareth and kids. Duw, they were terrible. Putting their fingers in all the trifles they were. And Gareth, well he just got drunk. And so did David. Well, what else could he do? There were no speeches of course and when all the food was eaten, everybody went home. I think your mam and dad were very worried. I wasn't, though. I just knew in my bones you'd got cold feet. I wish I'd done the same as you.'

She put her arms round me and started to cry.

'Men are horrible,' she said, and she sounded like my Auntie Annie.

'I think David was different,' I said. 'It's just that I wasn't ready.'

'Well, it doesn't matter now, does it,' Molly said. 'You've got me and I've got you.'

I was glad to be with her. We had all our pasts in common, all of it that we could share, all except the back lane, and that I could share with nobody.

Around midsummer I started to look for a job. I didn't want to re-apply to my old school. I wanted to start afresh. But my old headmistress was happy to give me a very good reference and she told me of the high school that had been bombed in the Blitz and had now been relocated just outside Cardiff.

'You'd like it there,' she said. 'It's almost in the country.'

So I made an application and I was invited for interview.

I was excited as I entered the school gates, and I realised how much I loved teaching. Inside I could smell the chalk and the red ink, and I heard the noise from the gym, and the practice of the school choir. My interview went well, and after a tour of the school, I was offered the post of English teacher and I knew that I would stay in that school until I had to retire.

I then entered into a rare period of happiness. I had much to look forward to. I could live at home with my mam and dad, and I could go every day to a wonderful place and do what I most wanted to do. I considered myself very lucky. But there was more luck to come. All his married life, with the exception of the war years, weekly and dutifully, my dad had posted his football coupons. And every week, with regular and more or less expected monotony, he failed to win. But about a month before the winter term was to start, he received a small windfall. I heard him shouting in the kitchen as he pored over the *Echo* for the weekly results.

'I've done it, missus,' he yelled. 'Duw, duw, this week I've done it. Duw, duw,' he kept saying, not believing his luck.

We rushed into the kitchen, my mam and me, and he proved his win by showing us the results. But neither my mam nor I understood anything about football and we just had to take his word for it.

'How much did you win, Dad?'

'Don't know. They'll send me a cheque, I suppose.'

'We'll have to wait then,' my mam said, not believing a word of anything. 'Now don't you get your hopes up, Dai Davies,' she said. 'Don't count your chickens.'

'We could all have a holiday,' my dad dared to say.

'We'll have nothing,' my mam said. 'We'll just wait and see.'

But she couldn't hide her excitement. I knew that it was her ambition to go abroad. 'Abroad' was a magic word for her, part of the language of her day-dreams. I knew she was thinking about that word, but keeping her mouth firmly shut.

'There's work to be done,' she said, as she started to clear away the breakfast things.

So for the whole of that day we kept our mouths shut and we didn't even tell Auntie Annie when she came for tea. And later on my mam wouldn't let my dad go down to the pub, in case he spent more than he could afford in anticipation of his win.

Early next morning the three of us rushed to the letter-box and we all pretended that we were just passing. But nobody was passing when the second post came, and it was not until my dad himself came home from work that he noticed the letter in the letter-box.

'It's come,' he shouted.

I was in my room and my mam was in the kitchen and we both rushed to his call. We followed him into the parlour. I don't know why he led us in there, considering we never entered the place unless it was Christmas or an engagement that was never fulfilled. Perhaps he considered his auspicious news required an auspicious setting. And there we were, seated around the table, my mam and me, and looking at him as he held the envelope in his trembling hand.

'Go on then, Dai. Open it,' my mam said.

'Afraid I am,' he said simply. He was close to tears.

'Shall I open it for you, Dad?' I said.

He clutched the letter to his chest. 'No, girl,' he said. 'I'll do it. Get me a knife for to open the envelope.'

Even for the few letters we received, an opener had never been necessary. We made do with our thumbs. But my dad had the greatest respect for that envelope and he was going to give it a clean and decent opening. I fetched him a knife and laid it in front of him. He stared at it for a while.

'Come on, Dai,' my mam said. Her voice came out in a squeak. She was as nervous as my dad.

At last, aware of the growing pressure around him, and fearful of it perhaps, he thought it wise to assume a debonair manner. He urged the point of the knife into the fold, and with a flick of his wrist, he unveiled what he had come to consider his long-earned due. He withdrew a folded letter, and as he opened it, a cheque fell face-down on to the table. This time he did not hesitate. He simply turned the cheque over where it lay so that all of us could view our windfall.

'Two thousand six hundred pounds,' we read, slowly and in astonished chorus. And then again to make sure that it was true. In those days, two thousand six hundred pounds was a great deal of money. It was equivalent to almost four years of my dad's gas-fitter's salary. He took my mam's hand, his face wreathed in smiles.

'We'll take a holiday,' he said, 'before our Bron starts her new job. The three of us. And we'll take Auntie Annie too.'

'Where'll we go, Dai?' mam whispered.

'Somewhere hot. Get a bit of sun for a change.'

'Abroad?' she dared.

To say the word aloud took infinite courage, for with its utterance she was translating a silent day-dream into a spoken reality. It took courage, for if it failed, it could no longer be the stuff of fantasy.

'It has to be abroad,' I said. 'It's the only place where there'll be any sun.'

'You can both go to the travel agent tomorrow to arrange it,' my dad said. 'A fortnight we'll have. The four of us.' He giggled with pleasure.

'There'll be lots to do,' my mam said. 'Tell your Auntie Annie, and passports and things. Abroad,' she marvelled again, but no longer in a whisper, for the word had come out of the closet of her dreams.

In those days, the package holiday business was in its infancy. It was still cheap, reliable and luxurious. The choice of holiday sites was limited, and Spain and the Balearic Islands seemed to be the most popular destinations. The following day we called first on our Auntie Annie. She was delighted with the news and our invitation.

'Will we have to go in an aeroplane?' she said.

That thought had never occurred to my mam and for a moment she might have wished 'abroad' back in the closet.

'It's nothing,' I said. 'It'll be fun.' I spoke like one who had a few flying-hours to her credit, but I had never been anywhere near a plane, and I was as terrified as they. I wondered whether my dad had envisaged a flight, and whether, at the thought of an aeroplane, he would cancel everything in sheer horror. I urged them not to worry about it, that millions of people all over the world travelled by air, but it was a fatuous argument. They were not concerned with the millions. They were concerned with themselves. 'It'll be an adventure,' my mam said, but with little confidence.

There was much to do, but after a few days we had secured passports for everybody and a package tour for four to Majorca. At such little notice, there was not a great deal of choice, so we opted for a place we'd never heard of, because the pictures looked so pretty.

When we left Cardiff station, it was still cold and raining, and we were glad of that because the contrast of Majorca would be more defined. We had a carriage all to ourselves, and our luggage was neatly stacked on the racks. Hanging from each case was a 'Friendly Travel' label and I gave a fond thought to that hopeful 'Sea-bank' label of mine and my nostril was still. It's over, I thought. All our yesterdays. Except in my heart and in my hands and in my fingers. And my nose.

A bus picked us up at Paddington station for to take us to the aerodrome. There were no jet-planes in those days. Just the old-fashioned propellors so they didn't need a big airfield for to take off and land. But for my mam and dad and Auntie Annie, the field was big enough and so was the single lone aircraft which gave us a mean stare as we alighted from the bus.

We were assembled in a waiting hall. There were many passengers there already and we had an opportunity to examine those who would be our companions in our fortnight's sunshine. The wrong side of thirty as I was, I was still the baby of the group. They were men and women of a certain age, couples who had seen their children off the premises into marriage and who now, faced only with each other, sought an event that would produce words and memories between them for a time. No couple talked to another. Perhaps each felt superior, or perhaps not good enough. Though it was probably terror that silenced them all. Our little quartet was silent too, eyeing the rain that slashed the windowpanes and the menacing shape on the field beyond. It was a relief when our flight was called, so that the general alarm might or might not find cause. My mam took a small bottle of brandy out of her handbag – for medicinal purposes, she insisted – and ordered each one of us to take a good swig. She was embracing us all into her own fear. I took her arm, and my Auntie Annie took my dad's and we stood in line, brandy-brave, and slowly moved out into the rain. It was a good hundred yards to the aeroplane across the open field. Most of the passengers were well past running, so they resigned themselves to the down-pour, raising their umbrellas, hopefully for the last time until their return. Despite the rain, it was exciting. We'd never been inside a plane before, so there was much novelty to take our minds off our fears. My mam sat next to my dad, and I sat behind them with my Auntie Annie. She offered me the win-dow seat. Indeed she insisted I take it. I think she was afraid of falling out. And she asked that the stewardess help fasten her seat belt, not trusting herself. Then she asked her to do the same for my mam and dad. She allowed me my own fas-tening, for which I was grateful. Then she shut her eyes, but her lids did not fall gently. They were screwed up in her stress. I held her hand.

'Tell me when we're up, girl,' she whispered.

My mam reached the medicine bottle over her seat. I noticed that it was half emptied. My mam hardly ever drank spirits. Neither did my dad and I supposed that their fear must have been acute. I didn't like brandy very much and I was pretending I wasn't frightened for my Auntie Annie's sake, and I passed the bottle to her, placing it in her hands. She drank it blind. By the time we took off some half-hour later, she was mercifully fast asleep and woke only when her lunch tray was put before her. She looked out of the window and saw cloud, and then she gave a little scream. I don't know what she expected to see but she could clearly not understand how we could stay up if there was nothing to travel on. But slowly she accepted that it was possible, seeing as how none of the other passengers seemed to mind, and she absorbed her fears in her lunch and the bottle of wine that came with it. My mam and dad had settled too. 'Nothing to it,' my dad said as if he were piloting the plane himself. And my mam was enjoying the luxury of being served.

After lunch, Auntie Annie stood up with confidence. She had seen others do so and come to no harm. And my dad took a walk down the aisle. But my mam didn't trust herself strapless and she stayed where she was. I went and sat by her side. 'I liked our dinner,' she said. 'We're lucky, aren't we?' Besides her talent for gratitude, my mam had an equal one for appreciation. I had the former in plenty, and would have had the latter had it not been for yesterday in the back lane. But appreciation was disallowed, for it inferred enjoyment.

We landed in Palma without incident, and as we left the plane, the promised sun was there to greet us. The hotel was not far from the airport and within walking distance of a sandy beach. But there was a pool in the hotel grounds, so the sea was an extra. Or that's how my dad saw it, who was not fond of sand and was seduced by the bright loungers and tables provided by the pool.

'Duw, this is the life,' he said, as he viewed how the other half lived. Then he realised that he was one of them and was possibly ashamed for he said, 'Must take presents back for my gas-mates. We'll go shopping. Nothing fancy. Nothing showoff. Greetings from Palma stuff. That sort of thing.'

My Mam had decided on a flamenco dancer for Mrs Pugh, and Auntie Annie on a pair of castanets for Blodwen. The presents that they would take home would be the only indication that they had been to Spain.

We had heard only a few words of Spanish, confined as we were to an all-English-catering hotel and an English tour guide. My dad even found an English pub, and apart from the climate and the luxury of hotel living, we need never have left home.

But none of that mattered. It was another life. The break-
fasts on the terrace, the private bathrooms, the balconies
overlooking the sea.

'We must do this every year,' my mam said. 'All of us
together. Something to look forward to.'

I was happy that they were happy and that should have
been enough for me. I had a good job to look forward to,
enough friends to take the edge off my loneliness. But it was
the future that worried me, that perilous tense that I had so
assiduously avoided, unworthy as I felt of its entitlement. I
avoided it because I thought that any vision of it would oblit-
erate my 'yesterday' and that would have been a betrayal. But
now I realised that the yesterday in my heart and in my hands
and in my fingers was permanent, unerasable, and that a thousand thoughts of tomorrow could do nothing to expunge that
undemolishable past of mine. And so, without fear of treach-
ery or lack of remorse, I dwelt on my future and what would
become of me. For my future spelt out a natural orphanhood,
and it was painful to envisage a life without my mam and dad.
For somehow their presence made yesterday tellable, although
never, never would it be told. But as long as they were alive,
they represented the only ears that would listen, if I cared to
impart, and perhaps they would understand. With them, my
yesterday was shareable, in principle if not in practice. But
once they were gone, I would have to bear it alone, so much
more alone than I bore it now. And I would have to live with
myself in the shadow of the back lane. And with my nose, as
if I needed any reminder.

No, I was not happy on that holiday, and in order to hide
my mood from my mam and dad, I spent much of my time
alone, going often into the old city of Palma, to lose myself,
and thereby feel anonymous, and in that anonymity, without
language, to find some freedom. And now that I could envis-

age the future, if not face it with some equanimity, it bothered me little that I was in a country of *mañana*.

I had never travelled before. My foray to Swindon had been my only sortie from home. But I had seen pictures in books of great cities with their cathedrals and monuments, and the old city of Palma offered them all. It was cool inside the cathedral, a welcoming relief from the sweltering heat outside, which is why I supposed most people sheltered there, rather than to offer worship. I sat there for a while, availing myself to awe, but if, like myself, you dare not believe in God, awe is not good for you. It makes you feel guilty, with or without reason. And I wasn't guilty. I had strayed inadvertently into yesterday and it was not my fault that another had strayed there too. Neither was it his fault, nor that of the tedious Mildred who had driven him there. And certainly it was no fault of Hugh Elwyn Baker whom the police had planted there. If it was anyone's fault, it was God's for His random mismanagement, and when I was sufficiently cooled, I left His house and His chaotic disorder.

Each day when I returned to the hotel and the pool, my mam and dad and my Auntie Annie were a little redder, and a little fatter, and wishing more and more that the holiday would never end. I told them in detail how I spent my days, inventing most of my stories, for in truth my sorties had been uneventful except in so far as they had given my yesterday different colours and meanings, and those I could not share with them.

Every evening we had dinner in the hotel conservatory, and afterwards, my dad would go to the pub, and my mam and auntie and me would walk along the seashore. One evening, the night before the end of our holiday, my Auntie Annie stopped suddenly on our sandy walk. She was trembling.

'What's the matter, Annie?' my mam said. 'White as a sheet you are.'

'I've got a sudden funny feeling about Blodwen,' she said.

'What sort of feeling?'

'Not a good one,' she whispered.

My Auntie Annie was known to have a prophetic streak, a trait not uncommon amongst Welsh women of her age. She'd had a 'feeling' about her Gwyn, long before he was taken ill, and no sign of the cancer that had carried him off. She'd had a 'feeling' long ago of the Sengennyd pit disaster. And now this Blodwen 'feeling'. It had to be taken seriously.

'We'll go back to the hotel and we'll phone her,' my mam said. 'Doesn't matter about the cost. Must put your mind at rest.'

But I feared that the call would not put my Auntie Annie's mind at rest. I believed in her 'feelings', and I feared for Blodwen too.

'We'll be home tomorrow,' I said. 'And there's nothing much we can do about it here.'

'Put her mind at rest it will,' insisted my mam, who tended to dismiss her sister's 'feelings'. I wondered if my Auntie Annie had ever had a 'feeling' about the back lane.

We hurried back to the hotel, my mam leading the way. I felt that my Auntie Annie was loath to make the phone call. She believed in her 'feelings' and she didn't want them confirmed miles away from home. But my mam was insistent. We went straight to her room, the three of us, and sat on the bed as she gave Blodwen's number to the English operator at the desk. She put the phone down. 'They'll ring us when we're connected,' she said. We sat and dreaded the bell. My Auntie Annie's lobster tan had disappeared, and now, apart from her sundry presents, there was no proof that she had left Cardiff at all. If her 'feeling' had been irrational, her colour would return, and I prayed for that as we waited for the phone to ring. And when it came, we all jumped in terror.

'Pick it up, Annie,' my mam said, loath as she was to answer it herself.

But my Auntie Annie made no move.

'I'll answer it,' I said. I picked up the receiver and heard Blodwen's voice. 'It's Blodwen, Auntie Annie,' I said.

'Thank God she's alive,' she said. Her colour returned slightly as she took the receiver from my hand. But I was frightened. Blodwen's voice had been full of panic and tears.

'I had one of my feelings,' my Auntie Annie was saying into the receiver. Or shouting, rather, conscious of the fact that Palma was a very long way from Abertillery. Then, 'Oh, duw. My God, my God.' She was paler now than she had ever been in Cardiff.

'What is it?' my mam said, believing at last in her sister's 'feelings'.

'Gareth's gone,' my Auntie Annie said. Then she waved my mam aside. Details would come later. But my mam was not satisfied. Gone could mean anything.

'Gone where?' she whispered.

'Dead,' my Auntie Annie said, then returned to the weeping Blodwen. 'Oh, there's terrible, cariad,' she said. Then she listened again for a while. 'I'll be back tomorrow. I'll ring you then. Bless you, cariad.'

She put the phone down and started to cry. 'I'm not crying for him.' She wished to make herself clear. 'Never liked him and I'm not going to change my mind now. It's Blodwen I'm sorry for. And the children. And what'll happen to them. Broken-hearted she is.'

'What did he die of?' I asked.

'What d'you expect? Drink of course. Choked on his own vomit, Blodwen said. The doctor's just left.'

'When did it happen?' my mam asked.

'When I had my feeling. About an hour ago.'

'Duw, Annie,' was all my mam could say.

We put our arms around her and comforted her as best we could. It didn't help matters when later on my dad came home from the pub very much the worse for wear. There was no point in telling him about Auntie Annie's 'feeling' or how it had been confirmed. He was too befuddled to understand anything. It would have to wait until the morning.

I was glad that we were going home, and grateful to Gareth that he had so well timed his death and thus my Auntie Annie's 'feeling' to coincide with the last day of our holiday. The morning would be spent in packing and preparing for departure. There would be much to keep us busy. My dad had sobered up by the morning and despite a monumental hang-over, he was able to comfort my Auntie Annie with his sympathetic chorus of 'duw, duw,' which descanted her own. And it was to the orchestration of these poignant vespers that we returned to Cardiff in the late evening of that day, and to further telephone calls to Blodwen.

She was still in tears. My Auntie Annie held the receiver away from her ear so that we could all eavesdrop on Blodwen's sorrow.

'Oh, mam,' she was saying. 'I loved him so much. He was such a good man. Such a good husband he was, and father. Oh, I miss him terrible, Mam.'

You liar, Blodwen, I thought. You didn't love him. You preferred the Hershey bars. He was not a good man. He was a wife-battering husband and an unspeakable father. Blodwen's weeping was prompted by guilt, and there is nothing like guilt to prolong grief. She would not be likely to marry again. For the rest of her life she would stew in Abertillery with her ter-rible children and choke on the aftertaste of Hershey bars. Poor Blodwen.

'I'll come up for the funeral I will,' my Auntie Annie said.

'I want you to stay, Mam,' Blodwen pleaded. 'I want you to come and live with me. Please, please, Mam.'

'We'll talk about it when I get there, cariad. I'll come up tomorrow. Help you prepare. Now don't worry. Duw, it's a terrible thing, cariad, what's happened. But time heals.'

Not if you don't give time time, I thought, and Blodwen was not likely to do that. Her guilt would forbid healing, however much time she was allowed. She would live out her life as the long-suffering widow of Abertillery, and she would get on everybody's nerves.

It was late, too late for my Auntie Annie to go home, and in any case we did not want her to be alone. We persuaded her to stay the night at our house. But we did not go to bed. We sat for a while around the kitchen table with the pot of tea that would make everything better, except bring the dead back to life.

'I should go there. Live there, I mean,' my Auntie Annie said. 'Blodwen needs me.'

We said nothing. None of us thought it was a good idea. Auntie Annie was no longer young and it would not be long before she would need to be taken care of herself. But we knew that her tie to Blodwen, her only child, was such that it called for sacrifice, and the need to sacrifice is not a topic one argues about.

'I could sell up here,' she said. 'House is too big for me anyhow. And Blodwen could do with the money. I don't suppose he left her very much. Enough for the funeral perhaps. Duw, duw.'

Again the vespers and my dad's echo.

We let her talk, rationalising the move she'd already decided to make. 'Put the house on the market tomorrow morning I will. Before I go to Abertillery. Be funny not living in Cardiff any more. Miss you I will.'

Then she started to cry and I hoped the realisation of what she was turning her back on would help change her mind. But she was adamant.

'It'll be a change for me,' she said. 'I haven't seen much of Blodwen since she got married. It'll be a chance to make up for lost time. And to get to know my grandchildren.'

My mam dared to suggest she sleep on it. It was not a decision to be taken in haste. But my Auntie Annie had clearly made up her mind. For good or ill, she was Abertillery-bound.

I stayed up a while after they had all gone to bed. Once again my future loomed and it saddened me. For my future was about death and loss of family and the terrible burden of my unshareable yesterday. My Auntie Annie's move to Abertillery seemed to me to be the very first stage of that dying future, and I feared that her absence from Cardiff would presage other absences, not of moving, but of final departure. I was glad that we had all been on holiday together. We had known and proved our loving and when death would come to any one of us, our grief would not be prolonged by guilt. It was something to be deeply grateful for.

When at last I went to bed, I passed my Auntie Annie's room and I heard her weeping. I knew that she was not weeping for Gareth, nor even for Blodwen's widowhood. She was weeping for loss, for time unused or misspent, and for herself perhaps and her shrinking years. I would miss her. Cardiff would be different for me now. My Auntie Annie's house had been the springboard for my yesterday, and in its absence, my back lane would lose its anchorage.

CHAPTER ELEVEN

After Gareth's funeral, Auntie Annie came back to Cardiff only to settle the sale of her house and to move her goods and chattels to Abertillery. My dad went back to work with his 'Greetings from Palma' ashtrays and a fading lobster tan. My Mam sat at her sewing-machine and stitched dresses for the summer. As her tan paled, it was her way of keeping the sun by her. And I started at my new school.

There were four teachers in the English department and, being the new girl, I started as a junior. I was in charge of the lower forms, the mercifully pre-*Middlemarch* stage. In those days, a great store was put by grammar, analysis and parsing and I enjoyed those lessons, considering them a discipline that would rub off on any subject to its benefit. Again I shall not dwell on those years. Teaching is a routine business and each day is much like another. In the ten years that I was there I was happy enough, and slowly graduated, through a combination of merit and dead women's shoes, to the post of head of the English department.

During that whole decade, I never once had a nosebleed. My nostril quivered from time to time, but it seemed satisfied with just that simple shiver. I don't know why my nose had suddenly decided to surrender, for yesterday was still in my heart and in my hands and in my fingers. As always. But it was a relief of sorts, and at times I ventured out without a hankie.

Over those ten years, my dad's football win, together with its interest, financed our annual holiday. More often than not my Auntie Annie joined us as a welcome relief from her miserable life in Abertillery. For miserable it was. None of us said 'I told you so' but it had turned out as we had predicted. My dear Auntie Annie, frail and ageing, was no more than a childminder, while Blodwen husband-hunted in vain. Each time I saw her, I wondered if I would ever see her again, and that pre-sense of orphanhood would finger me and the untellability of my back lane.

Most years we went back to *mañana* country, because of all the package tours it was the cheapest. Occasionally we tried the mainland where *mañana* was taken even more seriously, but on the whole, we stuck to Palma and that same hotel where we had first tasted how the other half lived, that half of which we were now a legitimate part. We did not bother with presents any more. Most gas-fitters were package-holidaying themselves, and Mrs Pugh had no more room on her mantelpiece for flamenco dancers. And after each *mañana* summer, I went back to school.

We had a dinner lady, Ellen, who had joined the workforce at the same time as myself. She was a good deal older than me and she was due for retirement. We had a whip-round for a present and a small after-school party to see her off. I would miss her. We had become friends over the years. Ellen was a daily encounter to which I looked forward. When she left, we promised to keep in touch, but somehow I knew that we would not meet again. Ellen's leaving marked the end of a decade and the onset once more of my yesterday.

The new dinner lady began work on the following Monday, and as I picked up my meal in the canteen that lunch hour, my nose began to bleed. I couldn't understand it. I was enraged. I could see absolutely no reason why my nose had once again declared hostilities. And of course, I was hankie-less. Surreptitiously I used my underskirt to stem the flow, but I was obliged to ask for a tea towel, for my nose was on attack with a vengeance. A patient store of ten years' blood would out, and would not be denied. I lay down on a bench and saturated the tea towel until the flow abated. I had little appetite for lunch and the headmistress suggested I take the afternoon off, and perhaps visit a doctor. But I knew that no doctor could cure my yesterday and I went home and to my room to try to understand my fickle nose. Hitherto there had usually been a nostril warning to a flow. But this time my nostril must have been sleeping. Moreover, a bleed had never occurred without some obvious association, some back lane reference, some turkey-carving reminder. But I could think of nothing in that canteen that made the slightest reference to my yesterday, and it worried me, because I imagined that perhaps the bleeding signalled the onset of a serious illness and had nothing to do with the back lane at all.

The following day, I armed myself with tissues, and prepared to enter the fray. I collected my lunch tray, and before I could set it on the table, I felt the flow. But I stemmed it and I ate my lunch. I would not be beaten. After a week of my resistance, I forced myself to connect the flow with some new ingredient in school dinners, introduced perhaps by the new dinner lady, and the smell of which must have prompted the flow. So for the next week I brought my own sandwiches, and went to the canteen solely for a cup of coffee. But it made no difference. My nose was still at war. I couldn't understand it. The continual bleeds were affecting my general health, and I felt myself available to all infection. And then the 'flu caught me and I was obliged to spend a week in bed. Each day of my indisposition I waited for lunchtime and the accompanying

flow. For some reason I associated the bleed with lunch hour.
But one o'clock came and went every day for a whole week, a
week in which my nose declared a truce. So it was quite clear
that the bleed was connected with the canteen. Yet for ten
years the canteen had never disturbed me and I was forced to
face the fact that the only new element in the canteen in all
those years was the dinner lady herself. And I couldn't understand it. I didn't know the dinner lady. I didn't even know her
name. I had never looked at her closely. I suppose I must have
had a natural resentment towards her because she had replaced
Ellen. I decided that on my return to school, and armed with
tissues, I would take a close look at Ellen's replacement and
find perhaps some flicker of recognition that would trigger the
back lane. It took some courage but I was not going to be
beaten. Although I fully accepted my yesterday and the atonement it entailed, it sometimes irritated me to the point of
frenzy and I would silently scream at the injustice of it all.

On the Monday I returned to school, and but for my ever-
watchful nose, fit and well. At lunchtime, I stormed into the
canteen in a mood of bravado, my tissues at the ready. There
was a small queue, and while waiting, I had ample opportunity
to study the dinner lady's face, and as I did so, my nostril
quivered. I was not afraid because, if for nothing else, I knew
now for certain that that face was responsible for my blood-
stained recall. When my turn came, I kept the tissue to my
nose and as she doled out my portion, I asked her her name.
I noticed that she paled slightly.

'Gloria,' she said.

'Gloria what?' I wasn't going to be satisfied with just a
Christian name, one that in any case seemed to my ears to
have been made up on the spot.

She paled even further and I feared for her stability. 'What
d'you want to know for?' she said. Her tone was hostile and
defensive at one and the same time.

'Just thought I knew you,' I said.

'Williams,' she gave me, 'and I've never seen you before.'

I kept staring at her and I noticed how her hand trembled as she doled out my portion. I had the impression that the woman had as much to hide as myself. I took my lunch to a table in full view of the counter, and I watched her carefully as she went about her serving business. Occasionally she caught my glance and was clearly unnerved by it, for she stumbled in her serving and she paled even further. At last I felt sorry for her and I turned my face away and left her alone with her secrets. But I had stared at her long enough to imprint her features on my memory, and all day I studied them, over and over again, in the hope of some flicker of recognition. And it was not until the middle of that night, as I tossed and turned in my restless bed, that a clue of sorts surfaced, and I knew that with a little more delving, I would discover the blood-stained connection.

The clue was simple. It related to fur. I concentrated on the fur, and out of it, I heard the sound of sobbing. And then the whole picture became terrifyingly clear. Gloria Williams, or whatever she chose to call herself, was none other than Mrs Hugh Elwyn Baker, last seen sobbing on her companion's fur collar on hearing of the passing of the sentence of death on her innocent spouse. No wonder she had paled. No wonder she had trembled. Since that terrible time, that 'Abide with Me' grey morning, she had hidden herself. Under a new address and her maiden name perhaps, she had wanted to start a new life for herself and for her children, and she didn't need snoopers like me staring at her with suspicion and asking for her name. I marvelled at the fact that my nose had recognised her well before I had, and I wondered what more tricks my nose had in store for me, or rather my mind, its stock of imprints long forgotten and put aside. I felt very sorry for Gloria Williams as she now called herself, but I realised that for five days a week, I could not share a roof with her. I didn't want to leave my job, but I had no choice. Had I stayed at the school, I would have simply bled to death. Even if I never, ever went into the canteen again, my mind would make sure that her school presence would forever haunt my nostril. I had to think of an excuse for leaving. I could hardly explain to the headmistress that every time I looked at the dinner lady, my nose began to bleed. I had taught at that school for over ten years. I had been happy there. I had reached the top grade, and had I stayed, there is no doubt that I would have been considered for the post of headmistress which was shortly due to become vacant through retirement. There was no reason on earth why I should wish to leave. I thought of pleading a chronic illness in the family, and their need for my care. But I was in hock enough to providence without risking any further calamity. Finally I decided to use my nose. For once it would come in useful. I told the headmistress that my health was failing and that the doctor had recommended a complete rest from work and stress for at least a year or else the bleeding would result in permanent incapacity. As I spun my sorry tale, I pictured the doctor and his look of concern, and for a moment I felt a chronic invalid, well cosseted and cared for. I rather hoped that my nose would oblige me at that very moment in the headmistress's study and bleed some proof of my story, but the little bugger was never there when I needed it and my nostril was defiantly still. In fact, I almost heard it laughing.

The headmistress was very sympathetic and promised that I could return to my job as soon as I was able. She put her arm around my shoulder.

'Poor Miss Davies,' she said, and her sympathy irritated me, because I liked her and I was angry with myself for having conned her so successfully. She told me she would arrange as much sick leave as possible and I felt even worse.

My story was good enough for the headmistress, but I had to dream up another tale for my mam and dad. The truth was impossible. I couldn't even use the nose-bleeding as an excuse for that would involve endless visits to the doctor to whom the truth was also untellable. So I told them that after almost fifteen years of teaching, I wanted a break, and that, with the permission of the headmistress, I was taking a sabbatical. I had to explain the meaning of the word to them, and they were suitably impressed, and accepted it without question. It seemed to them that I must have been very important to have been granted such a privilege. And after their acceptance of my cunning invention, I felt worse than ever before.

So there I was, on the wrong side of forty, jobless, and with little appetite to find another. My dad had retired some years back, and he and my mam were living on their old-age pensions. They were not poor. They had put money by over the years and they had long paid off the mortgage on the house. I was still able to help them with my sick-leave pay. But it was limited, and I knew that I would have to find another job. I didn't want to teach any more. Somehow that dinner lady episode had soured that instructive appetite of mine. But I couldn't think about that. I had other things on my mind.

My dad's health was failing. He had always been slightly asthmatic but lately, especially since his retirement, the attacks were more frequent and more severe. The doctor provided him with an inhaler which eased him for a time. It was sad to watch him so listless and without hope. But on good days, he was his old self, reading the *Echo*, watching television, going to the pub, and planning his next *mañana*. But on bad days, I dreaded a ring on the telephone in case my Auntie Annie had had one of her 'feelings'.

That summer, in spite of my joblessness, and my dad's precarious state of health, we managed another package holiday, and again to our old haunt in Palma. But this time my

Auntie Annie couldn't join us. Blodwen had chosen that exact fortnight to take a package holiday herself. Ever husband-hunting, she was going on a 'singles' jaunt to Portugal and my ageing Auntie Annie was to keep an eye on the children. Though they were quite grown up by now, they were still, as always, beyond anyone's control, and certainly beyond the control of a frail grannie.

So there were just the three of us on that holiday, and I had a room on my own. A twin-bedded room nonetheless, and at night I viewed the empty bed at my side and I missed my Auntie Annie terribly. I felt I was looking at an empty pair of her shoes.

But we had a wonderful holiday, the three of us, feeling safe in the familiarity of the place, doing the things we had always done. Lobster-tan gathering at the poolside, eating our fill on the terrace, walking at night on the sands with my mam, while my dad tippled in his regular pub. And as soon as we got back to Cardiff, my mam took to her sewing machine and summer dresses, and took to it with a vengeance, because she would not give up hope of another *mañana*.

And neither would my dad, and it was in the middle of one of his reminiscences around the kitchen table, when he was joking at the recall of some incident in the Spanish hotel, that his asthma choked his laughter. He grabbed at his inhaler, but this time it seemed to be of little avail, and my mam ran to the telephone and called the doctor. While we were waiting for him, we held my dad between us. I was crying, but I turned my face away so's my mam could not see. But her face was turned away too, and I suspected for the same reason. My dad kept saying, 'I'm all right. Don't worry. It'll pass like it always does. Duw, it's a bad one though.' He was fighting for his breath and groaning a little. 'Quiet now, cariad,' my mam said, rocking him, and I wondered how she'd manage without him. She started to sing to him, a soft lullaby, and I wanted to stop her because there was time enough for that. I feared he would fall asleep in her arms and not bother to wake up again. I was glad when the front door bell rang and interrupted her singing. I ran to answer the door.

'Mr Davies again, is it?' Dr Owens said. He'd visited a few times before. I led him into the kitchen.

'Duw,' he said. 'Bad this time is it, Mr Davies?'

My dad nodded his frail head.

'Let's have a look at you then. Open his shirt, Mrs Davies.'

My mam did as she was told and Dr Owens took out his stethoscope from his bag and listened to my dad's chest, both front and back. He said nothing and his face betrayed no prognosis. Then he took my dad's blood pressure with another contraption and when that was done, he said, 'Have to get you to hospital. Keep an eye on you there. Nothing to worry about. We'll just have to see how it goes. I'll use your phone,' he said.

My mam gave him twenty pence to put in the box. Rates had increased since the old tuppeny days. We'd gone metric anyway by then, though we still reckoned in the old money. 'It'll be here right away,' Dr Owens said as he came back into the kitchen. 'Only across the road, isn't it. You can get his pyjamas meanwhile, Mrs Davies, and things he may need.'

'I'll do it, Mam,' I said. 'You stay with Dad.'

I rushed upstairs to their bedroom. I looked at that old double bed of theirs, with its sagging mattress on which they had lain together for so long, had shared their pillows for so many years that they had begun to look alike, and it was hard to hold back my tears. I took clean pyjamas out of the drawer, and folded his dressing gown. And I was careful with his shaving kit and the special bottle of after-shave that he'd bought at the duty-free in *mañana*. I wanted him to take care of himself. I didn't want him to let himself go. I didn't want him to do anything except to stay alive and to be with us for ever.

I heard the ambulance draw up in the terrace, and out of the window I saw the net curtains rise. The terrace had never lost its appetite for gossip, but out of that gossip came sympathy and concern. So I welcomed those raised net curtains. They were token of one large if not so happy family.

I went in the ambulance with my mam and dad and Dr Owens. Dr Owens had insisted my dad be carried out on a stretcher. Though my dad protested that he could walk. I think he was ashamed of being ill. It took only a few minutes to reach the back of the hospital where my dad was offloaded and taken to a ward. My mam and me were told to wait, and we would be called when he was settled. As soon as he was taken away, my mam started to cry. 'I hate hospitals,' she said.

'They're not the end,' I told her. 'Auntie Annie's been in and out often enough.'

'He's not well though,' she said.

I let her cry. I held back my own tears and let her cry for both of us. And I held her close. Shortly Dr Owens returned.

'You can go and see him now,' he said. 'The nurse will take you. Don't stay long though. He's very tired.'

My mam dried her face and we followed the nurse down sundry corridors to Mansfield Ward on the ground floor. My dad was settled in the last bed on the left-hand side of the ward. He managed a smile when he saw us. I was angry that they had not dressed him in his own pyjamas. He was wearing the hospital hand-out, and already he looked institutionalised.

'We'll get your own pyjamas on you tomorrow,' my mam said. She couldn't bear to think of the man whose hospital uniform my dad had inherited. And whether he had lived to tell the tale. She held my dad's hand and I did the same on the other side.

'Tired I am,' my dad said. 'Gave me a pill they did.'

'You feeling better, cariad?' my mam said.

He nodded. We could see that he was close to sleep.

'Be better in the morning you will,' my mam said. She stood up and kissed him, holding his face in her hands. Then she turned quickly away to hide her anxiety.

'See you tomorrow then, Dad,' I said, kissing his forehead, but he was already fast asleep.

We walked home arm in arm and said nothing. When we reached our gate, 'I'll make some cocoa,' I said. 'Help us sleep.'

'Don't think I'll sleep a wink tonight,' my mam said.

'D'you want me to sleep in your bed?'

'That'll be a comfort, luv,' she said.

So we had our cocoa. 'He'll be all right, Mam,' I said. 'He'll be better tomorrow.'

I don't know why I said it. I didn't believe it myself. He had looked so resigned when we'd left him. It seemed that he knew what we were both terrified to believe. I watched my mam as she got into her side of the bed. I would have preferred it if she'd taken my dad's side, because I did not want to usurp his spousal status. I told myself I was keeping his place warm until his return. As I settled myself on his pillow, we sank down together, my mam and me, into the central crater, man- and woman-made over their many loving years. I put my arms around her. At first she stiffened, sensing an alien embrace. Then she knew that comfort was comfort, from whatever source, and she responded with her arms around mine. I think we must have fallen asleep quite quickly, not out of fatigue for neither of us was tired, but out of sheer sadness and the fear of facing reality.

My dad died that night. In his sleep. And while we were sleeping too. So nobody had noticed that my dad had passed away. None of his loved ones. Not even the nurse on duty. He did it when all our backs were turned. No doubt we had murmured in our sleep in the moment of his passing, and no doubt, too, that in Abertillery, my Auntie Annie had had a 'feeling'. But we slumbered on, my mam and me, wooing the dark, postponing the light of day.

Until the phone woke us. Its bell shrilled through the house with a certain urgency, breaking the silence of the long night with its scream. We sat up in bed, frozen in fear. Then my mam almost leapt out of the covers, her tears already flowing. I followed her downstairs, and stood by her side as she answered the phone.

'Mrs Davies speaking,' she whispered.

I didn't have to ask her who was calling or what they were saying. I could read the whole bulletin on her face.

'When?' I heard her say. Then, 'I'll come now I will.'

She put the phone down and took me in her arms. 'In his sleep,' she said.

The time seemed to matter to her. 'He never knew.' And that seemed to matter more.

'I'll go and dress,' she said. 'You'd better phone your Auntie Annie.'

I watched my mam upstairs. From her bent back and hopeless slippered tread, she had suddenly become an old woman. I didn't know Blodwen's number by heart. I had possibly put a block on it, resenting her commandeering of my loved Auntie Annie. I found the number in the telephone pad that hung on the side of the machine, and as I was sorting out the change, the phone rang once more. I wondered if my dad had come alive, or whether he had simply died again. But it was not the hospital on the phone. It was my lovely Auntie Annie with one of her 'feelings'.

'Our dad died in his sleep,' I told her.

'Due, duw,' she said softly, and the words sounded like a gentle requiem. 'I'll come down on the next bus,' she said.

I thought I'd make a cup of tea before we left for the hospital. My mam could never start a day without one, even such a day as this. In the kitchen I saw last night's *Echo* spread out on the table, and my dad's steel-rimmed reading glasses settled on the print like a spider. I would not clear the table. I wanted his glasses and his paper on the table for ever.

I boiled the kettle and brewed the tea and it was ready by the time my mam came downstairs. She saw the *Echo* lying there and she stroked the paper, touching what he had touched. Then gently she folded his glasses and put them in her bag. My mam didn't need glasses, but she would keep them by her. It wasn't as if she needed any reminder of him. She just wanted to touch a part of him from time to time, and to see his lips moving as he read.

'I'm hungry,' she said. 'I should be ashamed.'

But I was glad she had appetite. She was clutching after life. She owed it to my dad. I made her a fry-up, her favourite. An egg, some bacon and sausage. But when I placed it in front of her, she turned away. She could not eat a crumb of it. It was but the *principle* of survival that gripped her. Its practice seemed impossible. Neither could I eat it for her. In my time I had come to be more than familiar with the long distance between principle and practice. I cleared the plate away. We managed our cup of tea together. Then I dressed and we went to the hospital. Again our journey was silent. Not that we had no words. We had words in plenty. But in the numbness of our grief, each word seemed to have cancelled out the other.

We told our business to the receptionist at the desk. Or at least I told it. My mam couldn't find the words, and if she could, she dared not utter them. She told us to go to Mansfield Ward where the doctor would see us. But my mam didn't want to see any doctor. She wanted to see my dad. It was too late for doctors and their explanations. But I wanted to know the 'why' of it. I wanted to know why my dad who'd been alive on the Monday had been dead on the Tuesday. I

wanted to know who was responsible. I wanted to kill whoever
it was who had let him die. I dragged my grieving mam down
the corridor.

'I want to see the doctor,' I almost shouted. 'I want to
know how it happened.'

'He's gone,' was all mam could say.

When we reached the ward, the doctor was waiting for us,
together with the night-duty nurse who had been present at
my dad's death, but who had neither heard nor witnessed it.
The doctor took our hands, a gesture I could well have done
without. I felt he was trying to get us on his side.

'I'm very sorry,' he said. 'There was nothing we could do.
He died in his sleep.'

'You mean if he'd been awake you could have saved him?'
I asked. A death in sleep seemed to absolve everybody of
responsibility.

He noted my accusing tone and he responded likewise.

'Your father had a serious heart condition which was exac-
erbated by an acute asthma attack. There was nothing anyone
could have done.'

My mam didn't understand him. She wanted things simple. Simple questions. Simple answers. 'What did he die of?'
she said.

'A massive heart attack.'

I was suspicious of the word 'massive'. I felt the doctor was
using it in his own defence.

'The post-mortem will prove that,' he said.

'But doesn't a heart attack make a *noise*?' I insisted.
'Especially a massive one.' I turned to the nurse. 'How could
you not have heard it?' I asked.

She blushed a deep scarlet with a guilt that indicated she'd
been out of the ward, and probably on some private business,
when my dad, screaming with pain, had finally succumbed. I
was not satisfied, but there was little I could do about it.

'He died in his sleep. Quietly,' the doctor said. And again, clutching his life belt, 'The post-mortem will prove it.'

'Does there have to be one of those?' my mam pleaded.

'Hospital rules,' the doctor said. He put his arm on my mam's shoulder and I resented his familiarity.

'Would you like to see him now?' he said.

There was nothing more anyone could say. I looked down the length of the ward to the bed where my dad had died. It was stripped bare. No blanket. No pillow. Not even a mattress. Not a single trace of him. The nurse handed my mam a package. 'Mr Davies' things,' she said. The bottle of *mañana* aftershave stuck out from the carrier bag. My Dad's 'things'? Like my Auntie Annie's 'feelings', they were words that went nowhere and never came back.

The doctor came with us to the morgue. It was underground, a fitting transit lounge for burial. He held the door open as we entered. It was a vast cold room and around it were placed six or seven concrete slabs, all occupied and covered. Death had been busy at the hospital and my dad was not his only client. I had no doubt that they had all died in their sleep, and all from massive heart attacks, and all while the night nurse was about her private business.

'Mr Davies?' the doctor whispered to the morgue attendant.

The attendant led us over to the furthest slab. Gently he drew away the white covering sheet, then he stepped respectfully aside and nodded towards us. My mam was the first to see him, and again I read her heart on her face. And I saw her smile. I went to her side. My dad looked very peaceful, resigned and without regrets. I think it was this resignation of his that had brought a smile to my mam's face. It seemed to say that death did not bother him, so why should it bother anybody else who loved him? We stroked his face, my mam and me, with that kind of gesture that neither of us would have made when he was alive.

'Thank you,' my mam said to the attendant. She was a great one for manners was my mam. I took her arm and led her out of the morgue. She ignored the doctor who was waiting by the door. She hadn't liked his cover-up vocabulary, and arm in arm, we made our way back to the terrace. Mrs Powys was walking towards us. She'd been out for a loaf of bread from the corner shop.

'I saw the ambulance,' she said.

'He's gone,' my mam told her.

'Sorry I am, Mrs Davies. So sorry.'

We turned into the gate of our house, assured now that the whole terrace would be informed.

We sat at the kitchen table, my mam and me. She wouldn't have anything to eat. She even refused a cup of tea. For the first time in her life she accepted the fact that when the crunch came, a cup of tea would not make anything better.

'Have to arrange the funeral,' she said after a while.

'I'll see to it, Mam. Let's wait till Auntie Annie gets here.'

'Best draw the curtains,' my mam said. In the district where we lived, darkened windows were a sign of mourning. But if you lived in Cyncoed, a wreath on the door would do, and you didn't have to bother with the blinds. But the terrace was drawn-curtain country and you walked on tiptoe past the darkened houses.

'Run along and tell Mrs Pugh,' my mam said. She knew that no one in the terrace would inform her. The passing years had not softened their stern disapproval of the goings-on in the corner house.

'I won't be a minute,' I said.

I ran to the corner and rang Mrs Pugh's chimes and her blowsiness filled the open frame before their echo had died away.

'What's the matter, Bron?' she said, seeing from my expression that there was something very much amiss.

'My dad died,' I said, and I heard a questioning tone in my voice for I still couldn't believe that I was fatherless.

'Shall I come back with you?' she said.

'My mam would like to see you.' I hoped that Mrs Pugh would persuade my mam to eat a little. Her rejections of my offerings had been so adamant that I feared she had it in mind to starve herself to death. She had no interest in living without my dad. She had told me that on the way back from the hospital.

'What about me, Mam?' I had said.

'You're old enough to look after yourself, girl,' she said. But one is never old enough to make do without parents and I had often nurtured the hope that I would die before them, so that there would never be a time when I'd have to look after myself.

I waited on Mrs Pugh's front doorstep while she went into the kitchen and returned with a newly baked cake.

'Petal made it,' she said. 'She'll be glad to send it to your mother. I never knew him well,' Mrs Pugh was saying as we walked back down the terrace. 'Except through your mother. She worshipped him.'

I realised then that my mam must have felt very close to Mrs Pugh to divulge such a confidence. She was probably my mam's best friend. Best enough, unlike my Molly Smith who could only be just best.

My mam was still sitting at the kitchen table. She was not crying. She was staring dry-eyed into space. And even when that space was filled with Mrs Pugh, her vision seemed undisturbed. Mrs Pugh put the cake on the table and then her arms around my mam. And at last my mam started to cry, sobbing loudly into Mrs Pugh's ample blowsiness. Perhaps for a moment my mam might have thought her own mam had come back from the dead to comfort her. Mrs Pugh just held her and rocked her gently. She asked no questions. She didn't want to know the how, when, where and why my dad had died. All that was irrelevant. What mattered now was to help cushion the grief of his passing.

I left them together and I went to my room. I had not been alone since my dad had been taken to the hospital, and that time, unlike my back lane, seemed years ago. My dad had been alive for sixty-eight years, but now he seemed to have been dead for much longer. And still I could not accept that he was gone. I tried to recall the first moment that I had met him. Met him that is, and seen him as my dad. I had known my mam all my life. I actually recall feeding at her breast. But it was much later, when I was four or five perhaps, that my dad became part of my family picture. I used to go to the infants' school round the corner from our terrace. And every day at four o'clock, my mam would be waiting outside to take me home. And one day she wasn't there. I looked around the gate at all the aproned mams and I remember crying because I thought she might be dead. I didn't quite know what 'dead' was, but I'd heard about it and I knew it was a terrible thing. Then someone picked me up in his arms. I'd seen his face before. Often. And always in my mam's house.

'Where's my mam?' I screamed at him, for somehow I knew that he would know.

'She had to go out, cariad,' he said. 'She'll be back for our tea.' Then he kissed me and carried me all the way home. I think it was then that I knew he was my dad. Later on, much later it was, I discovered where my mam had been that day. She'd been up at my Auntie Annie's because my Uncle Gwyn had just died. I was still in the infants' school at that time but by the time I had left it and gone to the big girls' school, I fully understood what 'dead' meant, because it had happened on my Auntie Annie's doorstep. Now I come to think of it, it was from the first moment that I had recognised him that I felt that my dad had to do with dying. And perhaps that is why all my life, from that time, I had loved him with infinite care and protection, and as I thought of those infant days of mine, I was able to accept that he was gone and had himself assumed that label of death that he had first shown me. So I was able to cry, knowing with unbearable pain what I was crying for.

I heard the front door bell ring, and I thought it might be my Auntie Annie who, what with Uncle Gwyn and the unmentionable Gareth, was pretty well schooled in the dying discipline. I went downstairs and answered the bell. It was Mr Thomas from next door.

'So sorry I am to hear about Mr Davies,' he said.

I had the feeling he'd been practising that sentence for a long time. I smelt the beer on his breath that he'd no doubt taken to give him courage for his visit. I asked him inside.

'D'you want to see my mam?' I said.

'If she's receiving. Wouldn't want to disturb her.'

I showed him into the kitchen. He was slightly thrown by the sight of Mrs Pugh. He fidgeted and said he would come back later.

Mrs Pugh stood up. 'I'm off anyway.' Then to my mam, 'I'll be back, Betty. Later. I'll see myself out.' Then she kissed my mam right in front of Mr Thomas, who turned his face away.

When she'd left the room, Mr Thomas took her seat at the table. The comfort seat it had become, but Mr Thomas was in no way capable of Mrs Pugh's compassion.

'Sorry I was to hear about Mr Davies,' he said again. And then he did the most extraordinary thing. He actually put his hand on my mam's arm, and squeezed it a little. I swear there was a little smile on his face as he did so. And it was not difficult to guess exactly what was in his mind. I thought he might at least have had the decency to let the grass grow a little. I knew that, since hearing the news, Mr Thomas had fantasised a new future for himself. He would marry the girl next door, and he would tear down the wall dividing them, so that meals-on-wheels would have free passage for them both. My mam swiftly took her arm away and poor Mr Thomas's dream was rudely shattered.

He fidgeted in his chair. 'Well, I just wanted to say how sorry I was about Mr Davies,' he said yet again.

They were the only words he knew. He had the sense then to make to leave. 'If there's anything I can do,' he said to me.

'Thank you, Mr Thomas,' I said. I was sorry for him. Any man is entitled to his dreams, even if they were so ill-timed. Now he would have to go back to his lonely house and mourn his wife again, and consider her a far better catch than Mrs Davies could ever have been.

After his visit, there were many more. The terrace came to pay its respects and all with cakes or sandwiches and offers of help. And that whole day, my mam didn't touch a morsel of food.

It was not until the evening that my Auntie Annie arrived. She had missed the early bus and had waited two hours at the bus station for the next one. From the look on her face, she had cried herself out.

'He was good to me, your Dai,' she kept saying. 'A saint of a man. Always was.' Then she took my mam in her arms and didn't say another word.

Over the next few days, I busied myself with the funeral arrangements. The post-mortem on my dad proved what the doctor had said, but a post-mortem can give no evidence of neglect or oversight. We had to be satisfied.

On the third day they brought my dad home. The under-taker dressed him in his best suit and laid him out in the parlour. And still my mam hadn't eaten a thing. Occasionally she would take a cup of tea, that remedy that had lost all its remedial effects, while the terrace cakes and sandwiches piled up on the pantry slab. 'They'll keep for the wake,' my Auntie

Annie kept saying. She too had lost her appetite, but mine was shamefully in order. At night I would join my mam and Auntie Annie in the parlour and sit at the table and look at my dad. The Christmas decorations, the dusty streamers hung from the ceiling, were strangely at odds with what they over-hung, celebrating something that called for no celebration. My dad looked peaceful and much younger than he had looked in life, as if he had already begun a backward journey. The last time he had worn that suit had been in this very room, that night so many years ago when David Parsons had put a ring on my finger. My nostril quivered and I reached for my tis-sues. And for the first time since yesterday in the back lane, I welcomed the blood that followed. For it confirmed my stran-gled loyalty to yesterday, that loyalty which was my only *raison d'être*. I held my dad's hand, cold now and stiff, that hand that had trembled as it raised a glass to toast my engagement. I thought of David Parsons and with infinite regret, for because of him and my eternal yesterdays I had robbed my dad of so much happiness.

'Better go and lie down,' my mam said. 'Won't stop while you're sitting up, girl.'

I heard a slight tone of anger in her voice. She was fed up with my nose-bleeds and she might have thought they were the cause of all her troubles. And she would have been right. Though my nose had not killed my dad, it might well have contributed to his early demise.

I did as my mam told me. I went upstairs. But not to my room. I went to hers. I needed the comfort of her bed and the echoes of its years-long loving. I lay down on my dad's side and in a short while the bleeding stopped. For some reason I knew that, had I lain on my mam's side, there would have been no respite. I was astonished that such a thought had occurred to me, and it crossed my mind that, despite my mam's kindness to me throughout the years since yesterday, and the undeserved tolerance she had shown, there would come a time when her forgiveness would sour, and curdle into rage. I rose quickly from the bed, not wishing to dwell on such a possibility.

I busied myself with making her bed and tidying her room. I went to close her wardrobe which, in the rush of the morning's dressing, she had left open. Inside, I saw a hint of her jury attire and I opened the door wide to view the whole range of her justice dispensary. I needed no reminder of my yesterday, but I could do without chapter and verse, and I made to shut the door on all its details. And as I did so, I caught sight of a brown paper carrier bag, stuffed against her sparse row of shoes and slippers. What was inside the bag was none of my business, but I had an urge to discover its contents. My flickering nostril overcame my scruples and I put the bag on the bed and I looked inside. Whatever it was was covered with white tissue paper and the wrapping itself seemed to underline the peril of investigation. Nevertheless, I took it out of the bag and gently removed the tissue.

My nostril jolted as I viewed the white satin of my fall from grace. I lifted it from its wrapping and laid it on the bed. Or rather, what was left of it. The beautiful buttonholing was still intact, and the blood was yellowed with age and disappointment. But I dyed it yet again as my nostril dutifully flared with its donation. The skirt, though, was torn into ribbons, not scissor-cut, but ripped with a hand-made violence. I doubt if words accompanied its destruction – my mam's grief must have been beyond speech – but by the watermarks, I knew that there had been tears in plenty. I wondered how such rage had been bottled over the years, and I sensed yet again that soon enough it would detonate.

It rained on the day of the funeral, which seemed a fitting accompaniment to my dad's last journey into the earth. The terrace got out its black, and so did my mam and my Auntie

Annie and the three of us went into the parlour for to say our last farewells. I looked at my mam's face. It was gaunt and pale and I detected a hint of anger in her features. It was as if she had wept for him long enough, and starved herself in her sorrow, and now all that was left to her was a burning rage that he had deserted her. If she had slapped his face, it wouldn't have surprised me.

'Mam,' I said, taking her hand, 'it wasn't his fault.'

She turned and stared at me with a look of such hatred, even my nostril was petrified.

'No. It wasn't his fault,' she said evenly. 'If it was anyone's fault, girl, it was yours.'

And then I bled like I'd never bled before.

I don't know how I managed to get through the burial. My mam refused my arm in comfort. She preferred to take Mrs Pugh's. But my Auntie Annie stood by my side. She had said nothing after my mam's outburst. Perhaps she agreed with her. And perhaps my mam was right. That day I mourned not only the death of my dad, but the irrevocable passing of mother love, that love that had been so tender and so unshakeable all my life. She looked at me only once during the whole of that burial service and it was a look of such searing loathing that I shall carry it to my grave.

Not a word passed between us for the rest of that day. During the wake, I offered her food, but she turned away. Ever since my dad had died I had slept with her on his side of the mattress to comfort her. But that night I knew I had to sleep alone. My Auntie Annie took my place at her side, and I felt that I had been exiled from my family and home.

CHAPTER TWELVE

After a week my Auntie Annie had to go back to Abertillery. Blodwen needed her, she said. She didn't want to leave because my mam was still refusing to eat. It was her way of punishing my dad. And also myself. She was going to make sure that when she died, I would have two deaths on my conscience. She did not know that I already had two, thank you very much, and I had my insistent nose to prove it. I was innocent of that extra pair she would saddle me with, as innocent as poor Hugh Elwyn Baker. But there was a difference. Hugh Elwyn Baker *knew* that he was innocent, though accused, and I could not be too sure. Whatever. Since that hair-raising moment in the parlour when we viewed my dad's body for the last time, my life took a steep downward turn, for though my mam's presence haunted me daily, a silent and fasting ghost, I felt wholly orphaned. We passed each other on the stairs, and sometimes we sat at the same table, but never a word passed between us. At first I tried to talk to her if for nothing else but to beg her to eat, but a cup of tea was the only nourishment she would take and she was shrinking visibly before my eyes. I knew she could not live much longer, and my heart turned over as I looked into her sunken, unseeing eyes and at her dry, stubborn, unforgiving lips. And when I brushed past her, I could smell her mortality.

Then one day I could stand it no longer. I called the doctor. By that time, she had taken to her bed. I noticed that she had settled herself in the middle of the mattress, that crater full of sighs, as if in preparation for a deeper and more serious burial.

When I showed the doctor into her bedroom, she looked at me for a moment, with that same old look of loathing, but now it was tinged with one of irritation. I shut the door quickly and eavesdropped outside. I heard the doctor say, 'Let's have a look at you then,' and my mam told him he wasn't welcome.

'I'll look at you anyway,' he said.

I heard nothing more for a while, and then his gruff voice. 'You're letting yourself go, Mrs Davies,' he said, 'and that's not going to bring your husband back. You'll be joining him if you don't look out. And pretty soon,' he said. I felt the hot tears on my cheeks, but I was glad the doctor had shouted at her. I had hopes she might listen to him.

'I'll give this prescription to your Bronwen,' he said, 'and you must promise me to take it. For a week anyway. Three times a day and then we'll move on to something else. You're to stay in bed now, Mrs Davies, and I'll come and see you again in the week.'

I waited for him to come outside and he motioned me to follow him down the stairs. Once in the kitchen, behind the closed door, he said, 'Your mam's not well, Bronwen. And only she can make herself better. Can't you talk to her?' he asked.

'I've tried,' I said. I didn't want to go into it further.

'Well, see she takes this,' he said. 'Go to the chemist and get it now. It will keep her going at least.'

I saw him out, then I rushed down to the chemist shop and

rushed back again, clutching my mam's life-saver and praying
that she would take it from my hand. I prepared it carefully in
the kitchen. Three spoonfuls it was, in a small bowl of hot
water. I put it on a tray and I picked a flower from the garden
and laid it beside the bowl. It was my love token, too late for
that I knew, but since I could do nothing for my mam, I had
to do something for myself.

I took it upstairs to her bedside. 'Drink it, Mam.' I said.
'While it's hot. Please, please, do it for me.' As I said it, I
realised I was the last person she would do it for.

'Leave it on the side,' she said.

'No.' I was firm. 'I want to see you take it,' I said.

'Then you'll have to want.'

I sat by the bed and looked at her. And I watched the bowl
of nourishment grow cold.

'I'll go and heat it up again, Mam,' I said.

I went back to the kitchen and I warmed the bowl in a pan
of boiling water. I had left the flower on the tray upstairs, and
when I returned, I saw that she had crushed its petals into a
pulp. I was glad she had the strength enough for that, but the
hurt tore at my heart. I put the bowl on the bedside table. 'It's
hot, Mam,' I said. 'Drink it while it's hot.' I felt I was talking
to a child, but to a child who did not acknowledge its own
mother. I left the room. I had hopes that she would drink it
when I wasn't there.

I let three hours elapse before I prepared the second dose.
This time I did not include a flower. I knocked before I entered
the room, something I had never done before, but already I felt
a stranger in my own home. There was no answer, so I opened
the door gently. I heard a slight snoring, and on approaching
the bed, I saw that she was fast asleep. On the table beside her,
the bowl of nourishment stood stone-cold and untouched. I
didn't know what to do. I didn't know whether sleep was good
for her or bad. But I feared her sleeping. I feared that in her

weakened state, sleeping was a door to coma. And with that thought, I shouted at her.

'Mam,' I shouted. 'Mam, Mam.' I was screaming in my despair.

She opened her eyes and shook her head, bewildered.

'What is it?' she said. 'Why d'you have to wake me?'

The sole strength in her voice was made of her anger, her rage that I dared to interfere with her dying.

I did not lower my voice. I had to make a stand against her. 'You didn't take your medicine,' I shouted at her. 'And I've brought you another. And you're bloody well going to drink it even if I have to force it down your throat.'

'Go away,' she said.

I was helpless. I didn't know what to do. I felt like shaking her. But if I did, I feared she might rattle, skin and bones that she already was. I put down the tray and took hold of her shoulders. I tried to be gentle with her, as I lifted her into a sitting position. Then I sat on the bed and held the bowl in front of her. She did not even look at me. She simply slipped down into the crater once more and turned her head to the wall.

I put the bowl of nourishment next to the one that had cooled, and I thought of the row of Auntie Annie's brooches on the bookshelf in my room. I had a goodly collection by now, and I wondered how many bowls would accumulate on my mam's table before I would start to dust them. I went downstairs and I sat at the kitchen table and I wondered what I should do.

I did not go to bed that night. Every three hours I placed yet another hot bowl on my mam's table, and in the morning, with each one untouched, I rang the doctor.

'You were right to call me, Bronwen,' he said. 'I'll come as soon as I can. She'll have to go into hospital.'

I felt a measure of relief. I already felt guilty enough in

being labelled the cause of her dying. I didn't relish the guilt of actually killing her by neglect. For had the doctor not agreed to come, I think I would have let her die, since that was what she so fervently wished.

I went back to her bedroom and knocked on the door once more. She was staring at the ceiling.

'The doctor's coming again,' I said. It sounded like a punishment and that's perhaps how I viewed it. 'You're going to have to go to hospital. They'll *make* you eat there. Put a drip in your arm they will, and you won't be able to stop them.' I hated the spite that had crept into my voice. Then I flung myself on her bed.

'I love you, Mam,' I said. 'You *know* I love you.'

And then she did a strange thing. She looked at me, examining every feature, and then she laughed in my face. I could not bear to look at her any more, nor she at me, and she turned her face away as I left the room. I think it was at that moment that I knew that I would never see her again. It's not that I had one of Auntie Annie's 'feelings'. I just knew that, in laughing in my face, in turning away her head, my mam had said goodbye to me, to all my bowls of nourishment, to all my doctor and hospital arrangements, and to all my pitiful atonement. She would not give me time to deserve her forgiveness.

I was not surprised to hear the phone ring in the hall. I knew it was my Auntie Annie with a 'feeling' and I did not want to acknowledge it. So I let it ring. In time, my Auntie Annie must have thought she was mistaken for the ringing stopped and the silence that followed it was like the grave.

I sat in the kitchen and I waited for the doctor to arrive. He'd said he would come as soon as he could, but it was over an hour before he rang the bell. He barely acknowledged me in the hall, but went straight away upstairs. I followed him, and somehow I knew what he would find.

My mam lay there as I had left her, cradled in the crevasse

of her marriage bed. Her eyes stared into nothingness. A small smile was frozen on her lips, her last message to me, that all my care and all my loving over the years had counted for nothing. The doctor took her limp wrist in his hand and after a while, 'She's gone,' he said. 'She did it to herself. I'm sorry.'

He put his arm around my shoulder. 'So much sorrow, girl, and in so short a time. What will you do?'

'I'll manage,' I said.

'Will your Auntie Annie come down?'

'I'll ask her,' I said. I wished he would go away. I wanted to be alone with my mam. I wanted to tell her about all those things she wouldn't listen to. But most of all I wanted to tell her about the back lane. Because that would have explained everything.

'I'll come back with the death certificate,' the doctor said. 'And you get hold of your Auntie Annie. You shouldn't be alone.'

I saw him out of the front door. I would wait before I phoned Abertillery. First I wanted to talk to my mam.

I went back to her bedroom and I sat on the bed and I took her frail wrist in my hand. I rested my finger on its silent pulse. My dad had been dead for just over a month and for over a month I had endured her rage and her hatred. I had caught her occasional glances of loathing. I had listened to her seething silence. I had sniffed the bitterness that exuded from her every pore. But it had made no difference to my love for her. And I only hoped that she had known it. But I told her anyway, squeezing her hand. Then I said I was sorry about David Parsons and the disappointment I had caused her. 'I had reasons, Mam,' I said. 'And it wasn't my fault. It all happened a long time ago. During the war it was, when I was seventeen and still in school.' And then I saw myself walking down the back lane like it was yesterday, and the four strides I took to cover each terrace dwelling. Until I reached number thirty-six.

Then I let go of my mam's wrist and I couldn't say another word. But my nostril twitched and there was blood in their stead. My dad had gone, and so now had my mam. Now there was only Auntie Annie left to whom I could not tell my tale.

I placed my mam's hands together and laid them neatly on the counterpane. Nice and tidy. Then I went downstairs and phoned my Auntie Annie.

She answered the phone herself. Blodwen must have been out husband-hunting.

'I phoned you before,' Auntie Annie said. She sounded quite cross.

'There was no reply,' she said accusingly.

'What did you want?' I asked her.

'I had a feeling.'

'Mam's gone,' I said.

'I had a feeling,' she said again. 'Starved herself, did she?'

I heard her tone of accusation. 'I tried,' I said, 'but I couldn't get her to eat.'

'Stubborn woman your mam,' she said. 'I'll be down on the next bus.'

It occurred to me that now I was the only one left in Cardiff to die, and that my Auntie Annie, if she were still alive, would have no one to ring and tell her 'feeling' to. And all the next buses would come and go, and there would be nobody on earth to bury me. But I could not afford such thoughts. For the moment I had to busy myself with burying my mam.

My Auntie Annie's tone on the telephone had been cold and abrupt. Perhaps she was stifling her grief. Since my dad's funeral there was no doubt that, taking her cue from my mam, she had looked less kindly upon me, and I doubted that after this funeral visit I would ever see her again.

I felt the need to tell somebody about my mam's passing. I didn't want people to think that I was keeping it a secret. My mam was entitled to as honourable a funeral as was my dad.

The terrace had to be told, and that included Mrs Pugh. I think that she was probably my mam's closest friend, so I would tell her first. But she could not be relied upon to spread the news, for no-one in the terrace would be seen talking to her. I would call on Mrs Powys who had done her courier bit by my dad and thus the terrace would be informed. I noticed I was wearing an apron. My mam's apron. I was still too young to wear an apron on the street so I took it off and went down to the house on the windy corner. I hadn't seen Mrs Pugh since my dad's funeral. I had often wondered why she hadn't come to the house to comfort my mam. And when I saw her at the door, I suspected the reason why. All her blowsiness had melted. She still wore the same bouffant attire but now it sagged on an almost skeletal frame. She was clearly very ill.

'Are you all right, Mrs Pugh?' I said.

She smiled. 'I've felt better in my time,' she said. She asked me in to her red-flocked parlour.

'I've been meaning to come and see your mother,' she said. 'But I've not been too well. I'm on the mend now though. Tell her I'll be round next week.'

'Too late,' I said. 'She's gone.' I was speaking like a telegram.

A thousand words were not enough to tell of my loss, and one was one too many. I sounded cold and uncaring. And perhaps that was exactly how I felt. At least in one layer of my mind. But underneath that layer, I knew there was an ocean of hot tears that would in time melt its frozen capping and spill out that sorrow that I could not face.

Mrs Pugh was shocked at my news. She sat down on her pink sofa and shivered. 'How did it happen?'

I told her, but I omitted any reference to the hatred my mam had suddenly conceived against me since my dad's death. It wasn't that I felt I deserved it. It was simply because I was ashamed of it. Ashamed above all for my mam, that once so kindly a woman who rarely found fault with anybody, had suddenly become so eroded with bitterness that she was unrecognisable.

Mrs Pugh was deeply upset. I think my mam was her only friend.

'I shall miss her,' she said. 'We were close, you know. She told me lots about herself, the sort of things you tell intimate friends.'

Curious as I was to know what those things were, I would not ask about them, and I wondered, close as I was to my mam in the old days, how well I knew her. You don't think of your parents as having secrets. They seem too old to have anything to hide. But I knew that however old I was obliged to become, I would have a secret inside me for ever.

'What can I do for you?' Mrs Pugh said.

'Just visit like you used to,' I told her. 'And bring Petal.'

I made to leave the house.

'Look after yourself, my dear,' she said. 'It's sad to lose one's parents.'

I wondered then whether she had any children. Perhaps in time, she would confide in me as she had so safely confided in my mam.

I went back home and waited for my Auntie Annie. I threw away the bottles of nourishment that my mam had refused, and I prepared something to eat for our dinner. For the first time in my life I was not looking forward to my Auntie Annie's visit. I had sensed her hostility on the telephone and I was in no mood to be shouted at. I wanted comfort and solace, and those two lifetime sources of mine had gone. When the door bell rang I thought it must be Auntie Annie, but it was the doctor come with the death certificate. I noticed a few raised nets on the opposite side of the terrace monitoring the comings and goings at our house.

'Will you be able to make all the arrangements?' Dr Owens asked.

'I already know the ropes,' I said.

Shortly after he had left, the door bell went again. This time it was Mrs Evans from the nets at number fifteen.

'Is everything all right, Bronwen?' she asked. 'I see the doctor coming and going.'

'My mam's gone.' Again the telegram.

Mrs Evans wanted to know the how, the when, and especially the why, but I felt that 'She's gone' was more than enough to be getting on with, and certainly enough to take around the terrace. 'She just died,' I said. 'This morning.'

This had to satisfy her, and full of 'sorrys', she left. I watched her out of the front window and saw how she went straight to Mr Thomas's. There she would shatter for ever his fantasy of the girl next door.

At last my Auntie Annie arrived. I could see that she had been crying, and I realised that she must now feel as alone as I. I took the risk of kissing her. I was glad that she responded so warmly. We smelt of loss. Both of us.

'I've made us some dinner,' I said.

'That's nice. I'm hungry. Got the first bus I did. Had no time for breakfast.'

It was such a relief to be with someone who had appetite, and I led her into the kitchen and sat her down at the table.

'I've made soup and salmon cutlets,' I said.

'I can't eat until I've seen her,' Auntie Annie said suddenly. 'Will you come with me, girl?' she asked.

She sounded like a child who was afraid of the dark. I didn't want to see my mam again. I did not trust my nose. 'I'll get on with the dinner,' I said. 'You'd best be with her alone.'

As she went upstairs, I wondered whether I really could not look at my mam again. I didn't need any reminder of her face, but I wanted to remember it as it had been before my dad had died, when there was loving in her face and not a trace of bitterness. If I were to look at her now, it would be to recall that loathing look she had given me as she turned her face to the wall. I wanted to erase that look, but I knew that it was firmly imprinted on my mind and possibly in my nose, as was the back lane of yesterday, so many years ago.

After a while, my Auntie Annie reappeared. 'She doesn't look peaceful, girl,' she said. 'Not as I would have expected.'

'She hadn't eaten for over a month,' I said, in the hope that fasting would explain the discomfort of her features. I couldn't tell my Auntie Annie what hate that look was made of. Perhaps she knew, because she said, 'Your mam was not the woman she was when your dad was alive. Full of grief she was, and in that state she said things she didn't mean. Couldn't help herself, d'you see?'

I was grateful for her attempt to console me, but I knew that my mam had meant every word she'd spoken, both before and after my dad's passing, and every look she had given me.

'We're both alone now, girl,' my Auntie Annie said.

'You've got Blodwen.'

'Yes. I've got Blodwen,' she echoed, as if debating whether Blodwen were an asset or not. 'I live with her, but I never see her. Gallivanting she is. I should never have left Cardiff.'

'You can come and live with me, Auntie Annie,' I said. I don't know how much I meant it, but it seemed that I had to say something, and it was to my great relief that she refused.

'I wish I'd had a daughter like you,' she said, 'but Blodwen, like it or not, she's my flesh and blood and she needs me.'

I did not argue. I knew that my Auntie Annie needed to be needed, no matter who was making demands on her.

We finished our dinner and I asked her if she would at least stay the night.

'I'll sleep by her side,' she said.

I shivered. 'You don't have to,' I said. 'There's plenty of room.'

'She was my sister,' she said. 'My baby sister. I should have gone first.' She started to cry then and I couldn't see how a restless night beside a restless corpse could comfort her. Perhaps it was her way of apologising for having outlived my mam.

I cleared the table and decided to start straight away on the funeral arrangements. But first I had to draw all the front curtains closed, and as I did so, I wondered, when my time came, who would draw them for me. I left my Auntie Annie in the house while I went to the funeral parlour. I warned her that there might be visitors because of the blinds and Mrs Evans's telegraph, but I begged her not to show them my mam's body. I was ashamed of the fury on her face. I hoped the mortician could give it a peaceful smile before we laid her out on the parlour table.

I rushed down to the undertaker's using the back lane, because I didn't feel like conversation with sympathisers in the terrace. The undertaker remembered me from my last visit, and his face expressed surprise at my swift return. He tendered his deepest sympathies and I wondered what shallow sympathies were. But that's all he offered me. In view of the good business I was bringing him, it crossed my mind to ask him for a discount, but it would have been like asking Mrs Pugh for a cut after more than one blossom visit. I ordered the same class of funeral as I had for my dad. I had no intention of stinting on my mam because of the looks and the words she had given me.

When I got home, I found my Auntie Annie entertaining Mr Thomas at the kitchen table.

'Duw, duw,' he was saying as I came in.

His conversation skills had not improved. I wondered with what words he talked to himself. He made to leave.

'There's sorry I am,' he said to me, thus exhausting his entire vocabulary.

He didn't look at all sorry to me. Indeed, I thought I saw an ill-concealed smile around his mouth. I forgave it, because poor Mr Thomas had had enough death in his time and it must have given him a singular pleasure to see it happening to other people. I saw him out and told him I would let him know about the funeral.

For the rest of that day, the callers came from the terrace and I left them to Auntie Annie, who told them of the how, where, and when. But none of them asked about the 'why' because all of them could guess at the answer. 'Couldn't live without him' was their simple explanation. 'Such a happy couple they were.'

That night I heard my Auntie Annie pacing my mam's bedroom. Her apologies for her own survival were clearly not comfortable, and in the morning she looked tired and very old.

'I'll sleep on the bus I will,' she said.

I took her to the bus station. I was sorry to see her go, but she promised to come back for the funeral and to stay with me for a few days.

'What will you do with that big house, girl?' she said as we waited for the bus.

I hadn't thought about it. 'What should I do with it?' I said.

'Well, you don't have a job now, do you, girl? You could take in lodgers. Need the money you will. I don't suppose your mam had much in the way of savings.'

I had no idea of what my mam had in her Post Office account. Or my dad for that matter. Whatever it was, it was put by for *mañana* holidays and lobster tans and sand-strewn toes. I liked to think of those times, those happy times together, when those last looks and words had never been dreamt of and there was only the untellable back lane between us.

When the bus came I kissed my Auntie Annie goodbye, and I waved to her woeful face through the window. On the way home I thought about her lodger suggestion. But strangers in the house did not appeal to me. I thought it best to sell it. There was nothing to keep me in Cardiff any more. The back lane and yesterday would follow me wherever I went. I had learned that lesson in dismal Swindon. With the proceeds of the sale of the house, I could go to *mañana* country and lie in the sun and think only of the good days with my mam and dad and Auntie Annie. I grew quite excited as I fantasised about my forbidden future, but as I turned into the terrace and the drawn blinds, and my mam's look of loathing behind them, I felt ashamed. I turned quickly and took the route down the back lane. If shame was my clothing, there was no better place to air it, and by the time I reached home, my reliable nose had obliged.

The following day the undertakers came to lay my mam out in the parlour. I took a while to decide what they should dress her in. There was not a great deal of choice. Her wardrobe was not large, consisting of her *mañana* clothes, her jury apparel, and the special dress she had barely worn for my almost wedding. And any number of overhead aprons. I considered them all. I had to assess her pride in them. By this criterion, her dress for my wedding was the first to go by the board, and I was left with a choice between her jury and her housewifely pride. In the long run it would have been the aprons that had the edge, but my mam would not have wanted to be seen dead in an apron. So I had the choice of her jury dresses. The one she had worn on her first day, the green flowered one, was her favourite, but it was also the one she'd worn at my engagement party, so that it was a token of both hope and disappointment which cancelled each other out. Finally I decided on the sober suit she had worn on the last day of the trial when, with all her just intentions, she had helped pass the sentence of death on an innocent man, and I liked to think that possibly she had regretted it. The suit would satisfy both my mam and myself, and I would dress it up with a flowery scarf to take the edge off its sobriety.

I waited in the kitchen while the undertakers went about their business upstairs. I hadn't looked at my mam since the day she died, and I didn't intend to view her until she was decently laid out in the parlour. I dusted the parlour table where my dad had so lately lain, but first I pulled down all the Christmas streamers and crunched them up and threw them away because I couldn't envisage a Christmas at that table alone. I heard the undertakers coming down the stairs and the knock of the coffin on the landing turning. I opened the parlour door wide, and stood aside as they entered. They laid the coffin on the table and invited me to view their handiwork.

What I saw appalled me. My mam's cheek was blown up on one side, possibly with a wad of cotton wool, in a vain attempt to soften that look of loathing. Not content with that, they had rouged her cheeks, and daubed layers of make-up on her face as well as lipstick and mascara. Horrified as I was, I was close to laughter, for my poor old mam looked like an unemployable clown. She bore no resemblance to the woman who had loved me and whom I loved still.

'Take it off,' I said. 'All of it. My mam never used make-up in her life.'

They looked at each other. 'You've paid for it, miss,' one of them said. 'We can take it all off if you like. But you'll still have to pay.'

'Take it off,' I shouted at them. 'Just take the whole lot off.'

They went to work quickly. 'Pity it is,' one of them said. 'Won't look half as nice, will she?'

'Duw,' said the other. 'After all our good work.'

When they had finished, my mam was at least recognisable,

even though her look of pain was undiminished. The men left, still grumbling. 'Never had any complaints before,' one of them said.

I said nothing. I simply shut the door after them. I shut the parlour door too. I wasn't yet ready to spend time with her.

I only had one more visitor that day. Mrs Pugh came with Petal and I noticed that Petal was looking more like Mrs Pugh than Mrs Pugh herself. It seemed that she had inherited all the weight that Mrs Pugh had lost. Her blowsiness too, and I doubted whether she wore a kimono any more.

I took them both into the parlour to get it over with. They stood, one each side of the coffin.

'She must have suffered, poor thing,' Mrs Pugh said.

Petal said nothing but I could see that her eyes were filled with tears.

'I'll make a cup of tea,' I said. I more or less forced them out of the parlour and into the kitchen where they sat silently at the table.

'What will you do now, Bronwen?' Mrs Pugh said after a while. 'This house is a bit big for you on your own.'

'I couldn't stay here,' Petal said. 'Too many ghosts for my liking.'

'Ghosts can be company,' I said. But not my mam's, I thought. 'I don't know yet what I'll do. It's all been so sudden.'

'You should go away for a while,' Mrs Pugh said. 'A holiday. You've had too much on your plate lately. You need to get away from it all.'

I told her I would think about it. Then I asked how she was feeling, and was she on the mend?

'I'm much better,' she said, but out of Mrs Pugh's line of vision, Petal looked at me and shook her head, and I had the feeling I was living on Death Row and all I could do was to wait until my own turn came. I didn't want Mrs Pugh to die.

She was the only remaining link with my mam. In time I hoped to come close to her too, close enough to qualify to be another ear which would never hear my untellable tale. I prayed that she would get better.

And indeed, she managed my mam's funeral a week later, and she seemed even more sprightly, despite Petal's nods and winks. My Auntie Annie was there too, and Blodwen came with her, welcoming an excuse to wear her attractive widow's veil. And the whole of the terrace came, as they had come for my dad, with the exception of the Griffiths, who had to make do with their net curtains.

I was happy with the turn-out. They had all filed past my mam's coffin, and everybody had said how peaceful she looked, but only because that was what you had to say on such occasions, but no doubt, later on, they discussed amongst themselves her angry, twisted features. I'd made lots of sandwiches and cakes for the wake, and although everything was eaten, it was a solemn affair, and almost silent. I had hoped they would talk about my mam and what a wonderful person she had been and how much she would be missed in the terrace, and though I'm sure most of them were thinking of these things, none of them could find the words to utter them.

My Auntie Annie and Blodwen stayed with me for a few days after the funeral, for my sake they said, and meant it, but I was relieved to see them go. I wanted to be on my own and without my mam for the first time. I wandered around the house where I was born, and which now belonged to me. I started in the attic and I visited every room, but I left that bedroom to the last, and it was not until late evening that I braved entry. I sat on a chair and I stared for a while at the bed, the bed in which I had been born. And I relived all my childhood years. Until that day, yesterday, in the back lane. And then I bled. But for once it seemed right and proper, for

with the blood came the tears and I threw myself into their pit
of loving and wept my heart out.

Then I heard myself speak. 'I loved you, mam,' I said. 'I
loved you more than anybody in the world. I know that I hurt
you. Both of you. And you said nothing. You forgave me
because you loved me. I couldn't help it, Mam, and I never
told you why. It's because I killed a man. Yesterday. In the
back lane.'

CHAPTER THIRTEEN

So there I was, on the wrong side of forty, with no job and no prospect of one. The only real asset I had, the only one that I really valued, was my stubbornly retained virginity. My atonement was well on course. But I had enough money not to need a job. For as I discovered, when all the bills were settled, my mam and my dad had left a tidy sum and a house free of mortgage. Their Post Office savings had been *mañana* ones and enough to buy a lifetime in the sun. But it was my own savings that I used to take myself on holiday as Mrs Pugh had suggested. But I would not go back to *mañana*. Any reminder of those happy times brought tears. I wanted to go somewhere where they had never been, which, apart from Spain, offered the whole world. I would find the sun elsewhere, I decided. Moreover, I would invite Mrs Pugh to come with me.

I went down to the house on the windy corner. I was glad that Mrs Pugh herself answered the door, still unblowsy, but with a smile that belonged to her billowing days. She called me into her wonderland parlour and asked Petal to bring us some tea. Then we sat there, the three of us, and I issued my invitation. Mrs Pugh was overwhelmed and so excited, her cup shook in her hand.

'Can I go, Petal?' she asked.

'Of course,' Petal said. 'It will do you the world of good.' She threw me a look of deep gratitude.

Then I asked Mrs Pugh what she wanted to do on a holiday.

'Nothing,' she said. 'I just want to rest and lie a little in the sun. And be waited on. I don't want to go sightseeing. I want to rest and build up my strength.'

So I booked a package holiday in Cyprus, in a four-star hotel on the beach in Limassol. For my mam's sake I was going to do Mrs Pugh proud.

Petal came with us as far as Gatwick Airport. The blossoms had been given time off, and the house on the corner suspended business for the day.

'First time in almost thirty years in that house that I've closed,' Mrs Pugh said. 'During the war, we even opened on Christmas Day. There's somebody, somewhere, who wants it all the time. But you'll open up tomorrow, won't you, Petal?' Mrs Pugh said.

It was clear that Petal was slowly taking over the madamship of the house. Her increased weight and blowsiness proved it.

'I don't know what all the punters will do when I'm gone,' Mrs Pugh was saying. 'There's not another establishment like mine in the whole of Cardiff. Not one that's respectable and has earned good will.'

It was sad to imagine the terrace without the dubious house on the windy corner, and I wondered what would happen to Petal and to all the blossoms once Mrs Pugh had gone. The terrace would be very different. It would become ordinary and respectable. Since I was one, but certainly not the other, there would no longer be a place for me in that row of houses, and it would be reason enough to take my back lane elsewhere. But I would postpone such thoughts, because I'd had enough of death in my life and I did not want to envisage Mrs Pugh's name in that dismal catalogue of mine.

Petal burst into tears as we left for the departure lounge, far more tears than were merited by a mere fortnight's absence and I imagined that she was probably weeping at the thought of a homeless future.

'Good girl that Petal,' Mrs Pugh said as we boarded the plane.

'What's her real name?' I asked.

'Myfanwy. Myfanwy Williams. From Bridgend. She came to me when she was fourteen. Soon after she left school. In those days, girls from the Valleys used to go into service. She was my all-purpose maid in the beginning. She was pretty eager to learn and gradually I trained her in the blossom business. But I wouldn't let her start professionally until she was eighteen and she was my best and busiest blossom. She doesn't do it any more now, except for special customers who've known her from the beginning. Now she helps me most of the time. She's good with the accounts. She'd make a wonderful madam.'

'Is that what she wants to be?' I asked.

'You need money for it,' Mrs Pugh said, ' and I don't think she's saved that much.'

I was confused. It seemed natural to me that Petal would inherit the corner house on Mrs Pugh's demise, and again I wondered if she had children.

She said no more about the business and she settled down and strapped herself in and showed no fear of flying, though as far as I knew, she had never flown before.

'When I first went up in an aeroplane,' Mrs Pugh said, 'they had propellors you know. Not like the jets we have now.'

She surprised me. 'I didn't know you'd flown before.'

'Oh often. Paris, Rome, Madrid.'

'For holidays?'

'No. Business. My girls are very popular you know. And old clients like to send for them from time to time. And new ones too. It's a word-of-mouth business. I insist on being chaper-one. They like that.' She laughed. 'It makes the deal more respectable. Once I took six of my blossoms to Paris. There was a big party for a foreign visitor. We had a grand old time. That was the first time that I left Petal in charge of the house. And she managed it very well.'

'You're full of surprises, Mrs Pugh,' I said. 'I never knew.'

'No-one ever did. I kept it very quiet. The terrace wouldn't have been happy to know about it.'

'Did you ever tell my mam?' I asked.

'Yes. Just after she came back from her first time abroad. She was telling me about her fear of flying. That's when I told her.'

'She never told me,' I said.

'That's because I told her in confidence. That's what I liked about your mother. I could trust her.'

I was happy to talk about my mam, my mam of the old days, that is, before my dad had died. 'She was a good mam to me,' I said.

'And you were a good daughter. She often told me so.'

All that must have been before my dad died and I was glad that Mrs Pugh had not talked to my mam in her widowhood. 'Did she confide in you too?' I dared to ask.

'Yes. We exchanged our secrets, but hers go with me to my grave, as mine did to hers.'

I didn't want to know what my mam's secrets were. I was simply astonished that she had any. She seemed to have gone through life at an even temper, undisturbed, rarely angry or frustrated, and certainly her nose had never bled. So her secrets must have been those of which she was not ashamed, secrets that she was able to live with, and the recollection of which she might even enjoy.

'If only children could imagine their parents as children once,' Mrs Pugh was saying, 'there would be such a greater understanding between them.'

I didn't know what she was getting at and again I suspected that she might have had children of her own.

She fell asleep shortly after our conversation, but woke up for lunch, of which she ate very little. But she drank, her wine and mine, and went to sleep again. I bought some duty-free liquor on the plane because I sensed that Mrs Pugh would have need of it.

A bus was waiting for us at Larnaca Airport for to take us to Limassol. Mrs Pugh was wide awake by then, and feeling much refreshed after her long if interrupted sleep. When we arrived at the hotel, the sun was setting but there was the after-sense of a very hot day. I had booked two single rooms because I thought that Mrs Pugh would want her privacy. We arranged to meet in the foyer for dinner.

Although she claimed to be hungry, I noticed that Mrs Pugh ate very little. But she did drink a great deal and I was glad that I had bought a supplementary supply. She was much taken with Greek brandy. I knew that she was not well, but I did not know the nature of her illness or whether brandy was good or bad for her. But she seemed to enjoy it so I did not interfere. After dinner I suggested a walk around the hotel gardens, but she claimed fatigue. Perhaps she was tired, but she was also drunk for I noticed that she was fairly unsteady on her legs. I suggested that we both make an early night so that we would wake refreshed in the morning.

We breakfasted by the pool and I noticed that for that meal, she showed a very hearty appetite. She was wearing a bathrobe which covered her bathing costume. At the poolside, she slipped it off and sat dangling her feet in the water. I looked at her body. Even if I'd never met her before, I would have known that that skeletal frame had housed flesh in its time. And much of it. I had seen my mam in a bathing costume but I'd never imagined that she had looked different at any other time. Neither fatter nor thinner, as if indeed she was born in that very suit. My dad too. They were as they were, born into my present time. One's parents are one's parents. And always have been. They bypassed their childhood in order to sire you. But in Mrs Pugh's body, I had seen growth and change, and not only change, but decay. She was smiling as she sat there by the pool, and when a waiter passed by, I ordered a Campari for her because I knew it was a favourite drink of hers. When it was brought to her, she looked over at me and smiled. 'This is the life,' she called.

My dad used to say that. In the *mañana* days. I went and sat beside her.

'I'd like to go into the pool,' she said, 'but I'll need a bit of help down the steps.'

I took both her hands.

'I can't swim,' she said as she immersed herself in the water. 'I just like to wallow.'

But she no longer had the body for wallowing or the weight that could make waves. All she could do was to splash like a skinny, excited child. I joined her in the pool. I didn't swim. I just wanted to keep her company.

'I'm happy,' she said. 'I want you to know that. And that you are the cause of it.'

Very rarely in my life had I felt that I was good for anybody. Mrs Pugh's compliment lightened the load of my mam's legacy of hatred.

One night at the end of our first week, we were having dinner together. As usual Mrs Pugh had eaten very little. But she had drunk.

'I'll tell you a secret,' she said.

'Can you trust me?'

'I trust you as well as I trusted your mother. It's not much of a secret,' she said. 'It's just a little bit of gossip.'

'What is it?' I asked.

'You know your neighbour Mr Thomas?'

In a way she didn't have to tell me any more. I knew from her mischievous smile that Mr Thomas was a visitor at her house on the windy corner. This she confirmed. 'And pretty regular too,' she said. 'At least while his wife was alive. I don't think he's been since she died. But while she was alive, he would come every week. On a Friday. Bit much, on his own doorstep, I thought. He was never very particular about which blossom he took. I think he would have taken anything. He was like lots of men. The only way he could have sex was to pay for it. He thought it was such a filthy thing to do. He couldn't function if he got it for free. My blossoms didn't like him very much. They tried to dodge him. But I could always rely on Dahlia. She would do for him. I think she pitied him. But then there came a time when he wanted the kinky stuff and even Dahlia wouldn't oblige him. I had to tell him not to come any more. I don't know where he went after that. There's a place in Queen Street caters for that sort of thing.'

I wanted to ask her what kinky stuff meant but I didn't want to reveal my ignorance. But at the same time I wanted to tell her that I was still a virgin. It was my triumph after all, and I wanted to show it off but I couldn't explain to her why it was such a victory.

'Nowadays,' she was saying,' when I see him in the street, he crosses the road. He's ashamed of everything in his life. I'm like Dahlia. I'm sorry for him too.'

She drank her third brandy. 'I love this stuff,' she said. 'I must take some home with me. Makes me sleep.'

Some mornings during our holiday, Mrs Pugh stayed in bed. I didn't know whether it was because she was unwell, or whether she was suffering from a monumental hangover. Whatever. I let her lie, and most days, we managed to have lunch together.

On the day of our departure, we were scheduled to leave very early in the morning, and the night before, Mrs Pugh decided not to go to bed at all. We had what she called a night on the town and she insisted on treating me.

We went into the main square in Limassol and into one of the more rowdy tavernas. She liked to watch the dancing and listen to Greek folk songs. And all the time, she kept her brandy glass full. The dancers were men and most of them were very fat, but they had a grace and elegance about them that one does not normally associate with obesity. I watched Mrs Pugh getting merrier and drunker and I had what my Auntie Annie would have called a 'feeling', a 'feeling' that Mrs Pugh was dying. And that, for whatever reason, she had chosen to drink herself to death, in the same way as my mam had starved herself, and I didn't see that it was my business to interfere. It was Mrs Pugh's choice, as it had been my mam's. So I let her drink away, and in the early morning when the coach arrived to take us to the airport, the courier had to carry her on to the bus. She slept most of the way home on the plane, waking up for the occasional pre- or post-libation. But by the time we arrived at Gatwick, she was surprisingly sober. Petal was at Victoria station to meet us.

She was delighted at our return. 'I missed you,' she said to Mrs Pugh and put her arms about her, and I thought that if indeed Mrs Pugh had no children, Petal could be as close to a daughter as she would ever find.

After that holiday, its calm and its pleasure, I sensed that a chapter of my life had come to an end, and a new one was about to begin. I set about cleaning out my mam's and dad's wardrobes. It was like the final burial. I knew it would be a difficult task, especially with my mam's, but I knew too that it had to be done. My mam's ghost wandered about the house day and night and needed no clothing.

I started with my dad's. There was more remembered loving there. And less confusion. My dad had been a tidy man. He'd not been a hoarder. There was little enough in his wardrobe and all that he had, he had worn. Three jumpers, four shirts, six ties, six pairs of socks, two vests, two underpants, and three pairs of shoes. One jacket, two pairs of trousers. His best suit had been buried with him. I was surprised to find that he'd kept his war-time fire-watcher's uniform. His only souvenir. And because of that, it was the only piece of his wardrobe that I would not give away. It was how he would wish me to remember him. I folded his clothes into an old suitcase and took it down into the hall. I would telephone the charity shop to come and collect it.

I postponed starting on my mam's wardrobe. My dad's had been simple, pleasant even, with its loving memories. But I knew that every article of my mam's clothing would be imprinted with that last look of hers, and all her loving which had suddenly soured. I wished that I could feel resentful, but I knew that I had earned that terrible legacy. At least in my mam's eyes. Because she never knew about the back lane and the torture it had done me. I postponed the chore for as long as I could, and then, when it was dark, I went back into their bedroom.

My mam had had her own wardrobe and it was as neat and as sparse as my dad's. The jury dresses hung neatly side by side, and probably in the order she had worn them. Then there was a space, and after that interval hung the dress that she had worn for my hoped-for wedding. But while every single item in that wardrobe struck terror in my heart, they were all of them as innocent as the wearer they had clothed. I didn't even bother to wipe the blood from my nose as I looked at them, and I let it spill over one of my mam's aprons that I was wearing at the time. I found another old suitcase and I folded the clothes inside it without even bothering to take them off their hangers. I did not look at what I was doing. My blood spread across her whole wardrobe and I felt close to her for the first time since she had died. Blindly I packed her

underwear and jumpers and even her aprons in the same way.
I wanted to get it all over and done with.

'I'm sorry, Mam,' I heard myself saying. Over and over
again. And when it was all done, the bleeding stopped and a
great wave of relief swept over me. I think I was beginning to
forgive her.

It was about a month after we returned from our holiday
that Petal came to the door. I had visited Mrs Pugh a number
of times since our return and had found her well and in good
spirits. So I wondered what it was that Petal wanted.

'It's Mrs Pugh,' Petal said. 'She wants to see you.'

'Is she all right?'

'She's not well today. She's in bed,' Petal said.

On our way back to the house on the corner, I dared to ask
Petal what was the matter with Mrs Pugh. 'Has she got some
kind of illness?' I asked.

'I don't know,' Petal said.

But she did know, I was sure, and she was keeping it a
secret. Or perhaps she was afraid of it and didn't want to make
it real by speaking it aloud.

Mrs Pugh was propped up on pink pillows beneath a pink
satin eiderdown. It struck me as a bed in which one could only
get better. But she did not look well. The healthy tan she had
acquired in Limassol had completely faded, blotted out by a
yellowish hue. She managed a smile. 'Shut the door,
Bronwen,' she said. 'And sit here.' She patted the bed at her
side. I did what I was told and I sat down and took her hand.
It was cold and its bones felt brittle. 'I want to ask you a
favour, Bronwen,' she said.

'Anything. What is it you want?'

'I'm dying,' she said.

I put my other hand on hers.

'I've been dying for quite a time,' she said, 'but now I know
the end is near. I want you to see to things when I'm gone.'

I didn't want to agree immediately, because in agreeing, I was accepting the fact that she was dying, and I didn't want her to die. In many ways, she had made the terrace bearable for me and I would be more alone than ever without her. 'It won't come to that,' I said.

'It will, dear,' she stressed. 'And quite soon.'

Then I kissed her. It was my gesture of acceptance.

'What d'you mean, see to things?' I asked.

'I think they call it an executor,' Mrs Pugh said. 'You have to see that the items of my will are strictly carried out.'

'Can you tell me what they are?' I asked her.

'I have very little to leave. Just the house, the business and the good will. Though I say it myself, the good will will count very little without me. And there's still a mortgage to be paid off and one or two small debts. I have left a little for you, just as a thank you, and £300 to Petal. She has been very good to me and I wish I could leave her more. You will have to sell the house and pay off what is owing.'

'And what about what is left?' I said.

She began to whisper. 'You have your secrets, I'm sure, Bronwen. So did your mother. And so have I. But my secret I cannot take with me to my grave. I have to tell it to you, because it's part of my will. And when I'm gone, I don't care who knows it. Come closer,' she said.

I shifted towards her.

'I have a daughter,' she whispered. 'Elizabeth. She's forty-five now and she lives in London. Her father left me when she was a baby. He never sent me any money. He just disappeared. It was hard, but I found work. Different jobs. All kinds. But there was never enough money. She was clever at school and she got a place at Manchester University. I was so proud of her. We were close then. She was a lovely daughter. Bit like you, Bronwen. Well, she went up to Manchester and her grant nowhere near covered her expenses. I had somehow to get extra money for her. So I went on the game. It was the quickest way of earning enough. I didn't like men very much, so it was simple to use them just for the money. That was the way I put Elizabeth through her studies. With lots of extras too. She never asked me where the money came from. She must have assumed it came from my jobs. One day, she came home when I wasn't expecting her. I was soliciting a few streets away from where I lived. And she saw me. And watched me, so she said, for quite a while. She told me she never wanted to see me again. And she kept her word. I haven't seen her for twenty-five years, but I've kept track of her through someone I know. She's married and I've got a granddaughter I've never seen. I know that one day she will understand. I'm sorry that I have to die, that I can't give her more time to forgive me. But I want to leave her what I've got.'

She started to cry then and there was little I could say to comfort her. She had suffered far more than she had deserved. 'Perhaps one day you'll meet her,' she sobbed. 'and you could help her understand.'

'I'll write to her,' I said. 'Today. I'll tell her you're not well.'

Mrs Pugh shook her head. 'It's too late,' she said.

'She has a right to know,' I insisted.

'That is a right she is not entitled to.'

I though Mrs Pugh was wrong, but I admired her for that vestige of self-respect with which she was dying.

'I'll do everything,' I said.

She smiled. 'I'm tired now, dear. Come and see me again.'

I promised another visit, but she died the next day. I spent some time with Petal to comfort her, but I did not offer to help with the funeral arrangements. I'd had my fill of burials. I was the only terrace dweller who went to her funeral, but all the blossoms turned out in their finery and every net curtain in the terrace was raised.

The day after the funeral, I went to the office of the estate agents with the honest intention of putting Mrs Pugh's house on the market. But instead I put on my own. As I sat in the office waiting for some attention, it occurred to me that it was the most logical step I should take into my future. I would buy the house on the windy corner, and take up residence as the new madam, and I would appoint Petal as my assistant.

And so it was arranged. My house sold quickly. Mrs Pugh's debts were settled, and Elizabeth reaped her inheritance by proxy. She sent her husband to Cardiff to sign the papers, and when it was all settled, I made my move, to the astonishment and disgust of all the nets in the terrace. In the time-honoured long history of brothel ownership, I must have been the only madam in the whole of Christendom who was a virgin.

A few days after I had taken up my new appointment, Mrs Griffiths died. And that was one funeral I was happy not to attend. Thereafter I was afforded the same treatment in the terrace as had been offered to Mrs Pugh. Avoidance and disgust. Except for one brief encounter with Mrs Evans in the corner grocery store.

'Your mam and dad, God rest their souls,' she hissed at me, 'would turn in their graves.'

I did not tell her that my mam was already turning, and turning very nicely, thank you very much, for her restless ghost had followed me to the house on the windy corner.

I was happy there. I sensed I had found my true vocation. I left most of the administration in Petal's efficient charge. But I would go with her to the Valleys sometimes, in search of new recruits. Many of the blossoms whom I had met in the shelter days had wilted, and had left to graze on their savings. But they left their names behind and with them we baptised our new recruits. So it was still a house of flowers, in Mrs Pugh's memory.

I was happy in that house on the windy corner. But whatever I did for my nose, however diligent my atonement, it would not be satisfied. It never gave up on its bleeding protest, just in case I needed any reminder. Sometimes it would bleed without a nostril quiver-warning, and often without any apparent association, and I have to confess it was getting me down. So was my mam's ghost. It had no manners and an appalling sense of timing. It would appear at the door with a punter, and push past him to gain entry. Most nights it would sleep with me, and the only live thing about it was its look of loathing.

Petal was getting fatter and fatter and with my permission she had inherited Mrs Pugh's blowsy wardrobe. But she had kept some of her old Petal duties and each day she would serve me my tea in the wonderland parlour.

I will not dwell too long on those years. Like schools and teaching, brothels and whoring become routine. The punters came and went, and by word of mouth, we were busy most of the time.

When I had bought the house on the corner, I had written and told my Auntie Annie of my new address, and I did not hide from her my new profession. The news stunned her into a few weeks of stupefaction before she could reply. And not even in my Auntie Annie's hand. It was Blodwen who wrote on her behalf, stating that she shared her mam's disgust at my move. 'Disgusting' was the operative word. It salivated on the pages with its spleen. The letter ended with a request that I should not be in touch again.

I wasn't unduly depressed by the missive. I suspected it was Blodwen's hand, and I hoped that in time my Auntie Annie would write to me. Despite Blodwen's request, I continued to write regularly addressing my letters to Auntie Annie as 'Personal', and when after some months I still had heard nothing from her, I suspected that Blodwen had destroyed my letters.

One day, some months later, I had to go up the City Road

to collect some pillowslips that Petal had ordered. And I was close to the house where my Auntie Annie used to live, that home of the carving knife that had seen my downfall. I turned into the cul-de-sac, heedless of my nose, simply for a moment's nostalgia. And as I did so, I met her neighbour coming out of the house next door. I'd come across her from time to time when my mam was alive and we'd gone to visit my auntie before she moved to Abertillery. I stopped to say 'Hello' and I didn't like the look she was giving me. I thought she might have heard about my new profession. But it was not a look of disapproval; it was rather one of sympathy.

'Sorry I was to hear about your Auntie Annie,' she said.

I felt my heart leap. 'What about my Auntie Annie?' I whispered.

She looked astonished. 'You didn't know, girl?'

'Know what?'

'She died she did. Must be three months ago now. Buried she was, in Abertillery.'

There was no point in hiding the fact that I hadn't been told. 'I didn't know,' I said.

'Sorry I am,' she said. 'Would never have opened my mouth if I'd known. That Blodwen should have told you. Out of respect for your poor mam if nothing else. Can't understand it.'

But I understood it all right. Blodwen's revenge it was for my madamship.

When I reached home that afternoon, I fell into a deep depression, one that has haunted me from time to time ever since. With my Auntie Annie's passing, I felt that my banishment from home was complete. Now all of them had gone. My mam, my dad, and my Auntie Annie. There was no one left to whom I could not tell my untellable tale. They had gone and saddled me forever with my yesterday.

CHAPTER FOURTEEN

I have been in this house on the windy corner for almost thirty years. Each night in bed, I sleep with my mam's ghost by my side. Last night I had a new caller, one who had never come before, but who had bided his patient and innocent time. The amorphous shape of Hugh Elwyn Baker. I knew it was he because of his distinct middle parting. And when I awoke this morning, there was blood all over Mrs Pugh's pink satin sheets. Yet, in his presence, I felt purged and almost serene. It seemed to me that Hugh Elwyn Baker had at last forgiven me and that he, if nobody else, considered that I had paid enough.

And surely that is true. I have suffered for my sin. My mam died of it. My dad too. And so, marginally, did my Auntie Annie. It had taken Hugh Elwyn Baker over fifty years to visit me, and when I awoke this morning, I knew that his gentle coming was my amnesty. I knew too that I would never bleed again.

Today it is my birthday. And as always, my blossoms are giving me a party. They're out shopping, or busy in the kitchen, though Petal has insisted that a few remain on duty. Which is just as well because already, so early in the morning, the front door bell is ringing.

I make my way down the stairs. I feel a lightness in my

step, as if a great burden has been lifted. I pause on the stairs and view my domain. With a rush of affection I recall Mrs Pugh, and I am proud that I have loyally maintained her business of service. Proud too of my blossoms and the service itself. And bugger the terrace and its net-curtained disdain.

The bell rings again. I do not hurry. In the course of the past thirty years, I have learned to understand the nature of each ringing. A timid and short peal of the bell must be answered at once, lest the punter lose his courage and turn away. But an insistent ringing can wait, for behind those peals are arrogance and appetite enough. So I take my time as I walk towards the door and more time too as I detach the lock. I try to show no surprise when I view the punter. For it is none other than Mr Griffiths, one-time chief air-raid warden and king of the terrace. He must be over ninety now, though he looks spry enough, and he has, after all, pressed twice on the bell, which insistence proclaims a will and an appetite, if not an ability and wherewithal. I hope that Hyacinth is on duty, because she can always be relied upon to cater for the likes of Mr Griffiths. He shows no sign of recognition, though he must know who I am. Even if he has forgotten his little interference of so many years ago, he cannot help but know my name. For the name Bronwen Davies is a curse in the terrace, whispered behind ageing hands. I am the bad end their children will come to if they don't do their homework, or watch too much television, or fail to clean their teeth. I stare at him, and keep him waiting on the doorstep for a while. Then I put out my hand and up his admission fee, as a small but pleasing revenge for his war-time fumbling.

Once I settle him in Hyacinth's capable hands, knowing that it is only her hands she will need to offer him, I enter into my wondrous parlour. It has lost none of its allure that so mesmerised me when I was a girl, all fresh and bleeding from the back lane. I sit there at peace with myself, and for the first time since my girlhood, old as I now am, I envisage a future. A future that is free and without proviso and one which I myself can be part of, and with no sense of betrayal. Laughing to myself, I even toy with the idea of marriage. Just the idea.

Shortly I hear Mr Griffiths stumble his sated way down the stairs. Then I ring for Petal. She will wash the blood from the sheets, and for the very last time. Then she will bring my breakfast and with her eternal smile, she will kiss my gnarled hand in its seventy-third year of survival.

Today is my birthday. Tomorrow is another day which will breed another and another into a future. The past is over and done with. Yesterday in the back lane does not seem like yesterday any more. In my dimming vision, my harassed heart, and in my gnarled hands and fingers, it is well and truly over fifty years ago.

☐	AUTOBIOPSY	Bernice Rubens	£6.99
☐	BROTHERS	Bernice Rubens	£7.99
☐	THE ELECTED MEMBER	Bernice Rubens	£6.99
☐	A FIVE YEAR SENTENCE	Bernice Rubens	£4.99
☐	I SENT A LETTER TO MY LOVE	Bernice Rubens	£4.99
☐	KINGDOM COME	Bernice Rubens	£4.99
☐	MR WAKEFIELD'S CRUSADE	Bernice Rubens	£4.99

Abacus now offers an exciting range of quality titles by both established and new authors which can be ordered from the following address:

> Little, Brown and Company (UK)
> P.O. Box 11
> Falmouth
> Cornwall TR10 9EN.

Alternatively you may fax your order to the above address.
Fax No. 01326 317444

Payments can be made as follows: cheque, postal order (payable to Little, Brown and Company) or by credit cards, Visa/Access. Do not send cash or currency. UK customers and BFPO please allow £1.00 for postage and packing for the first book, plus 50p for the second book, plus 30p for each additional book up to a maximum charge of £3.00 (7 books plus). Overseas customers including Ireland, please allow £2.00 for the first book, plus £1.00 for the second book, plus 50p for each additional book.

NAME (BLOCK LETTERS) _____

ADDRESS _____

_____

_____

☐ I enclose my remittance for £ _____

☐ I wish to pay be Access/Visa Card

Number ☐☐☐☐☐☐☐☐☐☐☐☐☐☐☐☐

Card Expiry Date ☐☐☐☐